Michael O'Reilly

Author of "THE BRAVEST OF

Michael O'Reilly was bor.. ...   f
Donard, under the shadow of the Wicklow mountains and the Glen of
Imaal, where the United Irishmen, led by Michael Dwyer, made one of
their last stands against the British forces in the 1798 Rebellion. His
grandfather was a Fenian, his father a young member of the IRA in
the Irish War of Independence against the British which followed the
1916 Rebellion. His mother, principal of the local school, also had
strong nationalistic views and this family patriotism has always been
an important part of Michael's life. He firmly supports the ideal of a
United Ireland, a 32-county Irish Republic, as did Tone, Emmet,
Pearse, de Valera, where people of different religions and beliefs could
live happily together. He believes that it will be achieved within the
next ten years, initially under United Nations and European
Community supervision, following an inevitable British declaration of
intent to withdraw from the six counties of Northern Ireland.

Educated at Blackrock College, the Alma Mater of the late
President de Valera, he had a successful career in business
management before establishing his own public relations consultancy
in Dublin where he is now one of the best-known names in his
profession.

Since his schooldays, he has been writing in his spare time and
has had features and stories published in many different countries
including Britain and the United States. He wrote, for several years,
the popular weekly 'Friday Focus' personality profile page in the 'Irish
Independent', the country's largest selling daily newspaper. He then
joined the Irish Government's Industrial Development Authority to
establish the international publicity division which is now regarded as
a world leader in the attraction of overseas investment.

He is a member of the Public Relations Institute of Ireland, the
National Union of Journalists, the Foreign Press Association in
London and the United Arts Club in Dublin. This is his first book
and he is already hard at work on his second which will be published
next year.

Often combining two careers, business and writing, has meant
working many sixteen-hour days over the years, so he spends most of
his leisure among family and friends. He likes reading, listening to
music, stage shows, films, television, restaurants, walking alone by
the sea or in the countryside, watching Ireland compete in
international sports, and enjoying life to the full in the company of
good-humoured friends.

The Bravest of the Brave

MICHAEL O'REILLY

ANNA LIVIA

First published in 1991 by
Anna Livia Press Ltd.
5 Marine Road
Dun Laoghire
County Dublin

Copyright © Michael O'Reilly 1991

1SBN 1 871311 14 4 Paperback
1SBN 1 871311 15 2 Hardback

Typeset by The Works

Cover design by Bluett

Printed and bound in Ireland by
Colour Books Ltd.

All rights reserved. No part of this publication may be reproduced, copied or transmitted in any form or by any means, without the prior permission of the publishers.

DEDICATION

To all those brave Irishmen and Irishwomen who fought and died for Irish Freedom down through the centuries and to all those people who struggle for Freedom, Peace and Justice anywhere in the world to-day.

For Labouré Aishling and Emmett Michael Pearse without whose help this book might have been finished earlier but without whose love it would never have been written at all. God bless them both.

Michael O'Reilly,
Dublin. 3 May 1991.

CONTENTS

Down through centuries of oppression by a foreign power, Ireland produced many heroes, men and women, as confirmed in the 1916 Proclamation - "In every generation the Irish people have asserted their right to national freedom and sovereignty". Those featured in this book can only be regarded as representative of the many who lived, and died, for Irish freedom - The Bravest Of The Brave - and as a tribute to all of them.

INTRODUCTIONS by Sile de Valera T.D. and U.S. Congressman Joseph P. Kennedy..viii

THE MAN WHO BECAME A COUNTRY - the story of Eamon de Valera, born in New York, sentenced to death by the British in Dublin, who went on to become President of Ireland......................1

THE LONGEST FUNERAL - Roger Casement, knighted by the British for his humanitarian work in Africa and South America, hanged by them for his work for Irish Freedom in 1916 and buried in Dublin fifty years later..23

UNITED WE STAND-DIVIDED WE FALL - The British Duke of Wellington said of him - 'He landed in France with a hundred guineas in his pocket and had come near altering the destiny of Europe' - for Wolfe Tone had one burning ambition - 'To break the connection with England!'..43

TWO FIGHT OR DIE - The Famine of 1847 destroyed almost half the population of Ireland. Two men, John Mitchel and Thomas Francis Meagher, decided it was better to fight rather than let their people starve 73

AND THEN CAME NOVEMBER - The terrible Black and Tans were let loose on the Irish population, yet the nation stood still in prayer when Kevin Barry - 'just a lad of eighteen summers' - was hanged in Mountjoy Jail on Monday, November 1st., 1920.........................93

A MAN ABOVE ALL - Terence MacSwiney, Lord Mayor of Cork, died in Brixton Prison, London, after a hunger strike of seventy-five days rather than accept the right of the British to arrest him in his own country, Ireland **107**

THE BRAVEST OF THE BRAVE - Fifteen years in an English prison, most of them spent in solitary confinement, did not prevent the old Fenian, Tom Clarke, from returning after a successful career in America to become one of the leaders of the 1916 Rebellion, before facing a firing squad **125**

"IRELAND UNFREE SHALL NEVER BE AT PEACE" - These famous words of Pádraic Pearse form the final chapter which brings the struggle for a 32-county Irish Republic up-to-date; to 1991, the 75th. anniversary of the Easter Rebellion following which Pearse, and the other leaders, were executed in May of that year. It explains why and how the British should now leave the six counties of Northern Ireland and concludes that Pearse's words will remain valid until the last British soldier leaves the island of Ireland forever **143**

IRISH HISTORY AT A GLANCE - A brief guide to significant dates and events in Ireland from earliest times until the present day.... **161**

BIBLIOGRAPHY - A short list of other books which will be of interest to those who wish to know more about Irish History.

INTRODUCTION
by Sile de Valera

The age of revisionism in which we live has created and encouraged a prevailing negative view of things national. The revisionist theory feeds on self-doubt and a feeling of inferiority. It deliberately sets out to destroy history in its distorted and unfocused account. In wishing to evade the historical reality the revisionist projects his fear and if this fear is allowed to be transmitted unchecked it quickly becomes endemic. In Ireland over the last fifteen years it has become fashionable among some who would wish to be included among the intelligentsia to deride and mock our proud nationalistic past. As a result of this attempt by the revisionists many polititians have felt self-conscious in seeking to secure the legitimate right of the Nation to be re-united. Some have even felt embarrassed about commemorating the leaders and founders of modern Ireland.

Rather than allowing such feelings of fear and self-doubt to take hold we should break the bonds of dependency and eradicate the slave mentality from our midst. In order to achieve this we must be aware of our history, for a Nation who tries to divorce its present from its past quickly loses its way.

In this book Michael O'Reilly has very sensitively dealt with the lives of some of the giants of modern Irish history. Through the lives of these men we learn of the difficulties faced by the Irish people over so many generations which were as a direct result of being occupied by a foreign power. These men took on the might of the British Empire so that Ireland could find its destiny through freedom. This freedom was to be the enabling condition for the full expression of the mind and spirit of the Nation.

In mulling through these chapters the reader will delight in learning not just a string of historical facts but also something of the personal traits and characteristics of these towering personalities. In short it is a very human and sympathetic account. Such a book is particularly pertinent at this time as it attempts to give an honest and informative testimony to the personalities and events which will enable the reader to challenge his own views and opinions.

While I may not be in full agreement with Michael O'Reilly on every detail outlined in the last chapter of this book I would very much share the overall philosophy and trust of his thesis. As Pádraig Pearse proclaimed "Ireland unfree shall never be at peace". The only lasting solution to the Irish question is to allow the Irish people as a whole to discuss and decide on their own future without any outside interference. I look forward to the day when Ireland achieves its freedom and is at last at peace. In order that this aspiration and hope can be realised partition must be ended. Partition being at one and the same time the cause and symbol of division in our land. Any set of talks or agreements which do not accept this is doomed to failure. To be re-united is the inalienable right of the Irish people. Martin Luther King once told us he had a dream. The dream of the men portrayed in this book and indeed the dream of the Irish Nation is yet to be realised.

Sile de Valera T.D.
Dáil Éireann,
2 May 1991.

INTRODUCTION
by U.S. Congressman Joe Kennedy

The path to peace in Northern Ireland often seems hopelessly entangled by a thicket of tales and slogans from a bygone era. The future and the past are enmeshed in Ireland like few places on earth, leaving the present difficult to bring into the sharp focus that is a prerequisite for mobilizing the forces of political change.

The Irish nation stands today as the victim of a diplomatic fiasco created in 1921 that has proven to be unworkable. The fiasco has not only created oppression and injustice for the Catholic minority in Northern Ireland, it has also caused an erosion in the values and principles that lie at the heart of democracy in Great Britain.

To say that Northern Ireland does not work is only to state the obvious. The economy is chronically depressed. The security forces have been corrupted by the impossible situation into which they have been thrown. The judicial system has been compromised by the sacrifice of fundamental rights.

Efforts to preserve the status quo in Northern Ireland have been self-defeating for the British and degrading for the Irish. Internment, Diplock Courts, strip searches, plastic bullets, the "peace line" in Belfast - the list goes on. Each of these words and phrases stand before the world as evidence of the inhumanity that rules in Northern Ireland.

If only a fraction of the energy that has been put into preserving the status quo could be shifted to peaceful political change, then perhaps the cycle of violence that grips Northern Ireland could be broken at last.

New opportunities abound to harness the forces of economic development to forge a partnership with advocates of political change. Long years of economic deprivation can be supplanted by encouraging investment in the vast underemployed human resources of Ireland, poised at the gateway to the huge markets of a unified Europe. A secure investment environment can motivate people in ways that tanks and plastic bullets never could.

Ireland must be united and the British must withdraw to their own land if peace is to endure. The transition must be crafted with courage, wisdom, and discipline. The violence that Irish patriots of yesteryear employed in their struggles against the British must be replaced by modern tools of political change - diplomacy, public communications, organizing, and economic development.

In the final decade of the 20th Century, the world is very different than it was during the days of Wolfe Tone or even Eamon de Valera. Global communications have reshaped the politics of liberation. Random killings and other calculated horrors are flashed around the world instantaneously, creating a sense of repugnance toward the perpetrators that drowns out any political message no matter how meritorious it may be.

Today, to reach one's goal is not so simple. Guns and bombs must be replaced by word processors and video cameras. Guerilla fighting needs to be replaced by research and media analysis. Information is the weapon of our time.

The case for British withdrawal from Northern Ireland is a compelling one. For decades the world has not heard that case. Some argue that violence is the only means to bring attention to Northern Ireland, and that without violence the case against the British will not be heard. But that is a simplistic approach to a complex problem and that approach has not worked.

A new approach is needed. The time has come to utilize the information technology of the 21st Century to mobilize world opinion against the fundamental injustice and human rights violations that stem from the diplomatic fiasco which led to the partitioning of Ireland.

People around the world must hear the truth. The conflict in Northern Ireland is not an ancient battle of religious sects. Rather, it is an age-old story of one nation occupying another. The occupation has led to incalculable human suffering and it is the responsibility of the world community to bring it to an end.

The brave souls of Irish history should not act as straight-jackets forcing us to apply the tactics of previous generations to the challenges we face today. Instead, those souls can inspire to bold and ingenious techniques to captivate the imaginations of decent and honest people around the world. Then we can begin to right the wrong of Northern Ireland.

Joseph P. Kennedy II,
Congress of the United States,
24th April 1991.

Éamon De Valera — the Rebel Leader

1

THE MAN WHO BECAME A COUNTRY

The familiar tall, thin figure in the black hat and coat came down the steps of the regal mansion that was once a symbol of everything he hated and was driven quickly through the tree-lined Phoenix Park; perhaps remembering that February afternoon more than thirty years ago when his twenty-one-year old son, Brian, was killed there as his horse bolted under a low-branched tree.

The old Rolls Royce made its way towards Parnell Square, where a girl named Janie Flanagan, who was once a member of the Gaelic League, had taught Irish to a young man in his twenties who wore homespun Irish tweeds, a peaked cap and a dark moustache. He was twenty-eight and she thirty-three when they married in January 1910 and his sole ambition then was to be a good teacher. On his eightieth birthday, he had remarked: "If I were a young fellow again and were asked what I would like to do, I would say that I regard teaching as a fine profession. It is splendid to get to know things yourself and then teach them to other people".

Down now into O'Connell Street, the crowded centre of a busy capital. Dubliners, rushing to the theatres and cinemas, stared at the big black car and the man inside waved to the crowds he could hear but scarcely see. The modern stores were packed with bargain hunters with money to spend; the city's first skyscraper was a pillar of light above the dark waters of the Liffey; traffic jammed on the bridge as people hurried to enjoy themselves.

Elsewhere in the city, teenagers screamed to the music of one of the country's five hundred showbands and rock groups; hotels and bars were packed with spectators from the football and punters from the races; bearded ballad singers entertained in the lounges; late-night dine and dance clubs were filled with happy couples; it was the weekend and Dubliners were happy.

The man in the car could remember such a weekend more than half a century earlier, Easter, 1916, when he had marched along these same streets in his green uniform, his field glasses and his gun, at the head of a hundred men on their way to challenge an empire. At Boland's Mills, they had held off every attack and, by hoisting the Irish tricolour on an empty building and lighting candles in its windows, he had the big British guns firing at the wrong target. He exclaimed then: "If the people had only come out with nothing but knives and forks in their hands, they could have won the country." But instead, he was the last to surrender after a glorious week and was promptly sentenced to death.

The car passed at the bottom of the streets which led to Dáil Eireann, the Irish Parliament, the Mansion House and his old office in the government buildings; the scenes of many of the most memorable moments of his life long, long ago. "I felt it my duty to inform you immediately that I cannot recommend the acceptance of this treaty," and later, "I am sick and tired of politics - so sick that no matter what happens, I will go back to private life."

Then there was the 17th of May 1945, when, in one of his most devastating speeches, he made Winston Churchill appear very undignified and unstatesmanlike indeed: "I know the kind of answer I am expected to make. I know the answer that first springs to the lips of every man of Irish blood..... I know the reply I would have given a quarter of a century ago.............. allowances can be made for Mr. Churchill's statement, however unworthy, in the first flush of his victory...............he is trying to find in a crisis like the present, an excuse for continuing the injustice of the mutilation of our country............ meanwhile, even as a partitioned small nation, we shall go on and strive to play our part in the world, continuing unswervingly to work for the cause and understanding between all nations."

Some twenty-five years earlier, he had heard these words in the new Irish Parliament, as he was unanimously re-elected President of an Irish Republic still fighting for its very existence against the might of Britain; "In no generation for more than a century had any Irish leader equalled such achievements. No one has shown himself more fitted to deal with the traditional foe. He had not been deceived, nor intimidated by their threats. Eamon de Valera first met the English as a soldier and he beat them as a soldier. He has been meeting them now as a statesman. The honour and interest of our nation are alike safe in his hands." The car sped on past the circular American embassy at Ballsbridge.

America, the place where he was born; the time was October 14th, 1882. His father was a talented native of Spain; artist, linguist, musician. His mother, a beautiful young Irish emigrant, Catherine Coll, was from Bruree in the county of Limerick. When mother and child were well enough to leave the hospital on Lexington Avenue, young Eamon was baptised in St. Agnes' Church on 43rd Street, near Grand Central Station.

America, the scene of his triumphs: "Chicago last night gave rigorous and vociferous evidence of its desire for recognition of the Irish Republic. Eamon de Valera, President of Ireland, when introduced to an audience of one hundred thousand that jammed the auditorium and packed the street for blocks around, commanded one of the greatest ovations ever accorded an American or foreign statesman. For twenty-six minutes the President of Ireland stood unable to speak, while the huge crowd cheered in a frenzy of enthusiasm. The president was lifted to the shoulders of his uniformed bodyguard, composed of American veterans of the first World War; flags, American and Irish, rippled over the sea of faces; babies were handed up to be kissed by the Irish chieftain; and all the while the crowd yelled, screamed, clapped and, in many cases, broke into tears in the intensity of enthusiasm. No more genuine and heartfelt demonstration of love and admiration ever was accorded a visitor to Chicago."

Silently, the car passed the magnificent Dublin Horse Show grounds and this too held plenty of memories: "I believe that I owe my life to the fact that I was kept a prisoner in a horse-box at the Ballsbridge Show grounds instead of having been brought back to some of the inner city barracks. My American citizenship did not arise and I do not think it counted in the long run." But he had exclaimed years earlier: "How could I be accused of treason when neither technically nor otherwise am I a British subject and please God I will die without ever being one." The death sentence had, at the last moment, been commuted to penal servitude for life and he did not join the other Irish Republican leaders before the British firing squads.

The big car turned towards Booterstown, a fashionable suburb that was his home for many, many years, and where most of his large family were born. Around him and his wife Sinéad on his eightieth birthday were: Major Vivien, Managing Director of the Irish Press Group of newspapers, and his two children; his eldest daughter Máirín, a scientist at University College, Galway; his son Eamon, a gynaecologist, with his wife and two children; his son Rory, a professor of archaeology, his wife and three children; his younger daughter Emer with her husband and their nine children; his youngest son Terence, a solicitor, his wife and two daughters. That had been a happy day.

The car halted for a moment near Carysfort Teachers' Training College, where he had lectured until it was time to take part in the Easter Rebellion and life was never the same again. Then up the tree-lined avenue, past the Castle and the playing fields, and Eamon de Valera, President of Ireland, had come back on one of his regular visits to his Alma Mater, Blackrock College, that he first saw as a thin, sixteen-year-old boy in the nineteenth century. These sentimental journeys, from the Prime Minister's office, and later from the Presidential residence, to his old school were always regular features of Eamon de Valera's life in the late 1960's, just as they had been for almost half a century.

When his father died in America, his uncle had taken the three-year-old boy back to Ireland, to his home at Bruree village in County Limerick. Dressed in a velvet suit he was sent to the local national school, where he soon took first place in every class. By the time he was twelve, he was very studious, would always have a book on the table during meal times, and was teaching mathematics to boys in higher grades. He had an excellent memory and could repeat whole chapters of his favourite book "The Three Musketeers", without a mistake. Napoleon and the Irish hero, Patrick Sarsfield, fascinated him and he sometimes wrote essays about them. Taking an active part in school plays, he preferred the part of a uniformed officer and was so fond of guns that he once remarked: "I am afraid I shall be a soldier." An altar boy serving Mass, he liked to listen to the sermons and discuss them afterwards - but it was not all study. Hurling, Gaelic football and handball were his favourite games and he won many a hundred yards' race too. His uncle often related how young Eamon would sometimes return home without the household messages - having become so engrossed in a game of hurling that he had forgotten all about them. He liked to take the milk to the creamery for it offered him an opportunity to read a book without interruption. He had no interest in politics in those days and would take up a book when a political discussion started in his little home - "I was brought up in a labourer's cottage" - as the family sat around the turf fire in the kitchen.

His fourteenth birthday was one of the most important of his life; his teacher and the local priest arrived to ask his uncle to send him to the Christian Brothers School at Rathluirc. He had shown such promise at his studies and was such a pious boy that the priest may have thought he would follow in his footsteps while the teacher was convinced that he had a great future in that profession. Influenced by their arguments, his uncle, Patrick Coll, decided to spend the family's small savings to send the boy to the Christian Brothers and he was enrolled there on November 2, 1896.

He would go the six miles from his home every morning by train but, as the train did not leave until three hours after school ended, he would frequently walk home in the evenings and have his lessons finished before the train passed near his house. The confidence of the Bruree people in him was not wasted, for he quickly won a scholarship to Blackrock College, Dublin, where he arrived in 1898; a tall, thin, rather studious sixteen-year-old boy. He was now starting a brilliant academic career and, by the time he had matriculated there, had won many first prizes and exhibitions.

He became a part-time teacher at the college to finance his university career which was equally brilliant, resulting in his appointment as Professor of Mathematics and Physics at Rockwell College, County Tipperary, and later, Professor of Mathematics at the Teachers' Training College, Carysfort, Dublin.

A Bachelor of Arts, a Bachelor of Science, a master of six or seven languages, he became an examiner in the universities where he taught. The heads of the institutions put on record that: "He was devoted to learning and was extremely popular both in the classroom and the athletic field.... his success as a teacher was due to the admirable care, punctuality and zeal with which he devoted himself to the work as well as the great knowledge he possessed of the subject matter... his devotedness to duty and his manly piety was an example to all in the college."

Fate takes many strange turns. In 1907, his mother visited Eamon de Valera in Blackrock College in the hope of persuading him to return to America with her. He declined because he had been very successful at his studies and had hopes for a good future in education in Ireland. In 1912, he was a candidate for the Chair of Mathematical Physics at University College Cork and it is said that a Limerick County Councillor, whose vote would have been the deciding one in his favour, missed the Cork train by one minute. Instead it happened that he joined the Gaelic League in Parnell Square, Dublin, where regular classes were held in the native Irish language; that he met Pádraic Pearse and Thomas MacDonagh there - two of the seven who later signed the 1916 Proclamation - that he met the girl whom he married in 1910; that he joined the newly established Irish Volunteers, more to defend Ireland than to take part in a revolution. He still liked to read, to play chess, to be with his family, but his teaching, language classes and volunteer training became more demanding.

From the Howth gun-running in June 1914 to the rebellion against British rule in Ireland at Easter 1916 was a logical conclusion. That fateful Easter Monday morning Commandant Eamon de Valera was one of less than a thousand Irishmen who challenged the might of the British Empire at the height of its power, and the forty thousand soldiers it soon had in Dublin. After the leaders who had surrendered had been shot by the firing squads and de Valera had been reprieved, he was sent to Lewis Prison in England where he helped the rebels during a prolonged struggle against their captors, wrecking the cells in protest against the ill-treatment they received. In June 1917, when Eamon de Valera led the released prisoners from the boat that had brought them back to Ireland, he was a comparatively unknown teacher no longer, but was making his first public appearance as a leader of the Irish Republicans. Circumstances, fate, or what you will, had changed his life and, almost before he realised what was happening, he was elected a republican member of Parliament for County Clare and thus, in 1917, began a long political career without parallel. By then a confirmed revolutionary, he made no secret of his purpose at Tullamore: "Get every rifle you can and those of you who cannot get rifles, get shotguns and if you cannot get these, get the pike, a row of ten-foot pikes will beat a row of bayonets any day."

At the Mansion House, Dublin: "If England is out for the cause of small nations, she should prove it by giving Ireland freedom.... Until the full account is paid to the last penny, the Irish people will never be satisfied. We will do our best in our lifetime. We shall not sell our birthright for a mess of pottage. If we do not succeed, we will pass on the fight as a sacred duty to those who come after us."

Then, the inevitable happened, he was arrested and once again sent to prison in England. He was in Lincoln jail when the end of the war was announced in November 1918 but, for him, on the night of February 3, 1919, there was a much more important announcement - he had escaped!

The story of his escape reads like a modern thriller. By now the acknowledged leader of the Irish Republicans, he had been closely guarded, was allowed no visitors, and had been taken to an English jail for safety. However, he was allowed to serve Mass in the prison chapel and had managed to make an imprint of the jail door key in a soft wax altar candle. At Christmas, prisoners were allowed to send cards, passed by the authorities, to their relatives outside and the one sent by de Valera had an amusing picture showing a drunken man trying to fit a big key into a lock. What the prison officials did not realise was the fact that the key in the picture was an actual scale drawing of the key required to open the cell door. The key was made by his comrades outside and smuggled into the jail in a cake. On the appointed night, de Valera slipped quietly from his cell, had a terrible moment when the outer door would not open; then he met Michael Collins and Harry Boland according to plan, and disappeared!

The hunt was on for the "Professor, aged 35, height 6ft. 3ins., a tall, thin man with light brown eyes" and roadblocks were set up and ports watched; the newspapers had him in America, in Holland and in Dublin on the same day. All the time 'Dev' as he had now come affectionately to be known, stayed quietly in Manchester, England, sending a message home: "I have escaped from Lincoln to do the country's work and I am doing it."

A few weeks later he came back home to Ireland, undetected, to Greystones where the family were now living and a newspaper correspondent was granted a secret interview. "De Valera is a pleasant man to talk to. The familiar photograph carries a slightly forbidding suggestion that is wholly misleading. Here is the face of a man that has known much nervous strain and physical suffering; but as he talks, a very human light beacons from his eyes and now and then a little humorous smile plays around his mouth." That was a well-known British journalist of the time but an American writer quoted him in a more important story:

"England tries to bind and gag Ireland, to throw her into the obscurity of a dungeon. It is our duty to support all who would lend a hand to loosing her. We must strive at least to let in the purifying light to show Ireland as she is, struggling ever against the slavery in which England would confirm her, fighting through the centuries, maintaining in blood and tears communion with all who fight for liberty everywhere - battling for it as she ever is, with her foe upon the hearth at home. Ireland seeks nothing from England but the removal of England's oppressive interfering hand. Her only demand is the fundamental right to live her own life in her own way. England has no right in Ireland. Her 'de facto' government here rests solely on the number of her bayonets... We challenge her to allow the principle of self-determination to be applied to this island unit. Let her planted colonists and all be included.... the verdict, I, at any rate, shall abide by."

In April 1919, Dev was elected President of the Irish Republic; for in the general election in December 1918, his party, Sinn Féin, - popularly translated, 'ourselves alone', - had won a complete victory with seventy-three seats against six for the moderate nationalists and twenty-six for those who still wanted union with Britain. The first meeting of Dáil Eireann - Irish Parliament - was held on the 21st of January, 1919, and a Declaration of Independence on behalf of the whole thirty-two county Irish nation was issued by the democratically elected representatives of the people. The fight was on as the elected government of the Irish nation, through the Irish Republican Army, set to work to drive out the British forces that had occupied the country for more than seven hundred years, in spite of rebellions in every century. Ireland was cut off from the world by the British navy, troops were pouring in every day, and worse was to come in the next two years. But a moment of light relief was occasioned by the announcement that President de Valera, a wanted man, would appear at 5.30 p.m. on June 23, 1919, at the Waldorf Astoria hotel in New York to meet newsmen and world statesmen.

His escape from the island under siege was almost as dramatic as his escape from Lincoln prison. He had crossed to England on a boat, walked on board a ship bound for America, disguised as a seaman, and, once again through arrangements made by Irish

Intelligence Chief Michael Collins, was hidden by Irish members of the crew. He was now in America to get world recognition for the new Republic and to raise money for his fight for freedom.

An American journalist describes him: "Eamon de Valera is easily six feet tall and may be a little over. He is very straight in figure, and very active, and he gives one the impression of strength and health. His hair is light brown, with not a bit of grey in it; and he has the nicest pair of clear light brown eyes that I have ever had the pleasure of looking into. He was dressed in a suit of very dark grey, made by a very good tailor, and he had a little bit of white around the vest and his tie was black. Eamon de Valera is not in the least conceited or affected or full of his own importance. He is like all really great men: simple, kind, sympathetic and genuine. He laughed when I told him that I was far more interested to meet him than I was to meet the Prince of Wales. Even if I was not for Irish independence, I would be for Eamon de Valera, strong, strong, strong."

His triumphant tour of the United States is part of history; millions of dollars flowed in from people in all walks of life. Sometimes even American senators became overenthusiastic; "Ireland had educational institutions of a high order before Great Britain's people had ceased wearing skins of beasts and wisps of straw wrapped around their legs to protect them from the winter's cold. I do not say that to reflect upon the British. Ireland had the religion of Christ before the inhabitants of Great Britain ceased worshipping false gods." With that speech he was welcomed to Washington but, as this newspaper report shows, things were not always easy: "Smashing British propaganda as he goes, Eamon de Valera continues his tour. Never in the history of the United States were there so many paid, and unpaid, agents of Britain working in this country to undermine American liberty and prevent Irish independence, but this quiet, earnest leader of the new Ireland, armed with justice and clad in the armour of truth, treads steadily and methodically through their ranks, putting them to rout."

Travelling the length and breadth of America, working eighteen hours a day, the young President did not spare himself: speech after speech, town after town, statesman after statesman, then speech after speech again. "There can be no final settlement intermediate between union and separation. There can be no real peace between Ireland and England until Great Britain has assimilated Ireland and definitely annihilated the distinct national soul of Ireland, which England has failed to do after seven hundred and fifty years of effort, or until England has recognised that the soul has a right to seek its perfection in statehood. England says we can have self-determination within the British Empire. What does that mean?

You might just as well give a man his freedom but keep him inside the jail yard." And so on across the nation, until, after eighteen months in America, he was so hoarse he could scarcely speak.

The news from Ireland was bad. It was now late 1920 and the infamous Black and Tans had arrived to terrorise the civilian population. The I.R.A. were waging the guerilla warfare that was to be copied later in so many other countries under foreign domination.

Terror was let loose on the people of Ireland. Nobody was safe. The civilian population did their best to hide the fighting men who had to go 'on the run' into the mountains and the woods. The 'hit and run' ambush tactics of the guerilla army was too much for the Black and Tans who hit back at their relatives and friends. If the I.R.A. member of the family was not at home when they called, they would often shoot his brother or father instead. Hostages were tied to their lorries as they patrolled during the night, to keep away the attackers. When there was an ambush, the nearest town or village was often looted and burned to the ground.

The Catholic Church, never officially on the side of the Republicans, had to take notice and, on October 20, 1920, issued a statement condemning the British action in Ireland: "Countless indiscriminate raids and arrests in the darkness of the night; prolonged imprisonment without trial; savage sentences from tribunals that command and deserve no confidence; the burning of houses, town halls, factories, creameries and crops; the destruction of industries to pave the way for want and famine, by men maddened with plundered drink and bent on loot; the flogging and massacre of civilians, - all perpetrated by the forces of the Crown, who have established a reign of frightfulness which, for murdering the innocent and destroying their property, has a parallel only in the horrors of Turkish atrocities or in the outrages of the Red Army of Bolshevist Russia.... men have been tortured with barbarous cruelty. There are cases of young women torn undressed from their mother's care in the darkness of the night. For all this it is not the men but their masters who are chiefly to blame... it is the indiscriminate vengeance of savages wreaked on a whole town or countryside without any proof of its complicity in crime by those who are employed by the British Government." Strong words from the Bishops of the Catholic Church who had been opposed to the 1916 rebellion and the Irish fight for independence down through the centuries; although individual priests, ignoring instructions, had always administered to the fighting men.

President de Valera decided that he was needed at home and, again undetected, he arrived in Ireland at Christmas, 1920, when the war was in full swing. The British had to evacuate country barracks and were now defending the towns with a ring of steel. Drunken Black and Tans had murdered the Mayor of Cork in front of his family and had set fire to that beautiful city, holding back the fire brigade at gunpoint while it burned. But the I.R.A. were winning and British military chiefs estimated that it would cost in the region of two hundred and fifty million pounds and some two hundred and fifty thousand men to wipe them out, a few thousand badly armed guerila fighters who had the support of most of the population.

He attended the meeting of the I.R.A. headquarters staff, at which the decision was taken to strike a decisive blow against the British occupation by destroying the very heart of its commercial and civilian administration in Ireland - the beautiful Custom House building on the banks of the River Liffey in the centre of Dublin. "I was a party to that decision and not without a certain sorrow and a certain sadness of heart," he said afterwards for it was, and still is, one of the finest examples of European architecture.

On May 25, 1921, the Dublin companies of the I.R.A., in a swift raid on the Custom House, set it on fire, destroying the records of the British administration in Ireland, but suffered heavy casualties when trapped by a large force of British military. But the job was done and another heavy defeat had been inflicted on the enemy. A few weeks later, a letter arrived that was to change the face of history:

"Sir; the British Government are deeply anxious that, as far as they can assure it, the King's appeal for reconciliation in Ireland shall not have been made in vain... the invitation to attend a conference here in London....safe conduct to all....convey this invitation to you as the chosen leader of the great majority....." The letter was signed: D. Lloyd George, Prime Minister of Britain, and thus acknowledged, for the first time officially, the Irish leader de Valera and the success of the fight for freedom. After much correspondence, the two leaders met in London but the Welsh Wizard, as Lloyd George was known, had met his match as he confessed afterwards: "When I tried to bring him around to the present day, back he went to Cromwell again. It reminds me of a circus roundabout when I was a boy. I used to sit on a rocking horse in front, and when the roundabout came to rest, I was still the same distance from the horse in front as when I started."

All the British Government would offer to the Irish leaders was the status of a British Dominion, with the British in occupation of the Irish ports, and the north-eastern counties of Ireland to remain entirely under British rule. This was not acceptable to de Valera and the Irish Parliament at home supported his rejection of Lloyd George's proposal, despite the latter's threat of "terrible and immediate war" with an additional two hundred thousand British troops ready to sail for Ireland, to wipe out the Irish rebels once and for all.

There followed weeks and months of letters, communications and meetings with a solution as far off as ever and both sides getting impatient. As had happened often in the past, the British now tried to split the Irish unity by intrigue. British agents in Rome, through their expert propaganda machine, succeeded in bringing about a series of telegrams between the Pope and King George V which ignored the Irish leaders and the nation's expressed vote for freedom. De Valera's telegram to the Pope put the record straight. "The independence of Ireland has been formally proclaimed by the regularly elected representatives of the people of Ireland and ratified by subsequent plebiscites. The trouble is between Ireland and Britain and its source is that rulers of Britain have sought to impose their will upon Ireland and by brutal force have endeavoured to rob her people of the liberty which is their natural right and their ancient heritage". It created a sensation in Britain.

In spite of the President's efforts, the cabinet and the country were beginning to split; weary after years of warfare, there were many who would accept the British King as head of the new State in the hope of unity for the thirty-two counties; while there were others who stated: "If you sign for the King, you split Ireland from top to bottom." The negotiations dragged on into December 1921 with Michael Collins, Arthur Griffith and other Irish leaders acting as plenipotentiaries in the London talks with Lloyd George, but instructed not to sign any final treaty without consultation with the President and the rest of the cabinet at home in Dublin, who were trying to keep the people united and the I.R.A. in readiness if negotiations broke down.

Then came the bombshell! In the early hours of December 6, 1921, Irish delegates signed the treaty with Britain, without consultation with their colleagues at home. De Valera sadly said: "There it was and I had to make the best of it... I feel it my duty to inform you immediately that I cannot recommend the acceptance of this treaty. The great test of our people has come. Let us face it worthily without bitterness and, above all, without recriminations. There is a definite constitutional way of resolving our political differences." For once, the President was wrong!

As a result of the treaty, Ireland had been given the same status as a British Dominion, like Canada, but six of its thirty-two counties remained under Britain, having a separate parliament with limited powers. The remaining twenty-six counties would have more independence but must allow British occupation of its ports and make an annual contribution to the British exchequer; Irish Republicans must also take an 'Oath of Allegiance' to the British monarch. The Six-County area - which was not a historical, economic, cultural or geographical entity - was kept under direct British control because it was then needed as a base for the British navy and, over the centuries, had been planted with British settlers who were in the majority in that particular north-eastern corner of the country. For that reason, too, it had been the only part of Ireland allowed to build up worthwhile industries.

The Irish Republican delegates admitted signing under renewed threats of immediate and terrible warfare - some of them signed very reluctantly, while others, like Arthur Griffith, justified it: "It is the first treaty, between the representatives of the Irish Government and the representatives of the English Government since 1172, signed on equal footing. It is the first treaty that admits the equality of Ireland. We have brought back the evacuation of Ireland, after seven hundred years, by British troops."

De Valera on the other hand was just as emphatic: "I am against this treaty not because I am a man of war but because I am a man of peace. It will not end the centuries of conflict between the two nations. I wanted a document that would enable Irishmen to meet Englishmen and shake hands with them as fellow citizens of the world. That document makes British authority our masters in Ireland. You will swear allegiance to the King. It gives away Irish independence. It brings us into the British Empire."

In January 1922, sixty-four members of the Irish Parliament voted in favour of the treaty and fifty-two against it, although the President had made a passionate plea: "I stand definitely for the Irish Republic as it was proclaimed in 1916" and later exclaimed sincerely: "I am sick and tired of politics and no matter what happens I shall go back to private life." When the vote was counted, all the spirit and colour was gone from his face, his hands trembled as he took up the documents from his desk, there were tears in his eyes as he saw the unity he had tried so hard to maintain, break up and he tried to speak. "We have had a glorious record for four years...." but his voice finally broke down.

As de Valera had foretold there followed two years of civil war, Irish against Irish, with himself in the unwanted position of being leader of those who opposed the settlement with Britain, and once again he was in jail, arrested by those who were once his comrades. Broken and dispirited, he had been 'on the run' searching for food in the fields; unable to return to his wife and family, moving from cottage to cottage, sheltered by friends, forced further south as town after town fell to the forces of the new Irish Free State. Griffith had died. Collins had been shot in an ambush.

Due to British pressure, the new Irish Government had attacked the Republicans and continued the executions. But de Valera had defied certain capture to address an election meeting at Ennis, in the county of Clare which had first followed his leadership. The banner over his head read: "Damn your concessions, England, we want our country." His face marked with sorrow, the thin, worn figure of the President addressed the crowd: "I have come to tell you that I have never stood for brother's hand being raised against brother." Then the soldiers arrived and, as he was dragged away, he shouted to the large crowd: "I am glad it was in Clare that I was taken. Whatever happens to me, maintain the Republic." Held by his ex-comrades in secret solitary confinement, the broken leader read books by Einstein in bad light which was to affect his eyesight permanently. He remarked, "I don't object to solitude." It was October 1923 and all seemed lost forever. Meanwhile, his wife was desperately searching for information as to his whereabouts and his teenage son, Vivien, was addressing meetings of Republicans in his absence. But the country had not forgotten him and although his Republican party only won forty-four seats in the following general election against sixty-three for the government, de Valera himself received more than twice as many votes as a government minister in Clare, and it was decided to release him after eleven hard months in a dark and gloomy prison cell.

In his famous long, black cloak and hat, he went straight back to the town of Ennis, in which he had been arrested, where thousands from the surrounding countryside, with lighted torches, waited to greet him with the cry "Up Dev". He mounted the platform and, seeing the enthusiasm of the vast crowd, smiled for the first time in many months, before beginning with the now famous historic greeting: "People of Ireland, as I was saying to you when we were interrupted....."

Soon he was to go to America again, raise funds for his new political party, gaining more seats in the new Irish Parliament all the time, and then, in August 1927, deciding to enter it as the official Opposition party in spite of the condition that an oath must be taken to the British King.

He had closed the Bible and put it away, then turned to the clerk of the Parliament and said: "You must remember that I am not taking an oath and I am prepared to put my name down here under these words in order to get permission to enter the Dáil and it has no other significance."

Arriving in his old Ford car, working sixteen hours a day, harrying the government on unemployment and social issues, de Valera soon got the support of the Labour Party and, in the 1932 election, his party was returned with a total of seventy-two seats, while the Free State Pro-Treaty Government Party, by now known as 'Fine Gael', could only get fifty-seven and, for the first time, he was in power in the new Irish State. He had fought the election on two main issues: the abolition of the Oath of Allegiance to the British King and the retention in Ireland of the five million pounds a year land annuity - then a quarter of the country's tax reserve - which the British insisted must be paid to them annually.

By this time, with the assistance of funds collected in the United States, de Valera had his own national newspaper, the Irish Press, which was helping him to consolidate public opinion for the fight that was ahead.

Once again, after the passing of more than twelve tragic years, de Valera went to London as the leader of the Irish. He told the British Prime Minister that the Oath could not be justified because the treaty had been forced upon Ireland under the threat of even more horrible warfare, and regarding the payment of the land annuities, it had never been agreed to by the Irish parliament or people.

The British refused to agree to de Valera's plea and again began to threaten, this time using the economic weapon in an effort to bring the struggling new state to its knees and thus put de Valera out of power. They imposed heavy duties and sanctions on all goods from Ireland to smash an economy depending on the British export market but the Irish Government retaliated by putting a similar duty on British goods into Ireland.

De Valera, forced back on the original policy of Sinn Féin, 'ourselves alone', of self-sufficiency, set up new industries to supply the home market. He asked the people to burn turf instead of British coal; slaughter the calves because there was now no export market; wear Irish tweeds and woollens instead of the imported materials; and fought the economic crisis at home with all the powers at his command. By this time, he had seventy-seven seats in the Parliament - his highest ever - more than all the other parties combined, and was the acknowledged leader of the Irish once again.

His speeches on world peace to the timid League of Nations in the 1930's made him a leader of international stature. At home, he set to work to bring the Republic into being, removing one by one, the pro-British conditions imposed by the 1922 treaty. In 1937, he framed the new Irish Constitution and had it approved by the people. The state was now a Republic in fact, but not in name, as he had been careful not to declare it in so many words. He always had hopes that the pro-British element in the six partitioned counties of north-eastern Ireland, who formed less than twenty per cent of the population of the island, might yet be enticed into a united Ireland which could then be friendly to Britain.

The following year accompanied by most of his cabinet, he was back at Downing Street, endeavouring to negotiate with the British Government a settlement on the outstanding differences. In April 1938, another agreement was signed putting an end to the economic war; the British agreed to evacuate the ports in the twenty-six counties and give up their claim to the land annuities, now worth some one hundred million pounds, on payment by the Irish of a final sum of ten million pounds; a trade settlement allowed many goods from both countries to be marketed duty free, but the main question of partition was as unsettled as ever. Prime Minister de Valera had even offered federal status - a continuation of their local parliament to the British backed government in Belfast, with the powers now held by Britain reverting to the all-Ireland parliament in Dublin, but to no avail. The settlers in 'the North' backed by the British, retorted - "Not an inch," and the unnatural border remained.

Soon came World War II, de Valera proclaiming neutrality as the only course open to Ireland, part of which was already occupied by British troops.

Those still remaining in the underground I.R.A. declared war on England to end partition and some were treated harshly by both the British and Irish governments. Many of them had been his comrades in the fight for freedom, which they were still carrying on in their own way, doing what de Valera himself had done not so long before. His small independent state was subject to pressures from all sides.

The Germans offered a thirty-two county republic in return for help against the British; the British threatened complete occupation of the thirty-two counties if he did not help them; even his American friends deserted and attacked him for his neutrality, forgetting that their own country did not enter the war until it was attacked at Pearl Harbour.

When the war ended, he had lost many friends at home and abroad, but he had brought his country safely through those dangerous years, free of intensive bombing, hunger and death. The largest Irish army, some two hundred and fifty thousand men, had answered his call to defend the Irish state against any invader, German or British, and sad but proud, he was still the undisputed leader.

He said in the Irish Parliament: "I am getting old and my time is short. My task has been to make our dreams come true" but in 1948, he once again went to America, this time on a nationwide campaign against the partition of Ireland, once again receiving the welcome that has only been given to de Valera. That year, too, it was decided to declare a Republic for the twenty-six counties, which then became known as the Republic of Ireland. De Valera's dream had come true, in part, but partition still existed and British troops and money still supported the local government in Belfast which ruled the six remaining counties still unfree. In 1959, after more than half a century as the political leader of the Irish, he resigned as Prime Minister and was elected President by the people - although his authority extended over only twenty-six of that ancient nation's thirty-two counties. Yet Ireland had come a long way from his early days when not even one county was free and the old man, and the young nation, were still full of a quiet, determined hope for the future.

Thus on his eightieth birthday, October 14, 1962, Eamon de Valera, President of Ireland, sat in 'Aras an Uachtaráin', Ireland's White House, and looked back over the events of his full life. That pleasant day was made even happier by the presence of his frail, white-haired wife, who had remained ever faithful and full of encouragement during all the dangerous difficult times he had faced. The Republic of Ireland in the 1960s was a very different place to the one he had known; the fiftieth anniversary of the heroic 1916 rebellion had a different setting.

The country was reasonably prosperous; the part of the nation under his care had taken its place among the nations of the world. Under the banner of the United Nations, soldiers in the uniform of the Irish National Army had fought and died for the cause of world peace. The people were well dressed, happy, well fed. The Irish tricolour flew proudly at Irish embassies in the capitals of the world; Irish men and women competed under it at the Olympic Games and international sports. Irish racehorses, Irish tweed, Irish cut glass, candy, electrical equipment, carpets, processed food, hundreds of other Irish products were selling well in many countries.

The town of Ennis in County Clare that held so many memories for him, had changed too; now new industries from overseas countries, especially America, were providing employment for the young people who would have had to emigrate not so very long ago. At nearby Shannon International Airport, jets landed regularly full of tourists on their first visit to 'friendly Ireland', while the factories on the industrial estate helped to keep the people working at home. Native Irish industries had proved their worth in world markets and were expanding. The people were happier than ever before.

That October 14, 1962, the Irish were thinking of their President too, for that eightieth birthday was one of those rare occasions when the press and television cameras of the world were allowed to join the happy family reunion.

At the races, in the bars, in the hotels, the people were talking about the days gone by; "Old Dev is looking well," they said, seeing his picture in the papers. The Irish Independent, which admitted in its editorial: "This newspaper has not been the least of Mr. de Valera's critics in the past nor has it escaped his shafts," went on to sum up the feelings of the Irish, "Eamon de Valera himself has risen above controversy and bitterness. With dignity and honour and utter appropriateness, he now personifies the nation. He has chosen to show personal concern for all that interests the Irish people. No parish has proved too remote for the President to visit it on a great occasion. We rejoice with him. May the evening of his life linger long and warm, now the storms of its noontide are still."

The scene was peaceful in the President's house where Irish turf burned cheerfully in the marble fireplace and Waterford cut glass adorned the table, resting on mats of Irish lace. Antique Irish silver and portraits of Irish heroes completed the pleasant picture as the President, old in years but not in mind, remembered other birthdays - several of them spent in prison, others in hospital for serious operations on his eyes and many with his wife and large family in their home. There, the native Irish language had always been spoken among the family and perhaps he remembered that day in Dublin when he said: "To save the national language is the special duty of this generation... our own distinctive, traditional, Irish tongue." He also remarked, "A lot of our people did not know how to go about learning the language. Now they are getting more language minded and, when they see every other country anxious to preserve and spread its own language, they will learn Irish if they have the interest and enthusiasm for it."

The fact that the majority of the people did not speak Irish was a disappointment to the old President but he never gave up hope for the restoration of the native tongue, crushed through centuries of oppression; a bilingual nation was now his ideal. The language was always important to him, almost as important as freedom itself and, half a century ago, a priest had described him thus in America: "He is an idealist glowing with the beauty and justice of his ideal, confident that men will come to see in the long run that vision of his dreams, in the meantime infinitely patient with their reluctances... his gentleness is his most striking trait.. the movement of which he is the living symbol...." Years did not change him much. The people remembered on his eightieth birthday.

The bus conductor: "My brother told me about being in the parliament one day when Dev was replying to a long debate with facts and figures, talking for ages, referring to sheets of paper on which there was nothing written. He had a wonderful memory and did not like anyone to know that his eyesight was almost gone."

The detective driver: "I was with him many times on his journeys through the country. He never forgot an old friend in a hospital, and even when he was Prime Minister, would often call into a little country cottage, unannounced, sit down and have tea, talking about old times. Once, we spent weeks searching for people he had known when he was going to school as he wanted to visit them. We found one man in South Dublin, who, when he was at school with him, had persuaded his aunt to confine young Dev to bed - "Measles are very dangerous,"- so that he could get first at mathematics just for once! Dev laughed at that. There was another time when we located a woman living in a very poor part of the city who, as a young servant girl, had befriended him during the 'troubles', and he went to visit her, too."

The teacher: "Did you hear about the time when he was 'on the run' from the British and he sheltered for a few minutes in a house, the owner of which did not support his policy? When the soldiers had gone, he escaped through the back garden. Twenty years later, as Prime Minister, he returned to thank the lady of the house for sheltering him and said, 'When I called on you before, I noticed the finest irises I had ever seen in your garden and wonder if you could give me a root to plant at home.' She did and they became firm friends."

The journalist: "He always had that 'mysterious something' which makes a world leader. You could go to his meetings hating him and yet find yourself coming away cheering him. He spoke in a quiet school teacher's voice, monotonous, full of figures and exactness, yet there was a sincerity about him that really got you. The personality of the man was immense, although you did not notice it at first."

This writer: When he heard I had gone to Blackrock College, he took my hand and said, "I spent some of my happiest days there." When I introduced some journalists from Chicago, he asked them: "Does the old Loop line still run there and are the people still as friendly?"

The President himself, on drink, which he had never been seen to take: "I never took a formal pledge against it but we all realised that intemperance was bad for the freedom movement. I think there is nothing that goes so well with dinner as a bottle of Guinness stout and I had one a few days ago."

On smoking, which he never did in public: "I gave it up on entering prison in 1916 and only tried it once after that when we were trying to encourage the growing of tobacco. I had an Irish cigar and never had a better smoke in my life, so I had to tell them to take the box away out of my reach."

On exercise: "I have gone to the dogs since I came up here to the President's residence. There is nothing but gravel around here and it is not practical for walking."

On television: "I can see the announcer by looking closely and I can see a person being interviewed but a hurling match would be too fast for me."

On life in general: "I never planned my career. You do not plan your own life. We are not so much masters of our own destiny as we like to think."

This was on the occasion of his eightieth birthday in 1962 and when he was asked what sort of a celebration was planned, he smiled, "I haven't the faintest idea but I expect they'll have something to eat." On that occasion he expressed a fear that the Irish might get too soft: "Modern life is getting softer and softer. All civilizations have fallen through softness and getting things too easily and without having to work for them. We shall succeed if we can avoid the dangers of getting too soft, if we can keep vigorous in body and mind."

He went on to speak about the international scene: "I would not like to see a future for this country in which we would be a small piece of cosmopolitanism; it is best that each nation should develop its own national personality, not just to be a molecule in a huge mass."

On his disappointment: "That our ancient nation is still partitioned." He had never given up hope that Ireland would be united and, as could be seen from his many visits to the United States, never missed an opportunity of bringing this injustice to the notice of prominent people everywhere.

A kindly, quiet, old man, surrounded by his children and grandchildren, still speaking in his deliberate, soft voice, he looked back on an achievement: "The great thing was to get the people to realise that they were as good as any other people, capable of doing as good as any other people if they worked hard enough. I believe that they now have got this confidence which will enable them to succeed."

He enjoyed that eightieth birthday, one of the very rare occasions when he allowed his private family life to become public. His wife, Sinéad, tiny by comparison, was at his side, herself a well-known author of children's stories. His eyesight had deteriorated but he could still walk briskly to inspect a guard of honour of his old comrades, just as he did half a century ago. He had outlasted in office all the major political figures in every democracy in the world and was still going strong, as happy as on that Easter Monday when he marched at the head of his men for the 1916 Rebellion.

The British Empire was then at the height of its power and he had lived to see it decline and disappear, helped to its death through the centuries by those brave men who challenged it for Irish freedom. Just as other rebellions and the resultant emigration had enabled Irish soldiers to play a major role in winning American independence from the British, the 1916 Rebellion and the Irish struggle for freedom that followed in 1920, had the same international after-effects. If little Ireland, close beside mighty England, could strike for freedom, so could far-away India, Cyprus, Egypt, Aden and many African nations, until the once great British Empire was no more. It was ironical that Ireland, the first to rebel in the twentieth century, should still be the last to get complete independence for its full territory, but the President, on his eightieth birthday, knew that, like the rest, it would come.

Late in 1965 at the age of eighty-three, he announced that he would accept another seven-year term as President of Ireland. 1966 was the fiftieth anniversary year of the 1916 Rebellion and he was once again elected President.

Peaceful and content nearing the end of his days, he could look around at a land which had come a long, long way since his youth with most of his people living full, happy lives under the Irish flag. The man whom, to people everywhere, had become the symbol of Ireland, an international statesman, could perhaps remember the words of the marching song sung by his old comrades in more troubled days long ago...." Soldiers of the Rearguard, answering Ireland's call... from Cork to Donegal... though their tasks be hard... de Valera, he will lead you, Soldiers of the Legion of the Rearguard....."

He could look back with pride, and forward with confidence, for the Irish nation had certainly come a long, long way towards its rightful place in the modern world. He had done his part and played his key role in Irish history. Soon it would be someone else's turn and the words he spoke in more distant days...." We will do our best in our lifetime. We shall not sell our birthright for a mess of pottage, and, if we do not succeed, we shall pass on the fight as a sacred duty to those who come after us."

On Friday, August 29, 1975, the Irish tricolour flying at half-mast over the General Post Office, Government Buildings and Boland's Mills - which he had successfully defended against British forces almost sixty years ago - told the nation that Eamon de Valera was dead.

People wept openly in the streets. Seventy thousand people, including the author and his mother, waited patiently most of the day to pay silent tribute as the President lay in state in Dublin Castle, once the seat of British rule in Ireland. Old comrades from the 1916 rebellion stood shoulder to shoulder with young men in Irish Army uniform. The Chief, as he was affectionately known, had made it possible and his people had not forgotten. As Cardinal Heenan, Archbishop of Westminster said to diplomats representing fifty-two countries gathered in Westminster Cathedral, London, in an impressive tribute: "Eamon de Valera found time to serve God as well as his country."

Roger Casement

2: THE LONGEST FUNERAL

The crowd had been gathering all day. Every space along the route was filled and the people were packed close together inside O'Connell Street. The monuments to heroes of days gone by, the branches of trees, and ledges of the office windows, all provided special vantage points as the hour approached.

Quietly, the guard of honour in their smart green uniforms with white trimmings took up position, many of them wearing United Nations medals from their service in the Congo, a place which now had a very special significance. A great silence had fallen over the busy city as a faint, slow sound of military music was heard in the distance.

"He's coming," whispers the crowd and edges forward just a little more. The slow, sad, music grows louder, the regular beat of the drum touches the heart. The escort battalion of infantry, their rifles reversed, their feet marching in the unfamiliar step, their heads slightly bowed, comes into sight.

Slowly, the procession makes its way through the capital. The soldiers, the bands, the national flag, the big cars with the President and the Government ministers, the old veterans of the fight for Independence, but all eyes seek out the solitary gun carriage draped in the Irish tricolour. Slowly, sorrowfully, it is drawn past the silent multitude; a woman mutters: "Thank God, he is home at last"; another softly says a prayer on her rosary beads; the men remove their hats and stand silent with grave faces; even the children are unusually quiet as the sun shines down on Dublin's fair city. Many a tear trickles down unnoticed, many handkerchiefs move quickly to wipe away the tell-tale grief; the sorrowful procession goes on its way.

As it passes the General Post Office, headquarters of the Irish Rebellion half a century before, there is a sudden and unexpected burst of thunder as though the heavens were moved to mark this historic occasion. On the gun carriage, surrounded by a special guard of honour and covered with the national flag, a solitary coffin holds the attention.

For days, the people of Ireland had filed past it as it lay in state beside the burial place of the executed leaders of the 1916 rebellion.

Tomorrow, a day of general mourning when the nation stands still, it will join the many other coffins of Irish patriots buried in Glasnevin Cemetery - but today is Dublin's day to pay homage.

It is Sunday, February 28, 1965, and the funeral of Roger Casement, hanged for Ireland on August 3, 1916, is now taking place.

Roger Casement was born at Sandycove, near Dublin, on September 1, 1863. His father, an Ulster Protestant, had resigned from the British army rather than take part in the evictions in Ireland and became a supporter of nationalist John Mitchel. Both his parents died when Roger was still young and, after his ninth birthday, he was sent to the Ballymena Academy, near Belfast, until he reached the age of seventeen. Living with an uncle, he studied many books on Irish history, especially the rebellion of 1798, and became interested in the struggle for freedom.

In 1881, he went to work in his uncle's shipping company in Liverpool and three years later, at the age of twenty, he was Assistant Purser on a big boat bound for West Africa and adventure - in the area then known as "the white man's grave." This was the period when European countries were helping themselves to territories rich in rubber, ivory, copper, tobacco, coffee, and many other lucrative products, which could be harvested with the help of millions of African slave workers.

Africa fascinated the youthful Casement and he soon joined an expedition, which lasted several years. They were led into the Congo, and hitherto unexplored parts of the continent, by a retired American general who on his return lectured in the United States of America and became well-known as an explorer.

By now, Britain was also very interested in what other countries - France, Germany and Belgium - were doing in Africa, and Casement, the expert, was offered a Foreign Office appointment in 1892. His reports from various parts of Africa raised his reputation still further and promotion was rapid; he became Consul at the age of thirty-two.

A well-known official in the British service when the Boer War began in 1899, he was to remark a few years later: "It is a mistake for an Irishman to mix himself up with the English. He is bound to do one of two things; either go to the wall, if he remains Irish, or become an Englishman himself. You see, I very nearly did become one, once. At the Boer War time, I had been away from Ireland for years; out of touch with everything native to my heart and mind, trying hard to do my duty and every fresh act of duty made me appreciably nearer to the ideal of the Englishman... British rule was to be extended at all costs because it was best for everyone under the sun and those who oppose that extension ought rightly to be smashed... the war gave me qualms at the end... up in those lonely Congo forests... I found myself, the incorrigible Irishman."

By 1901, Casement was deep in his Belgian Congo, although he had been ill, investigating the stories of exploitation of the natives, interviewing, writing, travelling, never sparing himself. His personal courage was evident as he made his way, a lone white man, through hostile territory, re-visiting villages where entire populations had been wiped out since his previous expedition six years earlier. He saw men and women workers in chains, evidence of mutilation for the slightest offence; hands cut off for absence from work were widespread.

Full of anger, Casement returned to London in December 1903 and immediately set to work on the report of his investigations which, when it was published in February, aroused worldwide indignation and made him famous almost overnight. Not yet forty, he was hailed in Britain as a great champion of freedom and the denials of Belgian cruelty were brushed aside by his compelling documented report. As they say, he had arrived!

Jealousy in the British Foreign Office, and international politics, made it expedient to 'reward' him with a promotion to Lisbon, but he was soon back in London on 'sick-leave'! "It is a dirty, cowardly, knock-kneed game the Foreign Office has played that puts me out of action. They know the truth and yet deliberately, for the sake of paltry ease, prepare to throw over an honest and fearless official whom they deliberately thrust forward last year when it suited their book. They are not worth serving - and what sickens me is that I must go back to them, hat in hand, despising them as I do, simply to be able to live."

The following year, Casement's allegations into the Belgian cruelty in the Congo were upheld by an impartial international commission, some reforms were carried out to improve the lot of the native workers, and he was vindicated. In the June Honours List of 1905, he was made a Companion of the Order of St. Michael and St. George, a decoration reserved for those who have distinguished themselves in the British foreign service. Casement was very reluctant to accept this decoration and made the excuse of ill-health when the time came to receive it from King Edward VII of England. Many years later, this pathetic souvenir was returned, unopened.

Earlier, in 1904, Casement had managed to return once again to his native Ireland and had written: "All the old hopes and longing of my boyhood have sprung to life again. What we are now fighting for in Ireland, more than anything else, is our national character. If we do not preserve that, or restore it rather, we shall cease to be Irish. The language alone could not restore it. We must recapture many other things England, or contact with her, has filched from us... I don't find Ireland depressing as you do; indeed I find it a tonic after this abominable place with its abominable people. The English beat the Irish solely because they had no music in their souls and were capable of any cold-blooded crime; and they are just the same race today... Do you know what Michael Davitt wrote of them? The idea of being ruled by Englishmen is to me the chief agony of existence. They are a nation without faith, truth or conscience, enveloped in.... an incurable hypocrisy.... their normal appetite is fed on falsehood... they profess Christianity and believe only in Mammon'."

Yet, in 1906, Roger Casement sailed to Brazil as Consul for, as he put it, Great Britain and Ireland "All my thoughts are really with Ireland." And, two years later, he was again promoted - to be Consul-General in Rio de Janeiro. Here, along the banks of the great Amazon river, he discovered that history was repeating itself with conditions similar to those he had experienced in the Congo.

On a journey back to London for consultations and leave, Casement again travelled home to Ireland, met many of the revolutionary leaders, visited the scenes of his youth, and was tempted to remain there. But the determination to help the suffering Indians of the Amazon sent him back, at the head of a special commission of inquiry, in 1910. They found the workers mostly naked; their bodies marked with scars from regular beatings; their ankles worn away from chains; and the population of the Putamayo district reduced, through murder, deaths from hunger, and other causes, by some two-thirds inside three years. The companies harvesting the rubber had grown rich on the London market and, as in the case of the Congo, Casement was once again to make bitter, powerful, enemies.

The journeys under the most difficult conditions taxed his health but he was determined to go on. Soon he was to meet Armand Normand, the most degenerate of the local 'bosses' who kept a harem of captive native women as presents for new white workers. Murder, rape, and every kind of sexual depravity were the accepted mode of life among Normand and his associates and Casement made careful notes in his diaries of their actions to build up, once again, an unanswerable case:

"Flogging was one of the least of the tortures inflicted on the failing rubber-gatherers, but it was the most universal. All classes of the native population: young and old, women and children, youths and girls were marked on the buttocks and thighs, some lightly, some with broad and terrible scars... they were chastised with strokes of the machete... held under water until they became insensible and half drowned, kept prisoner in the station stocks until they died of hunger... the ears were cut off living Indians...

they had known Indian women to be publicly violated... Senor Normand, it was clear from the evidence of the Barbadians, had for years been engaged in the inhuman cruelties he inflicted on them in his efforts to make them work rubber for his profit...pouring kerosene oil on men and women and setting fire to them; burning men at the stake; dashing the brains out of children; and, again and again, cutting off the arms and legs of Indians and leaving them to speedy deaths in their agony."

Back in London, pressure was exerted on Casement by the Foreign Office to tone down the report and they sent him to South America again for further confirmation. On the return journey, he had a favourable meeting with President Taft at the White House and on July 17, 1912, his second famous report was published. The effect of this was even more remarkable than his Congo exposé. The London company of the Putamayo business was forced into liquidation; large sums of money were subscribed for the relief of the natives; religious missions were organized; and, once again, Casement won world acclaim for his achievements in the cause of suffering humanity. He was now entitled to sign himself 'Sir Roger Casement' for the British Government had rewarded his work with a knighthood: "There are many in Ireland who will think of me as a traitor." He always disliked the title and afterwards regretted that he had accepted it, although it was for services rendered in the cause of suffering human beings, rather than for anything done for Britain itself. The London Times, in an editorial, stated: "Sir Roger Casement has deserved well of his countrymen, and mankind, by the ability and zeal with which he has investigated, under very difficult conditions, such appalling iniquity."

His career at the Foreign Office was now drawing to a close. The long years under difficult conditions in the Congo and South America had left a legacy of bad health; his own words of years earlier may have come back to his mind: "The man who gives up his family, his nation, his language, is worse than the woman who abandons her virtue. What chastity is to her, the essentials of self-respect and self-knowledge are to his manhood."

After a brief visit to South Africa to see his brother and to restore his own shattered health, Roger Casement, in 1913, retired from the British service, on pension, at the age of forty-nine.

Always a prolific writer, Casement had been writing articles supporting Irish nationalism under various noms de plume while in the British Foreign Service and had met many of the Irish revolutionary leaders. He was a tall, thin, handsome man, his black hair and beard giving a marked distinction to a striking face. Those who knew him found: "A charming, wonderful personality, an able and cultivated man with a clear low well-modulated voice, full of sincerity." With few interests outside his work, apart from a game of cards, a walk in the country, and intelligent conversation, he made many friends, even in England, where his success had also made him powerful enemies. Now free of his official duties, he flung himself wholeheartedly into the cause of Irish independence and was at the Rotunda in Dublin when the Irish Volunteers were launched. He travelled the country addressing meetings and, in mid-1914, went to America to meet the Irish revolutionary leaders, including the old Fenian John Devoy. There they celebrated the good news that the rifles for the insurrection had been successfully landed at Howth, near Dublin.

In America when the world war broke out, he agreed with the other Irish Americans that this was the opportunity Ireland had been waiting for - although he regretted it had happened at a time when he seemed assured of future American financial and other support for the Irish cause.

In October, Casement, who was now known to the British as a prominent figure in the Irish revolutionary movement, decided to go to Germany to seek aid for the forthcoming rebellion.

He travelled disguised in a Norwegian ship, bound for Norway, and was fortunate to be accompanied by a native of that country, Adler Christensen. The ship was stopped by the British who arrested half of the dozen passengers but Christensen, who had been sent by the Irish Republicans in New York to assist Casement, helped him to evade capture and they reached Oslo safely. In neutral Norway, British agents, having made an unsuccessful attempt to capture or kill Casement, tried something different. The British Ambassador in Norway, Mr. Findlay, sent for Christensen and, after several meetings and much polite conversation, gave him the following signed letter, on notepaper headed 'British Legation, Christiania, Norway': "On behalf of the British Government, I promise that if, through information given by Adler Christensen, Sir Roger Casement be captured either with or without his companions, the said Adler Christensen is also to enjoy personal immunity and be given a passage to the United States should he desire it."

Although the Norwegian and his family were in poor circumstances, he resisted this offer to betray Casement, even when it was raised to double the amount mentioned by the British official, who had remarked that if he killed Casement - "Gave him a knock on the head" - he would never have to work anymore.

Christensen told Casement of the plot against him in Norway, helping him to escape the British agents and arrive in Germany safely. Meanwhile in London, Scotland Yard had in vain searched Casement's diaries and papers in the hope of finding anything that would discredit him; agents also investigated his life in Africa, North and South America, Britain and Ireland, without result. Everywhere, he had behaved perfectly and there was not a stain on his character. There was anger in London that the man whom they once proudly displayed to the world was now taking Ireland's part against Britain. Worse still, he was in Germany with whom they were at war.

Casement now got to work trying to recruit an Irish Brigade from the Irishmen in the British army who had become prisoners of the Germans. He was also negotiating for arms to be sent to Ireland but was finding conditions difficult. His health was still giving him trouble, a relic of his days in the tropics; there were not many volunteers for the Irish Brigade to fight against the British in Ireland and the Germans were delaying a decision about the arms. Sometimes, he almost gave up hope; but, as always, he was determined to do what he had set out to do. Offered the opportunity of returning to America and safety, as the United States was not then in the war, he refused and decided to stay in Germany to complete his mission.

Almost a year and a half had gone by, he had spent some time in a hospital and now the fateful message arrived: "The general uprising in Ireland has been decided for Easter Sunday, 1916." Casement wanted two hundred thousand rifles, the Germans would only give twenty thousand, which left there on April 9th for the journey to Ireland.

The story of the ship that carried them, and its commander, Captain Karl Spindler, makes thrilling reading as they ran the British naval blockade which, by this time, held Ireland isolated from the world. Exactly as originally planned, they arrived in Tralee Bay for the Good Friday rendezvous, but there was nobody to meet them. The Aud carried no wireless and Captain Spindler was unaware that the day fixed for the arrival had been changed to Easter Sunday. The hours went by. The Aud was discovered by the British, surrounded by thirty destroyers and cruisers and forced to proceed under heavy escort to Cork. When the convoy had almost arrived, the Captain gave the order. The crew threw off their Norwegian disguise, hoisted the German flag and blew up the ship - and with it, the rifles so badly needed for the Irish Rebellion.

That was a day of tragedy. Roger Casement, convinced that the arms on the Aud were insufficient for success, had insisted that the Germans send him to Ireland by submarine in order to advise the leaders to postpone the rebellion. Three Irish revolutionaries on their way to signal the Aud took the wrong turning in the dark and two were drowned. Nobody knew that Casement was coming home at all; he had been at sea, cramped in a tiny cabin, almost without sleep, for more than a week. When he struggled ashore from the

German submarine on lonely Banna Strand, he was exhausted and half-drowned. The captain of the German submarine sighted another vessel, thought it was a British destroyer and hurried away - not knowing that it was his own ship, the Aud, waiting in the bay.

Casement lay on the strand exhausted in a makeshift hiding place, and waited patiently while his two companions, also landed from the German submarine, went for assistance. A few hours later, before they returned, the police had found him and he was arrested. Once again Roger Casement was in a position to alter the course of history. The local volunteers had a hurried meeting to discuss the possible rescue of Casement but it was decided to follow the strict order they had been given from the capital - not to do anything that week which might alert the British to the plan for a general rebellion on Sunday. So the prisoner was left to his fate for the sake of the country that he loved.

When Easter Sunday, the day scheduled for the start of the Irish rebellion, dawned in Dublin, Roger Casement was in Scotland Yard, London, for the first of several 'third-degree' examinations. He was later secretly lodged in the dreaded Tower of London. Expecting to be taken out and shot every minute - as the fifteen leaders of the rebellion in Dublin had been after they had surrendered as prisoners of war - he was told that his friends had forsaken him. In fact, they had been searching London for his whereabouts for almost two weeks and when they eventually saw him, "He was terribly changed, his clothes were dirty, his face unshaven, and eyes red around the rims and bloodshot; his manner hesitating, and he was unable to remember names or words. His tie, bootlaces and braces had been taken away from him: he was collarless and had to hold up his trousers. I discovered afterwards that his cell in the Tower was verminous and his poor arms, head and neck were all swollen with bites. Thus does England chivalrously treat her enemies... in a cell to which daylight did not penetrate and which was lit by one dim electric lamp. Two soldiers were with him day and night. They were forbidden to speak to him... he asked me to procure some insecticide as he had become infested with lice in the Tower and it caused him torture."

Shortly after his friends discovered where he was held, the prisoner was moved to Brixton Prison. There the warders treated him with more humanity; his friends brought him some clothes and thus he took the stand on the Old Bailey in June 1916 on trial for treason: "I don't want to die and leave you and the rest of your dear ones but I must..... they want my death, nothing else will do. And, after all, it's a glorious death to die for Ireland." The trial of Casement was a farce insofar as, unknown to him, his defence counsel appears to have made a deal with the prosecution. The chief defender was Sergeant Sullivan whose one regret was that the trial was not held in Ireland, for then he would have been the prosecutor: "Casement was a liar, a rogue, a paid spy, a lunatic, a sex maniac, a traitor and a murderer.. he did not deserve a trial but should have been shot at sight..." said the man who was defending him. In actual fact, he had little defence prepared because, unknown to Casement and his other lawyer, Sullivan seems to have agreed with the prosecution suddenly to plead insanity and have Casement immediately committed to an asylum, out of the way. The reason for this was that legal minds did not agree that the treason act of 1351, under which he was charged, applied to his case at all. But the insanity plea had to be abandoned when the other lawyers on the case heard about it by accident and opposed it. Sullivan had prepared little defence, did not call the witnesses Casement had suggested, crowned his performance by collapsing, or pretending to collapse in court, and did not appear at all for the last day of the trial. The night the Casement trial ended, Sullivan was out celebrating in London's West End and when the American lawyer on the case, Michael Francis Doyle, was asked why Sullivan had defended Casement, he replied: "He did it for the money." He had received more than one thousand pounds for the defence from Casement's friends, who included: Sir Arthur Conan Doyle (The creator of Sherlock Holmes); George Bernard Shaw (the author of Pygmalion); William Cadbury (the chocolate millionaire) and many other people prominent in Britain and America. Sullivan was later promoted to be a British judge in Ireland but during the war of Independence there, was given twenty-four hours by the Irish Republican Army to leave the country forever.

The Chief Justice at Casement's trial had been involved in a notorious scandal some years previously and he had been brilliantly defended by F. E. Smith, who was now the Attorney General prosecuting at the trial. Smith, and his colleague, Carson, had, two years previously, organized an army of Protestant Orangemen in the city of Belfast to resist Irish independence and they had brought in rifles from Germany - which was now Casement's crime. Smith hated Casement and all he stood for.

Thus faced with a hostile judge and prosecutor, and an unreliable defence, Casement had no hope, "They want my death, nothing else will do." The first morning, he fidgeted a little in court and appeared a bit nervous - not unexpected considering his ordeal in the dreaded, medieval Tower. But as the trial progressed, he was able to smile, take notes, and listen intently, "a tall slim figure, a classical head poised between slightly drooping shoulders, a dark, striped tweed suit, a narrow double collar, a bluish tie... his head held high.... he seemed to be as vigorous as a man of his tall, lithe form and apparently nervous constitution could be expected to be... his black, wavy hair was parted at the side and brushed with care; his black moustache and pointed beard were well-trimmed and curly... he smiled at friends and stood easily, and with dignity, as he heard the indictment against him."

A procession of British soldiers, from Ireland, gave evidence that Casement had approached them to join his Irish Brigade when they were prisoners of the Germans but they had to agree that he asked them to fight in Ireland and for Ireland, not for Germany. Evidence was given of his arrest and, near the end, came Casement's speech from the dock:

"From the moment I landed on the Continent until I came home again to Ireland, I never asked for, nor accepted, a single penny of foreign money, neither for myself, nor for the Irish cause, nor for any purpose whatsoever. I refute so obvious a slander. I left Germany a poorer man than I had entered it... the pension I had earned by services rendered and it was assigned by law. The knighthood it was not in my power to refuse... for the Attorney General of England, there is only England, there is no Ireland, there is only the law of England, no right of Ireland, the liberty of Ireland and of Irishmen is to be judged by the power of England. Yet for me, the Irish outlaw, there is a land of Ireland, a right of Ireland... if I did wrong in making that appeal to Irishmen to join with me in an effort to fight for Ireland, it is by Irishmen, and by them alone, I can be rightfully judged...our choice lay in submitting to foreign lawlessness or resisting it and we did not hesitate to choose... I, for one, was determined that Ireland was much more to me than Empire and that, if charity begins at home, so must loyalty... let me pass from myself and my own fate to a more pressing, as it is a far more urgent theme - not the fate of the individual Irishman who may have tried and failed, but the claims and the fate of the country that has not failed. Ireland has not failed. Ireland has outlived the failure of all her hopes - and she still hopes. Ireland has seen her sons, - aye, and her daughters, too - suffer from generation to generation, always from the same fate and always at the hands of the same power. Still, always a fresh generation has passed on to withstand the same oppression... the cause that begets this indomitable persistence, the faculty of preserving through centuries of misery, the remembrance of lost liberty - this surely is the noblest cause ever man strove for, ever lived for, ever died for! If this be the cause I stand here today indicted for and convicted of sustaining, then I stand in a goodly company and right noble succession... it is not necessary to climb the painful stairs of Irish history - to review the long list of British promises, made only to be broken; of Irish hopes raised only to be dashed to the ground... we are told that if Irishmen go by the thousands to die not for Ireland but in Flanders, for Belgium, for a patch of sand on the deserts of Mesopotamia, or a rocky trench on the heights of Gallipoli, they are winning self-government for Ireland. But if they dare to lay down their lives on their native soil, if they dare to dream even that freedom can be won only at home by men resolved to fight for it there, then they are traitors to their country... but history is not so recorded in other lands. In Ireland alone, in this twentieth century, is loyalty held to be a crime. If loyalty be something less than love and more than law, then we have had enough of such loyalty for Ireland or Irishmen. Self-government is our right, a thing born in us at birth, a thing no more to be doled out to us, or withheld from us, by another people than the right to life itself - the right to feel the sun or smell the flowers or love our King. It is only from the convicts these things are withheld, for crime committed and proven - and Ireland, that has wronged no man, that has injured no land, that has sought no dominion over others, Ireland is being treated today among the nations of the world as if she were a convicted criminal. If it be treason to fight against such an unnatural fate as this, then I am proud to be a rebel and shall cling to my 'rebellion' with the last drop of my blood."

Already convicted, Casement heard the words: "You are to be taken hence to a lawful prison, and thence to a place of execution and that you be there hanged by the neck until you are dead." He was unmoved, "Casement... withstood the shock of sentence like a sphinx... rested his arms squarely on the dock rail... he waved twice to women friends!" After the trial, he was taken to Pentonville prison, put in the condemned cell, dressed in a blue convict's dress and a prison cap. "A felon's cap, the brightest crown an Irish head can wear."

At this stage, although condemned to death, nobody believed that Casement would be hanged. His influential friends immediately started a petition for a reprieve which was signed by most of the prominent people of the day. But the real reason why Casement could not be hanged was America. The Americans had not yet entered the war which had been in progress for two years but American support was now vital to Britain if she was to defeat Germany. The British Ambassador in Washington had reported: "All are agreed that it will be dangerous to make Casement a martyr. The great bulk of American public opinion, while it might excuse executions in hot blood, would greatly regret an execution some time after the event. It is far better to make Casement ridiculous than a martyr...if he is executed, his execution would be an even more formidable weapon."

It was now the end of June, 1916, and the 'executions in hot blood' mentioned in the British Ambassador's letter were those of the fifteen leaders of the 1916 rebellion who were shot after they had surrendered. The Irish-Americans occupied a powerful position in American politics at that time and were naturally completely anti-British; the rest of the American public, as did the rest of the world, greatly admired Casement for his humanitarian work in the Congo and in South America. It was also pointed out that he had not ever fired a shot in anger. Bishops, politicians, prominent businessmen, authors, leaders in every walk of life in Britain, were petitioning for his reprieve. While this, in itself, might not have been sufficient to have the sentence commuted, the fact that the United States was officially considering a request along these lines, due to public demand, was vital, for Britain realised that American help was now necessary to win the war.

Thus, once again, Casement was making history - what happened to him could change the fate of the world. If he was hanged, America would be even more reluctant to enter the war on the British side; but if he was reprieved, it would bring down the British Government and many of its top officials would end their days in prison, for, behind the scenes, in a small room in London's famous Scotland Yard, one of the most infamous deeds known to history had now been completed. It was a gamble for high stakes, perhaps victory in the world war, and Roger Casement was to be the victim of this terrible crime.

F. E. Smith had publicly prosecuted Casement and later proudly exclaimed to the Boston Post: "After the trial of Roger Casement, I threatened to resign from the Cabinet unless this traitor was executed. You will remember what a tremendous effort was made to save Casement and for a time the Government was wobbling. I gave them the choice of Casement or myself. Nothing gave me greater delight than the hanging of Casement." But it was the back-room boys of Scotland Yard and British Intelligence that brought about his execution. When Casement had first been taken to London as a prisoner he was questioned there for several days and wrote of it: "I heard them later discussing the matter amongst themselves... they want more to hold me up to contempt and ridicule, than to hang me. To hang me would be to make a martyr of me in Irish eyes and they want to destroy my reputation as an Irishman." He did not realise then how near he was to the terrible truth.

When the campaign for the reprieve of Casement seemed certain of success, copies of the notorious "Black Diaries" were secretly distributed. His influential friends faded away; the President of the United States decided not to intervene; the Protestant and Catholic Archbishops in Britain withdrew their support; prominent people, with some honourable exceptions, were afraid to be associated with his very name and it can be truly said that those diaries caused his death.

Today, more than seventy years afterwards, the Casement Diaries are still one of the great controversies and mysteries. Casement was the victim of one of the greatest campaigns of calumny known to the modern world. Falsified documents, called Casement Diaries, full of every kind of sexual perversion and homosexual activities, were distributed by British ambassadors, secret agents, military and naval personnel, across the globe, and his supporters disappeared.

From the memories of a top British Intelligence officer: "Admiral Sir Reginald Hall, head of Naval Intelligence, brought me to see Sir Basil Thomson, Chief of the C.I.D. There were a lot of papers on Thomson's desk and they included the Casement Diaries... Thomson said, 'Sir Cecil Spring Rice, Ambassador in Washington, is very worried about the Irish-Americans over there and Admiral Hall wants you to take these copies to him...We are anxious to get hold of anything to quell the anti-British movement...' we were in a rather difficult position at that time and if the anti-British movement had been allowed to grow it might have had a very bad effect upon the war." The officer who was handed the documents had then been instructed to go to the Bank of England where he was to be given a million pounds for America - it cost a lot of money to ruin a man like Casement!

The names mentioned, Thomson and Hall, are of vital importance for it is probably these men, with one other, who may have forged the Casement Diaries. Basil Thomson was the Chief of the Special Branch at Scotland Yard whose main wartime job was dealing with spies and foreign agents. He worked in close co-operation with Reginald Hall. Both were knighted and Hall was the head of the Naval Intelligence Service which specialised in forgeries, false passports and identity papers for British agents; they were both experts at their jobs - the production of faked documents, the forwarding of faked messages to the enemy, in fact, all the now well-known secret agent tricks and devices. These are the two men who interrogate Casement on his arrival in London, the ones he overheard plotting, "they want to destroy my reputation..."

It was Thomson who claimed to have discovered the alleged diaries, but, unfortunately for him, over the years, he gave different accounts of where and when he got them. In the first account, when Casement was in prison, he said that after Casement's arrest in 1916, he had sent the police to his old lodgings where they found a trunk, and, when it was opened, the diaries were inside. This had been exposed as untrue because all Casement's belongings including his diaries, which he had left behind in London, were immediately sent to Scotland Yard and had been there since 1916. If there had been anything incriminating or immoral in them, they would have been distributed then, at the time when the British Ambassador in Norway was offering ten thousand pounds to get rid of Casement. F.E. Smith, who prosecuted at the trial and later became Lord Birkenhead, said they were discovered buried in the sand where Casement landed in Kerry; Thomson later said they were found by a man then dead; it was even announced that the diaries were discovered four days after Casement's capture. So the first essential for a document of this nature, proof of its origin, was missing.

Ben S. Allen, noted American journalist, was a member of Associated Press, London Bureau at the time of the Casement trial and was shown the document by Admiral Sir Reginal Hall. "I read it over rather perfunctorily until my eye caught passages tending to confirm the gossip I had already heard concerning the document... my own theory is that it was a diary copied by Sir Roger Casement during the Putamayo investigations." Allen was put under pressure to use the material in his despatches to America but asked permission to see Casement first and confront him with the alleged diary. This permission was refused. It is worth mentioning that Allen returned to see the diaries many years later and stated that the documents now said by the British to be Casement's were not those he was shown by the British in 1916!

One of the few reputable people who have been allowed carefully to examine, over a period of days, the alleged homosexual diaries in more recent times, the late Dr. Herbert Mackey, found definite evidence of forgery: "I noted many instances of words having been changed by the means of erasure of some letters and substitution of others. In other cases a complete word was erased or bleached out and a different word put in its place. The effect of these alterations is to change perfectly innocent entries into ones which are highly suggestive, where not frankly lewd. Elsewhere, whole phrases were removed and another set of words written in instead with the same object. Many short sentences, consisting of five, four or three words were added here and there, at the end of existing entries... Sometimes longer sentences were put in where space allowed. This course was followed where there was room at the end of the diarist's entry for the day. Here, as elsewhere, the words written in are quite at variance with the preceding text and, usually, in the language of the gutter."

Dr. Mackey identified many of the people innocently mentioned in the diaries and each of them was of blameless character, highly respected in their community. But with the addition of the forged material into the diary these people, who included Catholic priests, became male prostitutes walking the street for hire for a few shillings.

Many people believed what was written in the diaries was authentic because of the high position of those knighted gentlemen, Hall and Thomson, who introduced them to the world. In the British Foreign Office at that time there was a notorious homosexual whose job was the forgery of wartime documents. It is likely that he was a party to the plot against Casement; a short time later he was found hanged in his room.

While his alleged diaries were being hawked around the world, Casement knew nothing of the falsification and naturally accepted full responsibility for the contents of the diaries as written by him. He did not discover until July 6th - a week after he had been sentenced to death - that diaries, full of indecencies, had been presented as his at a press conference, given by Hall. An American lawyer, M.R. Doyle, told Casement of this in his prison cell and he replied: "Such entries I did not write. I am not the author of any single one of them." His letter to the British Home Secretary demanding to be shown the documents and to have the opportunity of a public inquiry, was never even answered and he wrote to his solicitors, "regarding any scandalous references alleged in my diaries, any such entries are false and malicious and can be nothing but wicked forgeries. Get my diaries back and do all in your power to expose this monstrous fraud."

But time was running out. Casement said to the prison chaplain: "The British must have touched the lowest depths when they carried out this forgery for the purpose of destroying my character. Can anything exceed this villainy?" Later, he exclaimed: "My dominating thought was to keep Ireland out of the war. England had no claim on us by Law or Morality or Right. Ireland should not sell her soul for any mess of Empire."

Father James McCarroll tells the sad story: "The years have not dimmed the memory of a noble, gentle, lovely soul. It was a lonely place, the condemned cell at Pentonville prison. We met on the evening of June 29th, 1916, Feast of St. Peter and St. Paul, and thus began a friendship which I know has lasted far beyond the third of August 1916, the day on which he went to God. We met on the 29th of June and we met daily until the 3rd of August, until his lonely burial in the prison yard, with all the rites and ceremonies of the Church. I was the sole mourner at his grave, yet we were not all alone, for around were the prayers of his friends - and the souls of noble men who thought the same thoughts and dreamed the same dreams as Roger Casement."

The two weeks before Casement's execution brought him more tortures of mind and soul. He had been baptized a Catholic - his mother was of that faith - and in recent years had felt himself being drawn more into this religion. "If I die tomorrow, bury me in Ireland and I shall die in the Catholic faith for I accept it fully now. It tells me what my heart sought long in vain; in Protestant coldness I could not find it but I saw it in the faces of the Irish. Now I know what it was I loved in them. The chivalry of Christ speaking through human eyes - it is from that source all lovable things come, for Christ was the first Knight - and now goodbye. I write still with hope - hope that God will be with me to the end and that all my faults and failures and errors will be blotted out by the Divine Knight and Divine Nationalist."

But even this consolation was to be denied him in his last few weeks. So effective had been the slander campaign against his name, that Catholic Cardinal Bourne refused permission for the prison chaplain to give Casement the Sacraments. The Cardinal insisted that Casement first sign a public document "expressing sorrow for any scandal he might have caused by his acts private and public." Naturally, Casement refused and replied to the Cardinal "in all humility" offering to make a sworn public profession of his faith but declining to accept a condition which would brand him as a man of ill-fame in his private life and give the enemies of Ireland further ammunition against the cause he held so dear. So the Cardinal refused to have Casement reconciled to the Catholic Church and it was now August, 1916.

As the minutes ticked away in that drab and lonely British prison cell, the man who had just a short time before been the toast of the world's capitals, prepared to meet his Maker. Although he had suffered a great deal, he was still the same man who prompted a British journalist to write, a few short years previously: "Imagine a tall, handsome man, of fine bearing; thin, more muscle and bone, a sun-tanned face, blue eyes and black, curly hair. A pure Irishman he is, with a captivating voice and a singular charm of manner. A man of distinction and great refinement, high-minded and courteous, impulsive, poetical. Quixotic, perhaps, some would say, and with a certain truth, for few men have shown themselves so regardless of personal advancement. Tall, muscular, lithe, with swing of the torso and limbs, chest thrown out, neck held high, suggestive of one who has lived long years in the vast, open spaces. Jet black hair and beard covering cheeks hollowed out by tropical inroads, and a chin prominent, narrow and square. Strongly-marked features. A dark, penetrating eye, a little sunken in the socket. A long, lean swarthy Vandyke type of face, graven with power and, withal, great gentleness. An extraordinary handsome and arresting face... I have never known such personal magnetism emanate from any man. It was felt by all."

Not much later, when he was in the service of Ireland instead of Britain, the popular British press screamed for the death of this `pervert' and `traitor' but some of the more respectable had a different theme in August 1916. "Of a man discredited otherwise before the world they will have made a martyr to live long in the traditions of Irishmen at home and abroad. They - the British Government - have set at naught the very unusual request of the Senate of the United States, disregarding utterly the sentiments of a nation on whose goodwill much depends. It was open to them to pay some regard to this man's notable services to his country and to humanity in the past..."

Another, The Times, traditionally anti-Irish commented: "...We cannot help protesting against certain other attempts which have been made to use the Press for the purpose of raising issues which are utterly damaging to Casement's character, but which have no connection whatever with the charges on which he was tried. These issues should either have been raised in a public and straightforward manner, or they should have been left severely alone... It would have been fortunate for everyone concerned, and the simplest act of justice, if he had been shot out of hand on the Kerry coast. But if there was ever any virtue in the pomp and circumstances of a great state trial, it can only be weakened by inspired innuendoes which, whatever their substance, are now irrelevant, improper and un-English."

But the death of Casement was now essential to Smith, - "I gave them the choice of Casement or myself. Nothing gave me greater delight than the hanging of Casement". If he was allowed to live, the whole story of the forgery would be exposed and the British Government might be forced to resign.

The final curtain was now coming down. On Wednesday evening, August 2, 1916, Roger Casement made his first confession and was reconciled to the Catholic Church, by virtue of the special powers held by a priest when death is imminent.

"And if I die as I think is fated tomorrow morning, I shall die with my sins forgiven and God's pardon on my soul and I shall die with many good and brave men. Think of the long succession of the dead who died for Ireland - and it is a great death. Oh, that I may support it bravely. If it be said I shed tears, remember they come not from cowardice but from sorrow - and brave men are not ashamed to weep sometimes.

"And I hope I shall not weep, but if I do, it shall be nature's tribute wrung from me, one who never hurt a human being, and whose heart was always compassionate and pitiful for the grief of others.

"The long waiting has been a cruel thing, three months and eleven days now..."

The long waiting was almost over and his life neared its end. "It is a strange, strange fate, and now, as I stand face to face with death, I feel just as if they were going to kill a boy. For I feel like a boy - and my hands are free from blood and my heart always so compassionate and pitiful that I cannot comprehend how anyone wants to hang me.

"It is they, not I, who are the traitors filled with lust for blood, of hatred of their fellows.

"These artificial and unnatural wars prompted by greed of power are the source of all misery now destroying mankind... God gave me into this captivity and death, and I kiss the Divine hand that leads me to the grave.

"Alas, so much of the story dies with me, the old, old story, yet, in spite of all - the truth and right lives on in the hearts of the brave and lowly. It is better that I die thus on the scaffold.

"It is a glorious death for Ireland's sake with Allen, Larkin and O'Brien and Robert Emmet, and the men of '98 and William Orr, all for the same cause, all in the same way. Surely it is the most glorious cause in history. Ever defeated, yet undefeated."

Fathers James McCarroll and Thomas Carey, the prison chaplains, take up the story.

Pentonville prison in England, August 3, 1916. "Mass was said in the prison chapel at seven-thirty on the morning of his execution. It was at this Mass that Roger Casement received his first Holy Communion which was also his Viaticum. It was a day of great spiritual joy for him. He expressed a desire to go to the scaffold fasting so, as he said, that God might be the last food he took on earth.

"The intervening time between Mass and nine o'clock was passed in prayer. I gave him the Holy Father's Blessing, with Plenary Indulgence attached, shortly before his execution and, for an hour before, he followed me in fervent and earnest prayer.

"He marched to the scaffold with the dignity of a prince and towered straight over all of us on the scaffold. He feared not death and he prayed with me to the last. Quietly he submitted to the attentions of the executioner, with his hands bound, repeating the words, 'Into Thy hands I commend my spirit'. It was an edifying Catholic death and it was wonderful how he grasped the Catholic faith at the end. I have no doubt that he has gone to Heaven. His last words were, 'Lord Jesus receive my soul'."

Thus, Roger Casement died on August 3, 1916, and thereby took his honourable place among the Irish patriots who had died the same death down through the centuries of British oppression. But the conspiracy to ruin his good name and his character still went on with the refusal of the British Government to have the Casement Diaries examined by impartial scientific experts.

Yet, those days in 1965, fifty years after his death when the whole Irish nation paid him the highest honours of Church and State as his body returned for re-burial in Dublin, were proof - if needed - that Roger Casement had taken his rightful place among the heroes in Ireland, where there is no doubt that he was one of the noblest men, of the highest moral character and integrity. His memory lives on whenever men fight, and speak out for `Right against Might', whatever the consequences, and will be remembered when those who sought to destroy him are long forgotten.

In that lonely, English prison cell, three weeks before his execution, Casement wrote, for his priest, the following verse which asks for remembrance in our prayers:

"Think of a long road in a valley low,
Think of a wanderer in a distance far, lost like a voice among the scattered hills.
And when the moon is gone and ocean spills its waters backward from the trysting bar.
And in the dark furrows of the night there tills, a jewelled plough and many a falling star moves you to prayer,
Then will you think of me on the long road that will not ever end."

WOLFE TONE IN FRENCH UNIFORM

3 UNITED WE STAND - DIVIDED WE FALL

"Who Fears to Speak of '98" is a folk ballad well-known in Ireland today, but, less than two hundred years ago, Lord Holland of England had this to say... "The fact is incontrovertible, that the people of Ireland were driven to resistance, which, possibly, they meditated before, by the free quarters and excesses of the soldiery, which were such as are not permitted in civilized warfare, even in an enemy's country.

"Trials, if they must so be called, were carried on without number, under martial law... floggings, picketings, death, were the usual sentences... many were sold at so much per head to the Prussians... families, returning peaceably from Mass, assailed without provocation, by drunken troops and yeomanry, and the wives and daughters exposed to every species of indignity, brutality and outrage..."

The year passed on and still the country submitted to the brutality and excesses of the British garrison, their yeomanry, and a new method of torture without trial... "The Pitch Cap was made of strong, brown paper or coarse linen. The linen or paper was smeared with hot, melted pitch and pressed down on the closely cropped head of the victim - when the pitch was hardened, the victim was turned loose amid the jeers of the soldiers: sometimes, if the pitch had got into his eyes, his blundering about would afford additional amusement. They devised the additional torture of rubbing moistened gunpowder into the cropped hair and setting it alight. The effect of all this was to drive the unfortunate victim insane or cause him to kill himself..." Half hanging, which is self-explanatory, was widely practised and it was a common sight to see bodies, with some life still remaining, hanging from a tree or a gatepost in the country... while villagers were afraid to sleep at home at night in case the soldiers arrived... homes were destroyed... men, women and children outraged in every way..."

Then, the little chapel of Father John Murphy was burned down and the young priest found himself the leader of a rebel army ready to follow him to the end.

Born in County Wexford about 1753, John Murphy had been educated in the local hedge-school - by a teacher hiding from the authorities - later making his way to the seminary at Seville, Spain, where he was ordained, took the degree Doctor of Divinity, and then returned home to the parish of Boolavogue in Wexford. The best ball-player in the parish, light complexioned, about five feet nine inches, Father Murphy went about his priestly duties. He was against armed resistance and had advised his parishioners to surrender their weapons. However, the continued outrages against innocent people left him no choice and he took up arms with his faithful followers - thus starting the planned rebellion prematurely, long before the United Irishmen were ready to fight. However, people from all over Wexford flocked to his camp, and, two days later, on May 26, 1798, the big town of Enniscorthy was in the hands of the rebels.

Onwards the insurgent army poured into Wexford town, the soldiers retreating after many bloody battles. Bagenal Harvey, a Protestant landowner, was now the Commander-in-Chief of the insurgents and two Catholic priests, Father Murphy and Father Philip Roche, were always near him in the centre of the fight. They laid siege to the town of New Ross. "The thundering of the cannon shook the town; the very windows shivered in pieces with dreadful concussion. I believe six hundred rebels lay dead in the street. They would often come within a few yards of our guns. One fellow ran up and, taking off his hat, thrust it up the cannon's mouth, the length of his arm, calling to the rest - `Come take her now, me boys, she's stopped'..."

More than two thousand rebels were killed in this unsuccessful attack as pikes, swords and old muskets were of little value against cannon fire from a defended town. The bravery of these gallant pikemen in the following days, as they charged against superior forces, carrying all before them, won widespread admiration. Meanwhile, a further five regiments of troops arrived from England and the days of the rebels were numbered. No mercy was shown to a rebel, or to anyone the soldiers suspected of being a rebel. The news items of the time make this clear... "Father Roche came down to parley with the troops but was taken and hanged after being fearfully beaten... the rebel General, Father John Murphy, experienced similar treatment from the army. He was desired to work miracles and otherwise scoffed at and insulted by a young officer, who went to the length of offering a most indecent insult to his person, which so irritated the priest's feelings that, though on the very brink of eternity, he doubled his fist and knocked down the officer at a blow; upon which he was unmercifully flagellated and instantly hanged... his body was burned and his head was fixed on the market house at Tullow... The betrothed of one young woman, and the husband of another, were cast into prison in County Wexford. The women were permitted to visit the captives, they exchanged clothes and the men escaped unrecognized... the women were then sentenced to be tossed naked in a blanket. Soldiers roughly tore the garments from the young women, stripped them stark naked and then prostrated them on the blanket which was prepared for their punishment. They were tossed unmercifully, amidst the brutal laughter of the assembled soldiers... the married woman was pregnant and died from the effects of the treatment she received. The younger girl, a person of great beauty, was seriously injured both in body and mind... Father Brennan fled, leaving a deaf and dumb girl in charge of the priest's house... mortified at not finding the priest, and irritated at the girl's silence, the soldiers cut out her tongue and placing her on a dunghill, slowly tortured her to death..."

Having surrendered their arms as requested by the military, some of whom were also members of the local hunt, many rebels found themselves in the position of the hunted fox or deer, to provide sport for the local gentry and English soldiers, on the great Curragh Plain in County Kildare. A woman there... "turned over at least two hundred dead bodies before she recognized that of her husband... that night, the military began searching every house in the district; wherever a rebel corpse was found, the house was consigned to flames..."

In Carnew, twenty-eight prisoners without trial, were brought out of the place of their confinement and deliberately shot in a ball-alley by the Yeomen. Another typical scene took place in the small town of Dunlavin, in West Wicklow. "The 26th of May, being market day of Dunlavin, these unfortunate United Irishmen prisoners were marched, without trial, from the market house to the fair green, on the rising ground above the little town, in a hollow on the north side of the Roman Catholic church on the Sparrowhouse Road, the victims were ranged, while a platoon of the Ancient Britons stood on higher ground on the south side of the green on the Boherbuoy Road. They fired with murderous effect on the thirty-six victims. All fell dead and dying, amid the shrieks and groans of the bystanders, among whom were the widows and relatives. After the murderous task was completed, the military retired to the market place for other acts scarcely less cruel and bloody... flogging and hanging was the order of the day, to stamp out disaffection and to strike terror into the hearts of the country people. Back at the green, when all was hushed, while the life blood was welling from the murdered victims, their friends and relatives powerless to soothe their pangs, and lurking in terror behind the neighbouring fences, the soldiers' wives came to rifle the mangled corpses of the slain. One poor fellow, who was only wounded, when he found his watch being taken from him, made a faint effort at resistance but in vain; the woman sent for her husband, who quickly settled the matter by firing a pistol into the ear of the wounded man. Another victim, Peter Prendergast, was also living, being wounded in such a manner as that his bowels were exposed. He feigned death, was also plundered, but escaped... a woman replaced his bowels, bound him round with her shawl... men were hanging in death's agonies between the pillars of the market-house..."

Another British 'Reign of Terror' raged in Ireland, an estimated seventy thousand people, some of them United Irishmen, many of them not, were killed. Catholics and non-Catholics fighting side by side for the same Irish cause; the country again terrorized into submission... for awhile. For within five years, in 1803, the leader of yet another unsuccessful rebellion, Robert Emmet, was to make his famous speech from the dock: "Let no man write my epitaph for no man who knows my motives dare now vindicate them, let not prejudice or ignorance asperse them. Let them and me rest in obscurity and peace; and my tomb remain uninscribed and my memory in oblivion until other times and other men do justice to my character. When my country takes her place among the nations of the earth, then, and not 'till then, let my epitaph be written."

Before this handsome, twenty-five-year old patriot was hanged, drawn and quartered in Dublin, his body swinging with terrible contortions for over half an hour before he died and his head and limbs hacked to pieces for public display, his faithful servant and friend, young Anne Devlin had steadfastly refused to betray him. "When threats and wheedling produced no result, the soldiers advanced their bayonets slowly until the points were at the brave girl's neck, shoulders and bosom. The bayonets advanced further and entered the girl's flesh. She was covered from head to foot in her own blood. She still refused to betray Emmet so the soldiers tilted up a common cart until the shafts were standing high in the air. Then they drew a rope across the chain or backband that stretched from shaft to shaft. One end of the rope they made a noose which they slipped over the girl's head and tightened about her neck, while the blood from a dozen wounds still ran down her body. 'I will tell nothing' cried the choking Anne as they pulled the rope until it became taut about her neck and she was lifted from the ground and swung between the shafts of her father's cart. She lost consciousness and then her body fell to the ground and lay there as if dead". But Anne was still alive and had not given away any information. Her battered and almost lifeless body was thrown across a horse's back and brought into Dublin. There, further torture and years of imprisonment awaited her followed by a lonely life of extreme poverty. The young girl who became an old woman almost overnight had not told but Robert Emmet was still to die.

Thomas Russell, Wolfe Tone's best friend, followed Robert Emmet into rebellion and he was also executed on October 13, 1803. Yet back in 1798, as terror raged through the land, it never seemed possible that another rebellion would come so soon.

In 1798, all seemed lost forever and, across the seas in far-off France, the one man who could have changed everything was nearing the end of his life too!

The Duke of Wellington, famous British hero, had spoken of him thus: "He landed in France with a hundred guineas in his pocket and had come near altering the destiny of Europe." How near he came, and how ill luck, the fates, destiny - call it what you will - stopped him, that is the story of Theobald Wolfe Tone, the father of Irish Republicanism who had fourteen 'In Memoriam' notices in the Belfast Telegraph on November 19, 1966 - just one hundred and sixty-eight years after his death and fifty years after the 1916 Rebellion.

"I was born in the city of Dublin on 20th June, 1763. My grandfather was a respectable farmer near Naas in the County of Kildare and my father, his eldest son, was in successful business as a coach-maker." The young Tone was first sent to the 'English Commercial' school kept by a man "to whose kindness and affection I was much indebted," and who recommended that he be sent to a 'Latin' school so that he could be prepared for entry into the university, Trinity College, Dublin. "I began Latin with ardour and continued for a year or two with great diligence, when I began Greek which I found still more to my taste." His father then had an accident and retired to live in the country, leaving Wolfe Tone lodging with a friend. "I became, I may say, my own master before I was sixteen and, as at this time I am not remarkable for my discretion, it may well be judged I was less so then. I do myself and my fellow students the justice to say that, though we were abominably idle, we were not vicious; our amusements consisted in walking to the country, in swimming parties in the sea, and particularly in attending all parades, field days and reviews of the garrison in Dublin in the Phoenix Park. I mention this particularly because, independent of confirming me in a rooted habit of idleness, which I lament most exceedingly, I trace to the splendid appearance of the troops, and the pomp and parade of military show, the untameable desire which I ever since have had to become a soldier; a desire which has never once quit me and which, after sixteen years of various adventures, I am at last at liberty to indulge. Being at this time approaching seventeen years of age, it will not be thought incredible that women began to appear lovely in my eyes and I very wisely thought that a red coat and cockade, with a pair of gold epaulets, would aid me considerably in my approaches to the objects of my adoration."

Wolfe Tone's son was later to say of him: "His character was tinged with a vein of chivalry and romance; and, lively, polite and accomplished, his youth was not entirely free from some imprudence and wildness."

One of these incidents of 'youthful wildness' took place soon after he had been persuaded to enter Trinity College University, when he was a second at a fatal duel and almost expelled. However, afterwards, he wrote: "I should have been more successful if I had not been so inveterately idle, partly owing to my passion for military life and partly to the distractions to which my natural disposition and temperament but too much exposed me. As it was however, I obtained a scholarship, three premiums, and three medals, from the Historical Society, a most admirable institution, of which I had the honour to be auditor and also to close the session with a speech from the chair, the highest compliment which that Society used to bestow. I look back on my college days with regret, and I preserve, and ever shall, a most sincere affection for the University of Dublin." At another time he wrote, like many another student since: "I continued my studies at College as I had done at school, that is, I idled until the last moment of delay, I then laboured hard for about a fortnight before the public examinations and I always secured good judgements. During my progress through University, I was not without adventures."

One of these adventures lasted a long time.

"About the beginning of the year 1783, I fell in love with a woman who made me miserable for more than two years. She was the wife of Richard Martin of Galway... passionately fond of acting... one of the finest actresses I ever saw... being myself somewhat of an actor, I was daily thrown into particular situations with her, both in rehearsals and on the stage... I have never met in history, poetry or romance, a description that comes near what I actually suffered on her account for the two years that our acquaintance continued..."

A note from 'The Theatre', Kirwan's Lane, Galway on Friday evening, eighth August, 1783, announces a farce 'All the World's a Stage' and lists Martin and Wolfe Tone in the cast.

But the wild life of the young student with its drinking parties, the theatre and his love affairs was nearing its end.

He was now twenty-one, "And about the beginning of the year 1785, I became acquainted with my wife. She was the daughter of William Witherington and lived at that time in Grafton Street in the house of her grandfather, a rich old clergyman of the name of Fanning. I was then a scholar of the house in the University and every day, after commons, I used to walk under her window with one or other of my fellow students; I soon grew passionately fond of her, and she also was struck with me, though certainly my appearance, neither then or now, was much in my favour, so it was, however, that, before we had even spoken to each other, a mutual affection had commenced between us. She was at this time not sixteen years of age and as beautiful as an angel."

The course of true love did not run smooth until Tone hit on a plan: "She had a brother some years older than herself; and, as it was necessary for my admission to the family that I should be first acquainted with him, I soon contrived to be introduced to him and as he played well on the violin, and I was myself a musical man, we grew intimate, the more so as it may well be supposed I neglected no fair means to recommend myself to him and the rest of the family, with whom I soon grew to be a favourite. My affairs now advanced prosperously; my wife and I grew more passionately fond of each other; and, in a short time, I proposed to her to marry me, without asking consent of anyone, knowing well it would be in vain to expect it; she accepted the proposal as frankly as I made it; and one morning in the month of July, we ran off together and were married. I carried her out of town to Maynooth for a few days and when the first éclat of passion had subsided, we were forgiven on all sides, and settled in lodgings near my wife's grandfather."

Now a young married man, happy with his beautiful Matilda, Wolfe Tone returned to the university, working hard for his degree. But life was not easy. "The tranquil and happy life I spent for a short period after my marriage was too good to last. My wife's brother, jealous of the affection which his grandfather bore her and of the esteem he was beginning to entertain for me... contrived by a thousand indirect ways to sow feuds between us, and at length succeeded so far that we were obliged to break off all connections with my wife's family..."

Leaving his wife with his relations in County Kildare, the almost penniless student went to London and entered his name as a student of law at the Middle Temple but, "This was all the progress I ever made in that profession." He seldom went to classes or did any study. Instead he began to write theatrical reviews and articles for various publications and, "At the age of four and twenty, with a tolerable figure and address, in an idle and luxurious capital it will not be supposed I was without adventures with the fair sex. The Englishmen neglected their wives exceedingly in many essential circumstances. I was totally disengaged and did not fail to profit as far as I could by their neglect, and English women are not naturally cruel."

He was again living the life of his old Trinity College days. Many of his friends were also in London, and studies were forgotten. He went to parties where good wine and good books, not about law, were in plentiful supply. He read all the books he could find on South America and the Buccaneers, - "who were my heroes" - and managed, with the aid of some friends, to write a novel, 'Belmont Castle', which was, "most relished by the authors and their immediate connections." He also managed to do a little work. "I wrote several articles for the 'European Magazine', mostly critical reviews of new publications. My reviews were but poor performance enough; however, they were in general as good as those of my brother critics; and in two years I received about fifty sterling pounds for my writings, which was my main object; for as to literary fame, I had then no great ambition to attain it."

He was delighted when word came from Dublin that his wife's grandfather, that - "rich old clergyman" - wanted him to return and was presenting his wife with five hundred pounds to help them establish a new home. He came back to Ireland, "As to the law, I knew exactly as much about it as I did about necromancy," purchased one hundred pounds worth of law books and, once again, settled down to study for the profession that he actively disliked. His progress now was quick and, in 1789, having successfully completed his Bachelor of Law studies, he was called to the Bar.

Here was success at last, at the age of twenty-six. Yet, the law, and those connected with it in Ireland, bored and annoyed him. "As the law grew every day more and more disgustful, to which my want of success contributed; though in that respect I never had the injustice to accuse the world of insensibility to my merit, as I well knew the fault was my own... As one or two of my friends had written pamphlets with success, I determined to try my hand at a pamphlet."

Though Tone did not greatly admire the newly-instituted Whig club, which had been formed to bring about some internal reform of Parliament, his first pamphlet in their defence was quite successful. Encouraged by this, he wrote another asserting that Ireland should be independent and neutral should hostilities break out between England and Spain or France. Soon his work in the Law began to take a second place. "My mind had now got a turn of politics... A close examination into the situation of my native country had very considerably extended my views... I made speedily what was to me a great discovery, though I might have found it in Swift or Molyneux, that the influence of England was the radical vice of our Government... we would never be either free, prosperous or happy until Ireland was independent... this theory which has ever since unvaryingly decided my political conduct..."

Slowly at first, and then almost suddenly, Wolfe Tone was becoming the Father of Irish Republicanism. In this he was helped by fate, destiny, providence or accident. "My acquaintance with Russell commenced by an argument in the Gallery of the House of Commons. We were struck with each other, notwithstanding the difference of opinions and we agreed to dine together the next day, in order to discuss the question. We liked each other better the second day than the first, and every day since had increased our mutual esteem... There cannot be imagined a more perfect harmony, I may say identity of sentiment, than exists between us. I think the better for being the object of the esteem of such a man as Russell."

Thomas Russell of Cork, a Protestant like Tone, who at one time had been a librarian in Belfast, became a frequent visitor to Tone's house at Irishtown, Dublin, where the latter had taken his wife, who was not then in good health, to enjoy the sea air during the summer of 1790. "Russell and I were inseparable and as our discussions were mostly political we extended our views and fortified each other in the opinions; to the propagation and establishment of which we have ever since been devoted. I recall with transport the happy days we spent together during that period; the delicious dinners in the preparation of which, my wife, Russell and myself were all engaged; the afternoon walks, the discussions we had, as we lay stretched on the grass. It was delightful."

But Tone's happiness was not to last for long. Events in Ireland and abroad were soon to force him into the leading role in one of the most dramatic, and tragic moments in European history. His days in Ireland, with his now beloved family, were numbered.

In September 1791, Tone published his best known pamphlet: 'An Argument on Behalf of the Catholics of Ireland' although, at the time, he did not know a single Catholic! "Enough has been done and suffered by us, the Catholics, to satisfy not only justice and law, but cowardice, malice, and revenge; it is time our persecution should cease..."

In recognition of Tone's defence of the Catholics, he was appointed the first Protestant Secretary of the Catholic Committee. "The fact is I was devoted most sincerely to their cause. I would have sacrificed everything to ensure their success. I would not have deserted my duty to the Catholics for the whole patronage of the Government if it was consolidated into one office, and offered to me as a reward."

The 'Catholic Church' mentioned by Wolfe Tone is perhaps difficult to understand today, but, the position in Ireland towards the end of the eighteenth century is briefly described in his own words: "...The Protestants, though not above one tenth of the population, were in possession of the whole of the government, and of five-sixths of the landed property of the nation... the Dissenters, were at least twice as numerous as the Protestants. Like them, they were a colony of foreigners in origin, but, being mostly engaged in trade and manufacturing, with few overgrown landed proprietors among them, they did not, like them, feel that a slavish dependence on England was essential to their very existence, ... they soon ceased to consider themselves as anything other than Irishmen... The Catholics, who composed the third party in Ireland, were above two-thirds of the nation and formed, perhaps, a greater proportion still. They embraced the entire peasantry of three provinces, they constituted a considerable portion of the mercantile interest and, from the tyranny of the Penal Laws enacted at different periods against them, they possessed but a small proportion of the landed property, perhaps not a fiftieth part of the whole. It is not my intention here to give a detail of that execrable and infamous code, framed with the art and malice of demons, to plunder, and degrade, and brutalize the Catholics. Suffice it to say that there was no injustice, no disgrace, no disqualification, moral, political, or religious, civil or military, that was not heaped upon them... This horrible system pursued for over a century with unrelenting acrimony and perseverance, had wrought its full effect and had, in fact, reduced the great body of the Catholic peasantry of Ireland to a situation, morally and physically speaking, below that of the beasts of the field."

Thus, the young, and now successful, Protestant lawyer championed the cause of the less fortunate majority and had begun to show the political genius which makes him one of the great figures in Irish, and even European, history for that period. The French revolution was in full reign and its new ideas of Liberty, Equality and Fraternity began to reach the shores of Ireland. By now a firm Irish republican, believing in complete independence as the only hope for his country, Tone, with a political wisdom far beyond his years, decided that it was first necessary to unite the three religious sectors under some common bond and against obvious injustices.

The Society of United Irishmen was founded by a small group in Belfast, in Northern Ireland, on October 14, 1791. "The Society is constituted for the purpose of forwarding a brotherhood of affection, an identity of interests, a communion of rights, and a union of power among Irish men of all religious persuasions." Present were eleven Presbyterians - Dissenters -, and two Protestants: Wolfe Tone of Dublin and his friend Thomas Russell of Cork. The Society was named by Samuel Neilson, a Belfast businessman and the resolutions written by Tone. To win support from fair-minded Protestants and Presbyterians, he stated the aims of the new Society to be: reform of the corrupt local parliament; justice for the Catholic majority; unity, of all classes and creeds, for the common good.

Tone saw that a popular movement could be established on this basis and was careful to point out in confidence to a friend, "I have only proposed to set up a reformed parliament... I have not said one word that looks like a wish for separation...".

Of his resolutions and declarations for the new Society, he remarked: "..they contain my true and sincere opinion of the state of the country, so far as in the present juncture it may be advisable to publish it. They certainly fall far short of the truth but truth itself must sometimes condescend to temporize. My unalterable opinion is that the bane of Irish prosperity is the influence of England;... nevertheless, as I know that opinion is for the present too hardy, though a very little time may establish it universally, I have not made it a part of the resolutions."

Wolfe Tone was now the bridge between the different religious groups in Ireland - their religious differences being carefully fostered by the British to keep Ireland divided and occupied: "... the depression and slavery of Ireland was produced and perpetuated by the divisions existing between them; and consequently to assert the independence of their own individual liberties, it was necessary to forget all former feuds, to consolidate the entire strength of the whole nation, and form for the first time, but one people."

Soon closely associated with the religious leaders, particularly the Presbyterians of the North and the Catholics, Tone concentrated on bringing them even closer together for the purpose of local and national reforms. United Irishmen clubs were formed in other parts of the country and he was confident that the ultimate goal could be achieved in time. When the Dublin Society called the citizens 'to arms' in 1792, Tone, "laboured in vain to check this folly... acting revolution before it was made." In his political genius, he knew that the ideas, and success, of the French Revolution could be duplicated in Ireland, provided the people were united. "It was necessary to forget all former feuds... form for the first time but one people."

Having at last found his true vocation, Tone worked ceaselessly towards this end, yet keeping his personal convictions always in his mind. "...To break the connection with England, the never-failing source of all our political evils; and to assert the independence of my country: these were my objects.

To unite the whole people of Ireland, to abolish the memory of past dissensions and to substitute the common name of Irishman in place of the denomination of Protestant, Catholic and Dissenter - these were my means."

His efforts on behalf of the downtrodden Catholics brought results and a Relief Bill, which fixed the legal position of the Catholics, was passed in 1793. The Catholics, in gratitude, voted Tone a large sum of money and a gold medal but, by now, he was determined that Ireland must be free.

The following year, 1794, an envoy of the new French Revolutionary Government was sent to Ireland to discuss the situation with Wolfe Tone, as a leader of the United Irishmen. However, he was accompanied by an English spy and soon the British Government, long aware of Tone's opposition, were now certain that he was an active revolutionary. Betrayed, he refused to implicate his companions and, on the understanding that they would not be harmed, reluctantly agreed to leave the country that he loved. Having sold everything he owned, except his books, he left Dublin, in the company of Matilda his wife, his three children and his sister, on the 20th of May, 1795 and arrived in Belfast to await a boat to America. The United Irishmen of that city wanted to greet him and several weeks were spent visiting his Presbyterian friends, now all Irish republicans like himself. He remembered, all his life, that day when they climbed to Cave Hill, overlooking Belfast city, and there, with hands clasped together, pledged themselves: "Never to desist in our efforts until we have subverted the authority of England over our country and asserted our independence."

Then came that fateful day of June 13th, when a sad Wolfe Tone embarked with his wife and family for America, little knowing what was in store for him in the short time left. "Our friends loaded us with presents on our departure, and filled our little cabin with sea stores, fresh provisions, sweetmeats and everything they could devise for the comfort of my wife and children. Never, whilst I live, will I forget the affectionate kindness of their behaviour."

Although forced to leave Ireland he had no intention of forgetting it. "I am an inflexible Irishman and I will never by any act of mine divest myself of that name." In fact, he already had plans for the next step towards freedom. "Before my departure, I explained... to the United Irishmen... my intentions with regard to my conduct in America, and I had the satisfaction to find it met, in all respects, with their perfect approbation; and now I looked upon myself as competent to speak fully, and for the Defenders of Ireland."

Thus, as he left Ireland to go into exile, the first part of his plan had been successfully completed, Tone was now an acknowledged leader, and would not rest until his main purpose was achieved, "To break the connection with England... to assert the independence of my country..."

On board the vessel 'Cincinnatus', bound for Delaware, the voyage was not uneventful. After about five weeks at sea, three British frigates surrounded the ship and took away the crew, and some fifty passengers, all struggling violently, to serve in the British navy. Tone had a narrow escape. "The insolence of these tyrants, as well to myself as to my poor fellow passengers, in whose fate a fellowship in misfortune had interested me, I have not since forgotten and I never will. At length, after detaining us two days, during which they rummaged us at least twenty times, they suffered us to proceed."

Having left Ireland on June 13th, it is not difficult to imagine the scene on August 1st, when, at last, they landed on American soil, at Wilmington.

"... Not one of us having been for an hour indisposed on the passage, not even seasick. Those only who have had their wives, their children, and all in short, that is dear to them, floating for seven or eight weeks at the mercy of the winds and waves, can conceive the transport I felt at seeing my wife and our darling babies ashore again in health and in safety... in a few days, we have entirely recruited our strength and spirits, and totally forgotten the fatigues of the voyage."

The Tones now moved to Philadelphia where he lost no time in contacting the French Minister, on whose instructions he prepared a lengthy document on the situation in Ireland. While this was sent to the government in Paris and a reaction awaited, there was nothing Tone could do but provide for his family's new life in a strange land. "At length I agreed with Captain Leonard for a plantation of one hundred and eighty acres, beautifully situated within two miles of Princeton, New Jersey, and half of it under timber. I was to pay one thousand, one hundred and eighty pounds currency and I believe it was worth the money. I moved, in consequence, my family to Princeton, where I hired a small house for the winter, which I furnished frugally and decently. I fitted up my study, and began to think my lot was cast to be an American farmer."

Happy with his wife, "and our darling babies," Tone went to work with characteristic enthusiasm; he soon had plans for starting a farmers' club in the area and wrote back to Ireland for seed. "...My farm is in a beautiful spot and, I believe, very healthy. The buildings are mean and I propose therefore erecting a mansion for myself in the course of the ensuing year, and, in the meantime, shall do tolerably. The soil is light and sandy and never has been properly cultivated but I hope to show the Jersey men a pattern. They are miserable farmers by all that I can see."

These happy, wonderful days for the Tone family ended suddenly. While a lesser man might have settled down permanently and successfully, with his family, in the new country which welcomed him, Tone did not forget his people in misery at home in Ireland. Once again he set out to see the French Minister in Philadelphia and there received the long awaited letter of introduction to the leaders in Paris. Full of joy, and sorrow, he returned home. "On the 13th December, at night, I arrived at Princeton, bringing with me a few presents for my wife, sister and our dear little babies. That night we supped together in high spirits, my wife, sister and I sat together till very late, engaged in that kind of animated and enthusiastic conversation which our characters and the nature of the enterprise I embarked on may be supposed to give rise to. The courage and firmness of the women supported me and them too, beyond my expectations; we had neither tears nor lamentations, but, on the contrary, the most ardent hope and the most steady resolution. At length, at four the next morning, I embraced them both for the last time and we parted with a steadiness which astonished me." And so, on New Year's Day, 1796, Wolfe Tone, unknown, with little money, sailed from America to France to free Ireland from England!

February 1, 1796, Wolfe Tone landed in France as Wellington later remarked: "With a hundred guineas in his pocket and had come near altering the destiny of Europe." After a brief rest he set off for Paris on his mission. His descriptions of life there are familiar: "My landlord is civil but dear as the devil... Comédie as usual; sad trash this evening... the beauty of France is in the country... a most blistering bill for supper... in great indignation because I could not scold in French... landlords have flinty hearts; no tears can move them... Paris; Grand Opera, Théâtre des Arts... walked out alone to see the sights; the Tuileries, the Louvre, Pontneuf, etc., superb. Paris a thousand times more magnificent than London, but less convenient for those who go afoot... saw two companies of grenadiers in the garden of the Tuileries... I think them equal in figure to any men I have ever seen of their number... Then women; only to think what a thing fashion is. The French women have always been remarkable for fine hair, and therefore at present they all prefer to wear wigs. They actually roll and pin up their own beautiful tresses, so that they become invisible, and over them they put a little shock periwig. Damn their wigs; I wish they were burnt, but it is the fashion, and that is a solution for every absurdity. In the evening, walked to the Palais Royal, filled with military, most of them superb figures..."

After he had met a heroine of the recent French Revolution, Tone wrote: "I wish my dearest love could see her. I think she would behave as well in similar circumstances. Her courage and affection have been in some, very nearly as critical..."

In spite of his interest in the French capital and its inhabitants, Tone had not neglected his main business and, within two weeks of his arrival in France, had an interesting meeting with the American Ambassador, James Monroe - later President of the United States - and had delivered his credentials to the French Minister for Foreign Affairs. Thus began many weary months of negotiations with French Government officials, military and naval staff; long discussions; large manuscripts and statements; as Tone tried to interest the new French revolutionary leaders in the freedom of Ireland. The usual 'red tape' and 'wheels within wheels' made rapid progress impossible and much of his time was spent waiting. "Dined alone in the Champs Elysées. A most delicious walk. The French know how to be happy, or at least how to be gay, better than all the world besides... March 17th, St. Patrick's Day. Dined alone in the Champs Elysées. Sad, sad. The French are a humane people when they are not mad and I like them with all their faults..."

Tone did not get discouraged as he: "Was sent spinning like a shuttlecock from one government department to another, and my mind grew dizzy from a round of apparently fruitless interviews." After more than five months of this weary round, his money low but his spirits still high, Tone at last began to feel he was making progress. He had a long meeting, the first of many, with the famous General Hoche, and they discussed Tone's plan for the disruption of the then most powerful British Empire. These two young men faced each other in Paris and General Hoche was won over to Tone's view that Ireland was the place to strike - not Egypt or India as many other French military men favoured.

Tone's plan was simple: "With twenty thousand men there would be a possibility of resistance for an hour, and we should begin by the capital - Dublin; with five thousand I would have no doubt of success, but then we should expect some fighting and we should begin near Belfast; with two thousand I think the business utterly desperate for, let them land where they would, they would be utterly defeated before anyone could join them or, in fact, before the bulk of the people could know that they were come."

General Hoche was only twenty-eight years of age, Tone was now thirty-two, and they formed a close friendship. Carnot, the President of the French Executive Directory, agreed with their plan and an Irish Expeditionary force - Armée d'Irlande - was formed, with General Hoche as its Commander-in-Chief and Wolfe Tone his assistant. Carnot remarked, at their last meeting, that the invasion of Ireland would be "a most brilliant operation" and Tone had firmly told them that, when the British had been defeated, the Irish would establish an independent Republic.

The scene was set. At the port of Brest, more than forty French ships were at last ready to sail, each ship carrying about five hundred soldiers. Tone's dream for the freedom of Ireland was becoming a reality. Now an Adjutant- General in the French army, he was leading a force to free his native land after centuries of terrible oppression and to strike a fatal blow at the connection with England, "The never- failing source of all our political evils."

On the eve of embarkation, he wrote his dear Matilda a long and tender letter - she was, at this time, already on her way to join him in France. "I fear for your safety, and that of our dear little babies, exposed to the inconveniences and perils of a winter passage. I trust in God you will get here safe and well and that by the time you receive this we shall have finished our business; in which case you and I will devote the remainder of our lives to each other, for I am truly weary of the perpetual separation... the first thing I shall do after our landing will be, you may be sure, to write to you.... I will also take care to remit you money for your occasions and the very moment that my duty will permit, I will fly with the utmost eagerness to embrace you all. God only knows how I long for that moment."

Wolfe Tone, the wild, fun loving university student, was now the serious married man who deeply loved his family yet determined to fulfil his life's purpose: "To assert the independence of my country."

Disaster struck from the start. In those days, Britain ruled the waves and, in their efforts to sail unnoticed, several of the French ships collided while one of the battleships was wrecked on the rocks. Some British frigates were sighted and, in the confusion and darkness, the great French fleet of more than forty ships was separated into small units.

Then came another difficulty: "December 18th: At nine this morning, a fog so thick that we cannot see a ship's length before us." To be followed the next day by yet another. "It is a stark calm, so that we do not move an inch even with our studding-sails, but here we lie rolling like so many logs on the water." When the winds did come, they were "right in our teeth", and made progress difficult. At night, the fleet continued to get separated and, each morning, it seemed to Tone that the number of ships was growing less.

"December 20th: Last night, in moderate weather, we contrived to separate again, and this morning, at eight o'clock, we are but fifteen sail in company, with a foul wind and haze. I am in horrible ill humour and it is no wonder. We shall lie beating about here, within thirty leagues of Cape Clear, until the English come and catch us, which will be truly agreeable. Let me not think. I amuse myself at night, when the rest are at cards, walking alone in the gallery and singing the airs that my poor love used to be fond of... Well, hang sorrow.... several sail in sight to windward; I suppose they are our stray sheep. It is scandalous to part company twice in four days in such moderate weather as we have had, but sea affairs, I see, are not our forte. Captain Bedout is a seaman which, I fancy, is more than can be said for nine-tenths of his confrères."

December 22, and Tone could now see his beloved Ireland. Sixteen French ships are anchored in Bantry Bay; others are coming, but a fierce storm is raging. "The wind is still high and, as usual, right ahead; and I dread a visit from the English, and altogether I am in great uneasiness. Oh; that we were once ashore let what might ensue after; I am sick to the very soul of this suspense... I am now so near the shore that I can in a manner touch the sides of Bantry Bay... yet God knows whether I shall ever tread again on Irish ground..."

The violent storm still prevents a landing as the Irish countryside begins to be covered with snow. The flag ship, with General Hoche, the plans and the money for the expedition, has been blown off course and lost, but Tone convinces the remainder of the French that the landing must be made: "We are not more than six thousand strong, but they are tried soldiers, who have seen fire, and I have the strongest hopes that, after all, we shall bring our enterprise to a glorious termination. It is a bold attempt and truly original... we have not one guinea; we have not a tent; we have not a horse to draw our four pieces of artillery; the General-in-Chief marches on foot; we leave all clothes on our backs, and a good courage, but that is sufficient."

The French officers and men were now eager to follow the one Irishman in this gallant adventure. "We are tonight, six thousand of the most careless fellows in Europe, for everybody is in the most extravagant spirits on the eve of the enterprise which, considering our means, would make many people serious. I never liked the French half so well as tonight...!"

Christmas Day, 1796: "The wind continues right ahead, so that it is absolutely impossible to work up to a landing place, and God knows when it will change... the enemy has now had four days to recover from his panic and prepare to receive us... had we been able to land the first day and march directly to Cork, we should have a footing in the country."

Christmas Day brings thoughts of his family. "I have, by a desperate effort, surmounted my natural feelings so far that I do not think of them at this moment." But he had no illusions about the future, "... If we are taken, my fate will not be a mild one; the best I can expect is to be shot as an emigré rentre, unless I have the good fortune to be killed in action; for most assuredly if the enemy will have us, he must fight for us. Perhaps I may be reserved for a trial, for the sake of striking terror into others, in which case I shall be hanged as a traitor and embowelled, etc. As to the embowelling 'je m'en fiche', if ever they hang me, they are welcome to embowel me if they please. These are pleasant prospects; nothing on earth could sustain me now but the consciousness that I am engaged in a just and righteous cause... I see nothing before me, unless a miracle be wrought in our favour, but the ruin of the expedition, the slavery of my country, and my own destruction. Well, if I am to fall, at least I will sell my life as dear as individual resistance can make it. So now I have made up my mind. I have a merry Christmas of it today."

"December 26th:... we have been now six days in Bantry Bay, within five hundred yards of the shore, without being able to effectuate a landing; we have been dispersed four times in four days, and, at this moment, of forty-three sail, of which the expedition consisted, we can muster of all sizes but fourteen. There only wants falling in with the English to complete our destruction......notwithstanding all our blunders, it is the dreadful stormy weather, and the easterly winds, which have been blowing furiously and without intermission since we made Bantry Bay, that have ruined us. Well, England has not had such an escape since the Spanish Armada, and that expedition, like ours, was defeated by the weather; the elements fight against us... it is lost, and let it go..."

On that day, his hopes dashed as the remnants of the French fleet dragged up their anchors and set sail for home, Wolfe Tone was deep in sorrow. "... I hope the Director will not dismiss me from the service for this unhappy failure... if God Almighty send me my dearest love and darling babies in safety, I will rent or buy a little spot and have done with the world forever. I shall neither be great, nor famous, nor powerful but I may be happy..."

On New Year's Day, 1797, seven battered ships, including the 'Indomptable', with Wolfe Tone on board, arrived back in France, the expedition a total failure and, once again, all hope for Ireland seemed lost. The only two items of good news that reached Tone were that his family had reached the Continent and that General Hoche was safely back in France.

Soon, Tone again started negotiations with French Government officials for another expedition to Ireland - but had much time on his hands in Paris. The theatre was his main relaxation and he liked to drink in the sidewalk cafés, his thoughts constantly on his wife and family. "I am sure nothing on earth has such an influence on me as my wife's opinion... it is inconceivable the effect which the admiration or contempt of a woman has on the spirit of a man... I owe so much to my wife for her incomparable behaviour on ten thousand different occasions that I feel myself bound irresistibly to make every effort to place her and her dear little babies in a situation in some degree worthy of her merit and suitable to my sense of it. I am not without ambition or vanity, God knows; I love fame, and I suppose I should like power; but I declare here most solemnly that I prefer my wife's commendations to those of the whole world... Oh, my little babies, if I was to lose my Will or my Little Fantom; poor little souls, I dote upon them and on their darling mother, whom I love ten thousand times more than my own existence... I lead the life of a dog here in Paris, where I am as much alone as in the deserts of Arabia... my mind is overgrown with docks and thistles for want of cultivation and I cannot help it, for I have not a soul to speak to whom I care a farthing about..."

At last, his luck changed. His friend, General Hoche had been appointed Commander of the army with headquarters at Cologne and had requested the Director that they send Tone as his Adjutant-General.

One might forgive Tone for now embarking on his new career in the French army - he was therefore a French citizen - and leaving behind his almost impossible task of getting aid for Ireland. Yet he delayed several weeks in Paris, contacting Government officials and high-ranking officers in the army and navy, without apparent result. So, at the beginning of April, 1797, Theobald Wolfe Tone, now a high and respected officer in the French Army set off to join his headquarters and arrived in Cologne to have an unusual experience: "I have been lounging these three days about Cologne; stupid enough. Yesterday, I entered a church alone, for I visit all the churches; there happened to be no one in the place but myself, and as I was gazing about, I perceived the corner of a green silk curtain behind it. I drew near, in order to discover who it might be, and it proved to be a nun, young I am sure, and I believe handsome, for I only saw her mouth and chin, but a more beautiful mouth I never saw. We continued gazing on one another in this manner for five minutes, when a villainous, overgrown friar, entering to say his mass, put her to rout. Poor soul, I pitied her from the very bottom of my heart, and laying aside all grosser considerations, should have rejoiced to have battered down the gates of the convent and rescued her from her prison. These convents are most infernal institutions..."

Soon, Tone got leave of absence and set off to meet his wife and family, whom he last saw in far-off America almost two years previously. He arrived at the rendezvous too early. "May 3rd to 6th: Tormented with the most terrible apprehensions on account of the absence of my dearest love, about whom I hear nothing; walked out every day to the canal, two or three times a day, to meet the boats... no love; no love;... I was never so unhappy in all my life."

Then came May 7, 1797: "At last, this day, in the evening, as I was taking my usual walk along the canal, I had the unspeakable satisfaction to see my dearest love and our little babies, my sister and her husband, all arrived safe and well; it is impossible to describe the pleasure I felt..."

During the next few weeks, Tone's happiness was great, for, not alone was he reunited with his beloved family, but two items of good news from Ireland brought him new hope - the United Irishmen were ready for rebellion and there was almost mutiny in the British Navy. Here was Ireland's opportunity and, with the support of General Hoche, Tone immediately interested both the French and Dutch Governments in a new expedition. Both agreed that Ireland was an excellent target against England and soon Hoche was at Brest and Adjutant-General Wolfe Tone with the Dutch making final arrangements.

A large force of Dutch ships gathered at the Rexel for the expedition to Ireland and the French had allocated more than three million francs to fit out the fleet at Brest. Everything was ready and Tone exclaimed: "There never was, and never will be, such an expedition as ours, if it succeeds;... it is to change the destiny of Europe, to emancipate one, perhaps three nations; to open the sea to the commerce of the world; to found a new empire; to demolish an ancient one; to subvert a tyranny of six hundred years!"

Yet, once again, his high hopes were to end in frustration; the English fleet appeared to block the mouth of the port, preventing the Dutch from sailing and, very familiar:

"July 18th: The wind is as foul as possible this morning; it cannot be worse. Hell; Hell; Hell; Allah; Allah; Allah; I am in a most devouring rage.

"July 19th: Damn it; Damn it; I am, today, twenty-five days aboard, and at a time when twenty-five hours are of importance. There seems to be a fate in this business. Five weeks, I believe six weeks, the English fleet was paralysed by the mutinies at Portsmouth, Plymouth and the Nore. The sea was open and nothing to prevent both the Dutch and French fleets to put to sea. Well, nothing was ready; that precious opportunity, which we can never expect to return, was lost; and now that at last we are ready here, the wind is against us, the mutiny is quelled, and we are sure to be attacked by a superior force. At Brest it is, I fancy, still worse... had we been in Ireland... the destiny of Europe might have been changed forever... we must now do as well as we can."

The days and weeks went by, provisions were running low, the season was growing late, and the Dutch general put forward a proposal for landing in England instead of Ireland. Tone was astounded but said he was willing to take part in a daring mission to attack even London itself!

The months dragged on, the Dutch now favouring an attack on Scotland with a simultaneous landing in Ireland by the French. Months had gone by and another bitter blow was to follow. General Hoche, the brilliant young French general who shared Tone's enthusiasm for a landing in Ireland in the war against the English, died. Sad at the death of his friend, disillusioned with the Dutch and discouraged by the endless delays, Tone journeyed again to Paris.

On the way, he stopped off at Bonn, and, badly needing some pleasant company, "I had promised a very pretty woman at dinner, whose name I know not, but whose person I reverence, to meet her tonight at a grand ball given by the Municipality, but I will deceive her, like a false traitor, and go to my innocent bed; yet she is very pretty for all that, and speaks very pretty German-French, and I am sure has not one grain of cruelty in her composition... I have just received a delightful letter from my dearest love, written three months ago, which has put me out of conceit with all women but herself; so, as before, I will go to my virtuous bed."

In Paris, towards the end of the year, Tone was reunited with his family and, once again, began the rounds of interesting the French Government in yet another expedition to Ireland.

He is overjoyed when, following Napoleon's Italian victory, he is placed in command of an army for the invasion of Ireland.

Tone had by now met a Dublin lawyer, Lewines, who had been

sent to the Continent by the United Irishmen and, in December, 1797, wrote: "General Desaix brought Lewines and me this morning and introduced us to Bonaparte, at his house in the Rue Chantereine. He lives in the greatest simplicity; his house is small but neat, and all the furniture in the most classical taste. He is about five feet six inches high, slender and well-made, but stoops considerably; he looks at least ten years older than he is, owing to the great fatigues he underwent in his immortal campaign in Italy. His face is that of a profound thinker, but bears no marks of that great enthusiasm and unceasing activity by which he had been so much distinguished. It is rather, to my mind, the countenance of a mathematician than of a general. He has a fine, and a great firmness about the mouth; he speaks low and hollow... Lewines gave him a copy of the memorials I delivered to the Government in February 1796, nearly two years ago, and which, fortunately, have been well verified in every material fact, by everything that has taken place in Ireland since... His manner is cold and he speaks very little... he is perfectly civil to us... we have now seen the greatest man in Europe three times and I am astonished to think how little I have to record about him."

Wolfe Tone made many more journeys to see Napoleon, who was very reluctant to make a third attempt for Ireland and was always more interested at striking at England through Egypt and India.

The frustration grew as Tone called, discussed, explained, pleaded, again and again. The great opportunity of certain victory that he once had - when the English navy was in mutiny, the United Irishmen in rebellion, and the French forces landing in Ireland - was now just a dream, or a nightmare, as he could no longer hope to have these ingredients for certain success happen simultaneously.

The British mutiny was over; many of the leaders of the United Irishmen were either arrested or in hiding; his country was under a reign of terror as bad as that experienced during the French Revolution and, as yet, there was no decision from Napoleon.

Later, near the end of his life of captivity on St. Helena, Napoleon is reported to have regretted that he did not listen to Wolfe Tone and to have exclaimed" "If I had made the expedition to Ireland, what would England have been today, and the continent, and the political world?"

Meanwhile the British navy became more daring and, May, 1798, found Wolfe Tone, as a French officer, an Adjutant-General, commanding a fort under siege at Le Havre; the English fleet was in full attack and, as the cannons roared and the shells flew overhead, Tone, manning a battery of guns, had some disturbing thoughts: "It was a fine sight and I should have enjoyed it more had it not been for certain speculations on futurity and the transmigration of souls' which present themselves to my fancy at times. I defy any man to know whether he is brave or not until he is tried, and I am very far from boasting of myself on that score; but the fact is, and I was right glad of it, that when I found myself at my battery, and saw the cannonade, though I cannot say with truth that I was perfectly easy, yet neither did I feel at all disconcerted; and I am satisfied, as far as a man in that situation can judge of himself, that I should have done my duty well, and without any great effort of resolution."

The joy Tone felt when the last English attack was beaten off, "Vive la République", did not last long when he received the latest news from Dublin: "Lord Edward Fitzgerald had been arrested in Thomas Street, Dublin, after a most desperate resistance, in which himself, the magistrate, one Swann and Captain Ryan, who commanded the guard, were severely wounded. I cannot describe the effect which this intelligence had on me; it brought on, almost immediately, a spasm in my stomach, which confined me all day. I knew Fitzgerald but very little, but I honour and venerate his character, which he has uniformly sustained, and in this last instance, illustrated. What miserable wretches by his side are the gentry of Ireland; I would rather be Fitzgerald, as he is now wounded in his dungeon, than Pitt at the head of the British Empire; what a noble fellow; of the first family in Ireland, with an easy fortune, a beautiful wife, and family of lovely children, the certainty of a splendid appointment under government, if he would condescend to support their measures, he had devoted himself wholly to the emancipation of his country, and sacrificed everything to it, even his blood."

Ireland is now in rebellion; there are reports of battle engagements from several counties; Lord Edward Fitzgerald dies from his wounds; the rebels have little arms or ammunition and rely, for their success, on frontal charges with their long pikes, or lances, into the British guns. Tone despairs of some old friends, "... the militia and yeomanry of Ireland concur with the English to rivet their country's chains and their own, and, to my great mortification, I see some of my old friends in the number... they may yet be sorry for this base prostitution of their character and talents. If ever the day of retribution arrives, as arrive I think it must, they will fall unpitied victims, and thousands of other parasites like them, to the just fury of the People, which it will be impossible to restrain. What must I do now?"

All this time, he had been patiently negotiating with the French for another Irish expeditionary force but now affairs in Ireland reached a climax. Sometimes, there is despair in his thoughts but he manages to shake it off.

"June 20th, 1798: Today is my birthday. I am thirty-five years of age; more than half my career is finished, and how little have I yet been able to do. Well, it has not been, at least for want of inclination, and, I may add, of efforts; I had hopes two years ago that, at the period I write this, my debt to my country would have been discharged, and the fate of Ireland settled for good or evil. Today it is more uncertain than ever. I think however, I may safely say, I have neglected no step to which my duty called me, and, in that conduct, I will persist to the last."

Persist he did, and, on August 5, 1797, General Humbert, with a small force of one thousand French soldiers sailed for Ireland, accompanied by Tone's brother, Matthew. They made a successful landing at Killala in County Mayo and inflicted such a defeat on General Lake at the town of Castlebar that the engagement became known as 'The Races of Castlebar' so quickly did the opposing English forces retreat.

Within a few days, the French had captured the entire county of Mayo and much of the province of Connaught. The General sent urgent messages to France for reinforcements. "Within a month of the arrival of this force, Ireland, I am convinced, will be free!" There were the usual delays and time was running out. Terrorized by the ferocious reign of terror on the insurgents in counties Wexford and Wicklow, the burning of Catholic homes, the slaughter of the occupants in the northern counties and the lack of proper leadership or arms, the local people did not rally behind the French forces in the West. Adding to their fear was the fact that the slaughter of the occupants in the northern counties had been carried out by a new organization, formed with British Government support, called the Orange Order and dedicated to maintaining religious discrimination and persecution. On September 8th, the gallant French forces had to surrender and, as can be expected from a study of that most unfortunate 'Luck of the Irish', the French reinforcements, a second expedition, sailed for Ireland a week later - too late to have any hope of success.

Theobald Wolfe Tone, Adjutant- General in the French Army, was on board - unaware that his brother Matthew had already been captured and hanged. He was to write no more in his famous journal which was completed by his son William, who became a French cavalry officer and later a United States army captain.

Wolfe Tone, on board the 'Hoche', accompanied by some three thousand men on eight frigates, thus sailed again for Ireland. The expedition, he knew, was doomed to failure - the Irish rebellion was already defeated and the other French force had surrendered.

But this was his life's work and he had declared: "If the French Government were to send only a corporal and twelve men, it would be my duty to go along with them."

A violent gale and heavy seas once again dogged the French expedition, which was soon being shadowed by ten ships of the British navy. The French Admiral Bombard urged Tone to go aboard one of the small frigates which were successfully making a dash through the cordon back to France but he refused. They both knew his fate if captured. "... If we are taken, my fate will not be a mild one; the best I can expect is to be shot as an emigré rentre, unless I have the good fortune to be killed in battle; for most assuredly if the enemy will have us, he must fight for us. Perhaps I may be reserved for a trial, for the sake of striking terror into others, in which case I shall be hanged as a traitor and embowelled etc. As to the embowelling, 'je me'en fiche', if ever they hang me, they are welcome to embowel me if they please. These are pleasant prospects; nothing on earth could sustain me now but the consciousness that I am engaged in a just and righteous cause..."

It was mid-October, 1798, when Wolfe Tone began to man one of the Hoche's big guns, as the British fleet closed in near Lough Swilly and the hills of Donegal he loved so well.

The account of the battle tells us the rest: "Three great English ships of the line, and three frigates, bore down on the Hoche, where it floated off the Irish coast, with its main mast crippled. Tone commanded one of the batteries throughout the violent contest that followed, when, for six long hours, virtually the whole English fleet poured its fire upon that solitary and valiant vessel. It is reported that Tone fought with the utmost gallantry and as if courting death; but, although twenty-eight of the Hoche's guns were reduced to scrap iron, he was not hit. The Hoche's gunmasts and rigging were swept away, the decks flowed with blood and the cockpit was crowded with the wounded and dying defenders of the flag of France; the rudder was gone and five feet of water was rising in the hold... only when every gun upon the Hoche was silent and the vessel was almost sinking, was the flag hauled down..."

Later, the French officers, including Tone, were landed and marched, as prisoners of war, to the town of Letterkenny. At breakfast with the British commmander of the district, Tone was recognized by a local Orangeman, and immediately seized. Bound in chains, the fetters fastened from foot to foot underneath his horse to prevent escape, Tone now began his last long journey to Dublin, under heavy escort, still in his French uniform.

General Hardy, the officer in command of the French army at

Lough Swilly, protested strongly to the British.

"The Adjutant-General Wolfe Tone is an honest man; his courage and distinguished conduct earned him the confidence of the government and the esteem of all soldiers who are governed by the principle of honour; I need not, therefore, conceal from you the surprise with which I learned that you have caused him to be treated ignominiously like a criminal." The last chapter in Tone's eventful young life was nearing its end. On a bleak Saturday in mid-November 1798, Tone, now a French citizen and officer, was brought before a court martial in Dublin and quickly sentenced to death. Appearing in his French uniform, he stood before the court and proudly admitted his efforts to free his native land. "I mean not to give you the trouble of bringing judicial proof, to convict me, legally, of having acted in hostility to the Government of his Britannic Majesty in Ireland. I admit the fact. From my earliest youth, I have regarded the connection between Ireland and Great Britain as the curse of the Irish nation, and felt convinced that, whilst it lasted, this country could never be free or happy. My mind has been confirmed in this opinion by the experience of every succeeding year and the conclusions which I have drawn from every fact before my eyes. In consequence I determined to apply all the powers which my individual efforts could move, in order to separate the two countries. In a cause like this, success is everything. Success in the eyes of the vulgar fixes its merits. Washington succeeded and Kosciuszko failed. I have laboured to create a people in Ireland by raising three million of my country men to the rank of citizens. I have laboured to abolish the infernal spirit of religious persecution by uniting Catholic and Dissenters. To the former I owe more than can ever be repaid. The services I was so fortunate as to render them, they rewarded magnificently; but they did more. When the cry was raised against me, when the friends of my youth swarmed off and left me alone, the Catholics did not desert me... I ask that the Court should adjudge me the death of a soldier and let me be shot by a platoon of grenadiers."

Instead, he was sentenced to be hanged within forty-eight hours. It was Saturday, November 10, 1798, and in the lonely death cell, Tone was writing his last farewell: "Dearest love, the hour is at last come when we must part. As no words can express what I feel for you and our children, I shall not attempt it; complaint of any kind would be beneath your courage and mine; be assured I will die as I have lived and that you will have no cause to blush for me... Adieu, my dearest love; I find it impossible to finish this letter. Give my love to my sister, Mary, and, above all things, remember that you are now the only parent of our dearest children, and that the best proof you can give of your affection for me will be that you preserve yourself for their education. God Almighty bless you all."

But all was not yet lost. The French Government had already promised to take care of Tone's wife and family and there was hope of direct government intervention to prevent the execution; he was a French citizen and senior officer.

In Dublin, hope was even higher when Tone's lawyer successfully applied to the courts for a writ of habeas corpus. As he had never held a position in the British army, his trial by court martial, while the civil courts were actually in session, was illegal, even under British law. At the Court of King's Bench, the Chief Justice immediately issued a writ that Tone be brought from the prison to appear before the civil court.

The Sheriff of the Court was quickly despatched to the prison but the military authorities refused to hand Tone over. The angry Chief Justice, on hearing this news, immediately instructed the Sheriff to return to the prison, to bring Tone to the Court, and to take the prison officers into custody for contempt if necessary.

When the Sheriff returned to the prison barracks for the second time, he was told that Theobald Wolfe Tone had attempted suicide by cutting his throat with a penknife. For almost a full week, Tone lived in agony; no friend or relative allowed to see him, until, on November 19, 1798 he died alone.

His death was officially declared 'suicide' but was this meant to disillusion the Catholics, who had looked on Tone as their leader? Was it suicide or was it murder?

No coroner's inquest was ever held on Tone's body. When the Sheriff of the Court first went to the prison with the Court Order for Tone's release, why was he not told that Tone had cut his throat? Why was the weapon described, on different occasions, as a penknife, a razor, a piece of glass?

Tone, a Protestant, was the man who had united people of different religions as Irishmen. "When the friends of my youth swarmed off and left me alone, the Catholics did not desert me", so an official 'suicide' would do as much harm to his memory as the forged Casement homosexual diaries. Parnell, another great Irish leader, was also the victim of a proven forgery and sudden mysterious death in prison was not unknown either. In fact Tone's death was not the only one in these circumstances at that time.

Oliver Bond, a remarkably robust United Irishman of thirty-five, in perfect health, was found dead, soon after his arrest, in the prison yard. He had just been given a free pardon if he left Ireland but an Irish rebel, even overseas, was always a danger. So

Bond died suddenly and mysteriously before he could leave the prison. It was officially stated that he died of `apoplexy' although it was said by other prisoners that he had been killed by an under-gaoler.

Suicide was repugnant to Tone. He knew the shame that word held for his Catholic friends and had he not written to his wife; "Be assured I will die as I have lived, and that you will have no cause to blush for me." Then, as the time of his execution drew near, Tone, happy with the news that his family would be well looked after by the French and by their relatives, may also have remembered what he had written as he travelled to raise a French army to free Ireland. "God knows whether we shall ever meet again. If I reach Ireland in safety, and anything befalls me afterwards, I have not the least doubt but my country will take care of them and my boys will find a father in every good Irishman; but if I shall happen to be killed at sea and the expedition shall not succeed, I dread to think on what will become of them. It is terrible. I rely on the goodness of Providence which has often interposed to save us; on the courage and prudence of my wife, and on the friendship of my brother to protect them. My darling babies; I dote on them. I repeat to myself a thousand times the last words I heard from their innocent mouths. God Almighty bless and protect them."

The official time set for his execution was almost upon him, the gallows was being erected near his cell, as he wrote a final message to his wife: "Adieu, dearest love. Keep your courage, as I have kept mine; my mind is as tranquil this moment as at any period of my life. Cherish my memory; and especially preserve your health and spirits for the sake of our dearest children. Your ever affectionate, T.Wolfe Tone."

A few hours afterwards, the official story given out by the gaolers who had refused to release Tone to the Civil Court, was that he attempted suicide but there was never any reliable evidence to support this - no coroner's inquest was held - and it is likely that Wolfe Tone was murdered. The Court of King's Bench might have banished him, a French officer from Ireland but back in France he would once again have worked for Irish freedom.

His tragic death was yet another set-back to the cause he loved so dearly. Wolfe Tone, the man who worked almost all of his adult life, "To subvert the tyranny of our execrable government; to break the connection with England, the never-failing source of all our political evils; and to assert the independence of my country: these were my objects; to unite the whole people of Ireland, to abolish the memory of past dissensions, and to substitute the common name of Irishman in place of the denominations of

Protestant, Catholic and Dissenter-these were my means," was dead.

It was November 1798 and Theobald Wolfe Tone was dead... But down through the years, his ideals and writings have since inspired young Irish men and women. Tone had become known as the `Father of Irish Republicanism'. Perhaps the best tribute to Tone came from Pádraic Pearse, one of the executed leaders of the famous 1916 rebellion. "He has spoken for all time, and his voice resounds throughout Ireland, calling on us from the grave when we wander astray following other voices that ring less true."

"This then is the first part of Tone's achievement - he made articulate the dumb voices of the centuries, he gave Ireland a clear and precise and worthy concept of nationality. But he did more than this. Not only did he define Irish nationalism, he armed his generation in defence of it. Thinker and doer, dreamer of the immortal dream and doer of the immortal deed, we owe to this dead man more than we can ever repay him by making pilgrimages to his grave or by rearing to him the stateliest monument in the streets of his city. To his teaching we owe it that there is such a thing as Irish nationalism, and the memory of the deed he nerved his generation to do, to the memory of 1798, we owe it that there is any manhood left in Ireland."

One hundred and sixty-nine years after his death, in November 18, 1967, Eamon de Valera, President of Ireland, as he unveiled "the stateliest monument in the streets of his city," to Tone's memory said: "It would sorrow Tone's heart not to have the whole nation united... let us have the hope and courage that Wolfe Tone had, let us work to see that his ultimate ideal will be realized."

JOHN MITCHEL

THOMAS FRANCIS MEAGHER

4   TWO - FIGHT OR DIE

"Six famished and ghostly skeletons, to all appearances dead, were huddled in a corner on some filthy straw, their sole covering what seemed a ragged horsecloth, their wretched legs hanging about, naked above the knees. I approached with horror and found by a low moaning they were alive. They were in fever, four children, and what had once been a man. It is impossible to go through the details. Suffice it to say, that in a few minutes I was surrounded by at least two hundred such phantoms, either from famine or from fever, such frightful spectres as no words can describe. Their demonic yells are still ringing in my ears, and their horrible images are fixed upon my brain. My heart sickens at the recital but I must go on. My clothes were nearly torn off in my endeavour to escape from the throng of pestilence around, when my neckcloth was seized from behind by a grip which compelled me to turn, I found myself grasped by a woman with an infant just born in her arms and the remains of a filthy sack across her loins, the sole covering of herself and the baby.

"The same morning the police opened a house on the adjoining lands, which was observed shut for many days and two frozen corpses were found lying upon the mud, half-devoured by rats. A mother, herself in fever, was seen the same day to drag out the corpse of her child, a girl about twelve, perfectly naked, and leave it half covered with stones. In another house, within five hundred yards of the cavalry station at Skibbereen, the dispensary doctor found seven wretches lying unable to move under the same cloak. One had been dead for many hours, but the others were unable to move either themselves or the corpse... I ventured through the parish this day to ascertain the conditions of the inhabitants, and altho' a man not easily moved, I confess myself unmanned by the intensity and extent of the suffering I witnessed, more especially among the women and little children, crowds of whom are to be seen scattered over the turnip fields like a flock of crows, devouring the raw turnips, mothers half naked, shivering in the snow and sleet, uttering exclamations of despair while their children are screaming with hunger. I am a match for anything else I may meet with here, but this I cannot stand... in one house, a man, still alive, was lying in bed with his dead wife and his two dead children; in another, four adults and three children were huddled in silence around the fireplace while in another room a man and his wife lay in bed, the woman shrieking for food, the man unable to speak. In many of the homes, corpses were lying for days, there was no one with sufficient strength to move them. Frequently they were being eaten by starving dogs, cats and rats. Never in my life have I seen such wholesale misery!"

This first hand account from an official in the service of the British Government does not tell even half the story of one of the greatest mass exterminations in history - the death of the Irish! Evicted from their homes because they could not pay the exorbitant rents; the people roamed the countryside looking for food. "Food which was so putrid and offensive so that in consuming it they were obliged to leave the doors and windows of their cabins open."

When their main food, the potato, was stricken with blight, the landlords, backed by the soldiers and the police, took the opportunity of evicting the starving people from their homes. "The tenants must be taught by the strong arm of the law that they had no power to oppose or resist."

In Waterford, the people were trying to live on blackberries, in Cork on cabbage leaves, in Mayo on turnips, but even these were soon gone. Typhus fever was now everywhere; the odour from the crowds of starving wretches was unbearable; dysentery, with diarrhoea, produced by eating rotten turnips, cabbage, and even grass, left the people too weak to move. Bodies swelled up to twice or three times their normal size; scurvy brought disintegration of the body with teeth falling out and legs turning black; children suffered the worst. "No words can describe the appearance of the arms. From below the elbow the two bones seem to be stripped of every atom of flesh. If you take hold of the loose skin within the elbow joint, and lift the arm by it, it comes away in a long, thin fold, as if you had lifted one side of a long, narrow bag in which some bones had been placed."

Their jaws were so swollen that they were unable to speak. Horrible creatures hardly resembling human beings roamed the countryside. The population became an army of walking skeletons.

Those quiet, proud people who loved their homes and families became maniacs in a wild rush to get away from the terrible death that awaited them. Mass emigration flowed out from every port in `coffin ships' not fit for animals. "Hundreds of people, men, women and children, of all ages from a drivelling idiot of ninety to a babe just born, huddled together without light, without air, wallowing in filth, and breathing a foetid atmosphere, sick in body, dispirited in heart, with the fevered patients lying between the sound, in sleeping places so narrow... living without food or medicine... dying without spiritual consolation and buried in the deep..."

A ship, Virginius, took nine weeks to cross the Atlantic, setting out with four hundred and seventy passengers, of whom one hundred and fifty-eight died at sea, and another one hundred and six were stricken with fever; of the rest, the harbour doctor reported: "The few that were able to come on deck were ghastly, yellow-looking spectres, unshaven and hollow-cheeked; not more than six or eight were really healthy and able to exert themselves."

Little better awaited them at the end of the journey; the ship Agnes arrived with four hundred and twenty-seven live passengers but, after two weeks in quarantine, only one hundred and fifty were still breathing. A Boston newspaper said: "Groups of poor wretches were to be seen in every part of the city with their weary and emaciated limbs, at the corners of the streets and in the doorways of both private and public houses."

In America and Canada, there are monuments still to be seen near the points where the Irish emigrant ships arrived. "To preserve from desecration the remains of six thousand immigrants who died from ship fever A.D. 1847-'48, this stone is erected by the workmen... in this secluded spot lie the mortal remains of 5,294 persons, whom, flying from pestilence and famine in Ireland in the year 1847, found in America but a grave."

On a Celtic cross over the St. Lawrence are these words: "Sacred to the memory of thousands of Irish immigrants who to preserve the faith suffered hunger and exile in 1847-'48 and, stricken with fever, ended here their sorrowful pilgrimage."

More than a million emigrated to escape death at home in Ireland; for another million, or perhaps even two million, there was no escape. They died in agony screaming for food. Their limbs falling apart, they lay down and died by the roadside and were never buried. They died in their homes with their families; they died everywhere... but meanwhile in the capital city, state functions and balls, with their glittering gaiety and banquets, went on as usual. Dublin society was enjoying life to the full.

By now, half of the country's eight million people were dead or starving to death. Was this the mass extermination of the Irish race that the British government had always been striving for?

Lord John Russell wrote that Britain would do nothing for Ireland and said in the British Parliament: "Rage against Ireland on account of its faction, its medicancy, its ingratitude, is extreme... we have subscribed, worked, visited, clothed for the Irish... the only return is rebellion and calumny. Let us not grant land, clothes, etc. any more and see what that will do."

While, in public, the government pretended to be concerned about the famine and made a show of help, often useless, in private it was regarded as a blessing which would rid Britain of the Irish who had always refused to be integrated into the Empire. A British Government adviser on economic affairs left no doubts about that, as the well-known

Benjamin Jewett remarked: "I have always felt a certain horror of political economists since I heard one of them say that he feared the famine of 1848 in Ireland would not kill more than a million people, and that would scarcely be enough to do much good."

And so the ships laden with food, grain and other produce, left Ireland for Britain under the protection of the soldiers and police while the Irish starved. A British civil servant estimated that at the end of just one harvest sixty thousand tons of oats alone left the country. The seas were full of fish but the people had no boats; expensive food was on sale but they had no money. "Poor wretched half-clad wretches howling at the door for food from morning till night." For the few who could get work, the pay was seven pence a day and a pound of Indian meal was seven pence, if it could be found - and if it could be eaten.

The miserable windowless cabins that housed the majority of the destitute population became living tombs. For the majority, there was no work, no food and nothing but death awaiting them. Yet ship after ship left the Irish ports for Britain and other countries. According to the official figures, in three months during the famine in Ireland, two hundred and fifty quarters of wheat; seven hundred thousand hundredweight of barley; one million quarters of oats, worth almost two million pounds had been sent out of the country while the people starved.

No wonder an English writer remarked: "The moment the very name of Ireland is mentioned, the English seem to bid adieu to common feeling, common prudence and common sense, and to act with the barbarity of tyrants and the fatuity of idiots."

No wonder monuments in Canada and America have inscriptions like: "Thousands of children of the Gael were lost on this island while fleeing from foreign tyrannical laws and the artificial famine in the years 1847-'48. God bless them. God save Ireland."

No wonder John Mitchel said as he watched the food produced in Ireland loaded on heavily guarded ships bound for England, while the Irish people died of starvation: "The Almighty sent the potato blight but the English sent the famine."

In an article headed: "2,000,000 Murders" and dated May 7, 1847, he exclaimed: "Think of it. Two million deaths in two years; Caesar in all his wars slew little more than one million men; the wars of the Romans against the Jews destroyed 1,350,000; the plague of Milan cost but 140,000; the plague of London but 680,000; the whole number slain in the Peninsular war did not reach 2,000,000."

We might add that even in the century and a half since the Irish famine, there has been no catastrophe, not even the two world wars, where one quarter of a country's population was wiped out in two years. Has there been any act, except maybe Hitler's mass extermination of the Jews, that could compare with this terrible massacre, a long, slow, agonizing death by hunger and fever, of the Irish race in 'Black '47'?.

That the Irish survived at all is a miracle; that they managed to fight again for freedom and independence is even more than that. In the midst of this death by hunger which ravaged the land, two men more than any others, spoke out for their dying people. This is their story:

John Mitchel, the son of a Unitarian clergyman, was born in County Derry on November 3, 1815. He became a Bachelor of Arts at Trinity College in 1834, and after a short time as a bank clerk, studied law to become a solicitor in 1840.

Defending many Catholics in the Courts, he hated religious intolerance and, on business trips to Dublin, frequently met leading Catholic nationalist leaders. Always interested in journalism, he accepted an invitation to join the staff of 'The Nation', a new journal dedicated to the cause of Irish nationalism, history and culture.

So it was that, in 1845, at the beginning of the Famine, John Mitchel, with his wife, whom he had married when he was a law student in 1837, and their children, moved to Dublin and he gave up his legal profession forever. At that time, he was: "Rather above the middle size, well-made and with a face which was thoughtful and comely, though pensive, blue eyes and masses of soft brown hair - a stray ringlet of which he had a habit of twining around his finger while he spoke, gave him perhaps too feminine a cast. He lived much alone and this training had left the ordinary results; he was silent and retiring, slow to speak, and apt to deliver his opinions in a form which would be abrupt and dogmatic if it were not relieved by a pleasant smile. He was already happily married, and lived contentedly among his books." When he came to Dublin, a colleague watching him work remarked: "When he had finished his thinking, he would go to his desk and begin to write. He wrote very rapidly, and without any apparent hesitation or effort."

Before long, Mitchel had made his mark on 'The Nation', making appeals to the Protestants to join their fellow countrymen, the Catholics, for the common good of Ireland - as Wolfe Tone had done half a century earlier.

On March 7, 1846, in an article entitled: 'English Rule' he made no secret of his feelings: "The Irish people are expecting famine day by day and they ascribe it unanimously, not so much to the rule of heaven as to the greedy and cruel policy of England. Be that right or wrong, that is their feeling. They believe that the seasons as they roll are but ministers of England's rapacity; that their starving children cannot sit down to their scanty meal but they see the harpy claw of England in their dish. They behold their own wretched food melting in rottenness off the face of the earth, and yet there are heavy-laden ships, freighted with the yellow corn their own hands have sown and reaped, spreading all sail.. for England; they see it, and with every grain of that corn goes a heavy curse."

While Mitchel was thus writing the leading articles in 'The Nation' and living happily with his wife and family at Charlemont Bridge, Dublin, another young man was making a name for himself with the spoken word as can be seen from his speech in July of that same year: "The soldier is proof against an argument but he is not proof against a bullet. The man who will listen to reason, let him be reasoned with; but it is the weaponed arm of the patriot that can alone avail against battalioned despotism. Then, I do not disclaim the use of arms as immoral, nor do I believe it is the truth to say, that the God of Heaven withholds His sanction from the use of arms... Abhor the sword? Stigmatise the sword? No!..."

Thomas Francis Meagher was born in Waterford city on August 3, 1825, the son of a wealthy businessman and parliamentarian. He was educated at the Jesuit College of Clongowes, County Kildare, and Stonyhurst in England which made him remark of the Irish Jesuits: "They never spoke of Ireland. Never gave us, even what is left of it, her history to read."

Leaving Stonyhurst in 1843, he went to Dublin to study law but soon found the big political demonstrations in the capital of more interest. At that time, he was: "Middle-sized and well made. The lines of his face were so round as to give a character of languor and indolence, till it was lightened up by enthusiasm, when it became impassioned and impressive. His voice was not rich or flexible but the genuine feeling with which it moved rendered it an instrument fit to express a wide range of emotion and passion with astonishing power. In the council of the Party he did not prove of much value... he stirred the judgement, he exercised less control... in private, he was a fast friend and a man of steady honour... nature had made him a great orator and training had made him a a great gentleman."

So it was that John Mitchel and Thomas Francis Meagher, one a writer from the North, the other a speechmaker from the South, both studying law, and both interested in the future of the country that gave them birth, met in Dublin. Mitchel gave his first impressions of his new acquaintance: "To me, at first, he seemed merely a rather foppish young gentleman, with an accent decidedly English, - which, however, was not his fault but the fault of those who sent him to be educated at Stonyhurst in Lancashire. We walked into the banquet room together... Dublin in those days, whatever may be the case now, had dazzling women to which my new friend seemed by no means insensible. I cannot say that in our first casual intercourse our impressions of one another were very favourable. I was from the extreme North, he from the far South, and no chord was struck in the one which truly responded to any chord in the other, until we spoke of Thomas Davis, then lately laid in his grave. Next day, he came to see me at 'The Nation' office in D'Olier Street; we walked out together towards my house in Upper Leeson Street; through College Green, Grafton Street, Harcourt Street, and out almost into the country, near Donnybrook. What talk. What eloquence of talk was his. How fresh and clear and strong. What wealth of imagination and princely generosity of feeling. To me it was the revelation of a new and great nature... he was always Irish to the very marrow."

Meagher disliked the society life in Dublin: "For its pretentious aping of English taste, ideas and fashions; for its utter want of true nobility, all sound love of country and all generous or elevated sentiment." So he became more immersed with the affairs of the ordinary people. With the famine raging in Ireland, he denounced the meagre help offered when nothing was being done to improve the conditions of the people. "Four Law Commissioners were appointed. They were Englishmen and Scotsmen for the most part. They came in for large salaries and grew opulent upon their mission of charity. The poor houses were built and were soon stocked with vermined rags and broken hearts, with orphaned childhood, fevered manhood and desolate old age."

Meanwhile, Mitchel had broken with 'The Nation' because he wanted a more vigorous policy against the English Government, "I had watched the progress of the famine policy of the government, and could see nothing in it but a machinery, deliberately devised, and skilfully worked, for the entire subjugation of the Island, the slaughter of a portion of the people and the pauperisation of the rest."

On February 12, 1848, the first issue of his 'United Irishman' newspaper appeared and made his policy clear: "To sweep this island clear of the English name and nation... The Irish people have a distinct and indefeasible right to their own country..." He began to address articles in his newspaper to the British Lord Lieutenant in Ireland entitled: "Her Majesty's Executioner General and General Butcher of Ireland" and continuing "I assert and maintain that in the island of Ireland there is no government or law. That which passes for 'Government' is a foul and fraudulent usurpation, based on corruption and falsehood, supported by force and battening on blood. I hold that the meaning, and the sole meaning, of that government is to make sure of a constant supply of Irish food for English tables, Irish wool for British backs, Irish blood and bones for British armies; to make sure, in one word, of Ireland for England, and to keep down, scourge and dragoon all Ireland in submission and patient starvation."

Mitchel's articles describing the horrors of the famine years make terrifying reading and soon he had become one of the leaders of a planned armed revolt against the British. The government acted and in his "Jail Journal" we read:

"May 27, 1848: on this day, about four o'clock in the afternoon, I, John Mitchel, was kidnapped and carried off from Dublin in chains, as a convicted 'Felon'. At Charlemont Bridge this evening, there is a desolate house - my mother and sisters who came up to town to see me; five little children very dear to me; none of them old enough to understand the cruel blow that has fallen on them this day, and above all, above all, my wife. What will they do? What is to become of them?... The possible sacrifice indeed was terrible; but the enterprise was great and was needful. And I know that my wife and little ones shall not want... my wife and children, they are the real martyrs."

Mitchel, charged with treason, felony and the writing of seditious articles, was sentenced, after a specially selected jury had found him guilty, to fourteen years transportation beyond the seas.

Still defiant of English rule in Ireland, he was confident that his writing in the 'United Irishman' and other publications would have their effect and sow the seed of rebellion. "For me, I abide my fate joyfully; for I know that whatever betides me, my work is nearly done."

A journalist later reported: "He wore a black frock coat, light waistcoat and dark trousers, and a light leather cap upon his head; the hair was closely cut. His hand and right leg were heavily manacled and fastened to each other by a ponderous iron chain." Thus Mitchel was rushed on board ship, heavily guarded for transportation to an unknown destination.

But, at home, Meagher was still active, in spite of close police attention, and he was determined to go ahead with the rebellion, although, "At that moment, I entertained no hope of success. I knew well that the people were unprepared for the struggle... We are driven to it. There is nothing for us now but to go out; we have not gone far enough to succeed, and yet too far to retreat."

The city was now an armed camp as troops poured in from England. The people, starving and struck with fever, were more interested in food than arms, but Meagher, with O'Brien, and the other leaders, began a tour of the country in the hope of leading the population in revolt.

As he tried to rally the people, his thoughts went back to April 15, in the Rotunda, Dublin, when, on his return from Paris, he had presented his comrades with a new emblem which was destined to become the national flag of Ireland.

"From Paris, the gay and gallant city of the tricolour and the barricades, this flag has been proudly borne. I present it to my native land and I trust that the old country will not refuse this symbol of a new life from one of her youngest children. I need not explain its meaning. The quick and passionate intellect of the generation now springing into arms will catch it at a glance. The white in the centre signifies the lasting truce between the 'Orange' and the 'Green' and I trust that beneath its folds the hands of the Irish Protestant and the Irish Catholic may be clasped in generous and heroic brotherhood."

So he went from Dublin, "To depend on the honour of another is to depend upon her will; and to depend on the will of another country, is the definition of slavery. No foreign hand can bestow the prosperity which a national soul had the power to create. No gift can compensate a nation for its liberty." To Wexford, which had been one of the strongholds of the valiant 1798 rebellion half a century earlier; then on to Kilkenny and later Tipperary. Everywhere the result was the same. Meagher, and the other leaders, were given a tremendous reception by the starving people but there were no arms, no supplies and little fighting spirit left in these weak bodies. After a few skirmishes with the police and soldiers, it became evident that a full-scale rebellion was impossible at that time - as Meagher had earlier stated - and the leaders were forced to go into hiding pursued by the British forces.

"Reward 300 pounds for the capture of Thomas Francis Meagher, no occupation; 25 years of age; 5 ft 9 ins in height; dark, nearly-black hair, light blue eyes; pale face; high cheek bones; peculiar expression about the eyes; cocked nose; no whiskers; well dressed."

In August 1848, he was arrested near Thurles, County Tipperary, and tried for high treason against Britain. "Did I fear that hereafter, when I shall be no more, the country I tried to serve would speak ill of me, I might, indeed, avail myself of this solemn moment to vindicate my sentiments and my conduct. But I have no such fear... No, I do not despair of my poor, old country - her peace, her liberty, her glory. To lift this island up, instead of being, as she is now, the meanest beggar in the world - to restore to her, her native powers and her ancient constitution - this has been my ambition and this ambition has been my crime. Judged by the law of England, I know that this crime entails upon me the penalty of death; but the history of Ireland explains that crime and justifies it. Judged by that history, I am no criminal... Judged by that history, the treason of which I stand convicted loses all its guilt, has been sanctified as a duty, and will be ennobled as a sacrifice... I now bid farewell to the country of my birth, of my passions, of my death; a country whose misfortunes have invoked my sympathies; whose factions I sought to quell, whose intelligence I prompted to a lofty aim, whose freedom has been my fatal dream. To that country I now offer as a pledge of the love I bore her, and of the sincerity with which I thought and spoke, and struggled for her freedom, the life of a young heart; and with that life, the hopes, the honours, the endearments of a happy, a prosperous and honourable home. Proceed then, my lords, with the sentence which the law directs. I am prepared to hear it, I trust I am prepared to meet its execution. I shall go, I think, with a light heart before a higher tribunal where a judge of infinite goodness, as well as of infinite justice, will preside and, where, my lords, many, many of the judgements of this world will be reversed."

So it was that, at the age of twenty-three, Thomas Francis Meagher heard those dreaded words: "You will be hanged, drawn and quartered..." but his good humour did not desert him and, back in his cell, he greeted fellow prisoners: "Hence I am and found guilty; and glad, too; that they did convict me, for if I had been acquitted, the people might say I had not done my duty. I am guilty and convicted for the old country... Come on in now to the cell and let me have my dinner... Let us have one hour's fun..." For fear of a national uprising, the sentence was commuted to transportation for life beyond the seas and in July, 1849, Meagher, with some companions, sailed away from Ireland, a convicted felon, on his way to Van Diemen's land... Tasmania... as had John Mitchel before him, leaving behind a country on its deathbed.

....

For seven hundred years, the Irish had resisted every attempt to subdue them, to make them British. Their lands had been taken away from them, settlers had been sent over from Britain, the natives had been driven to the bogs and the mountains. The butchery of Cromwell and his 'Model English Army' had reduced the native population to little more than a million two centuries before the famine yet the Irish nation still survived, unconquered and a source of continuous trouble to the British.

In 1801, after the failure of the United Irishmen's Rebellion of 1798 and the death of Wolfe Tone, the British had tried to end this dissension, once and for all, by passing the Act of Union, making the two countries one. Some Irishmen supported this because, on the surface, it looked as if it would benefit Ireland. Irish goods would have free entry onto the British market and the vast capital resources of Britain could be used to build up the smaller and weaker nation. But what actually happened was the destruction of the Irish economy, for the real reason for the Act of Union was to crush Ireland forever. English goods were dumped on the Irish market, the native Irish industries collapsed, most of the population became unemployed. What was hailed with a great fanfare, after much bribery and corruption to get it accepted, became yet another instrument for the destruction of the Irish nation and was one of the causes of the famine calamity which followed. Mitchel and Meagher had made their protest and their words were soon to become deeds with the Fenians in yet another Irish rebellion, but meanwhile they were both sailing away from the land they loved.

....

On June 1, 1848, Mitchel wrote in his diary: "It was a raw, damp morning that I took my last look of Irish land. The First Lieutenant of the ship 'Scourge', in full costume, with cocked hat and sword, came for me with a boat full of marines."

Soon he was on board a prison ship in Bermuda and he remarks: "Asthma; asthma; the enemy is upon me. For a few months I fondly dreamed that the fiend was shaken off... November: I have been sick and unable to write. Why do I not open my mouth and curse the day I was born? Because I have a proud hope that Meagher and I together will stand side by side on some better day... where is he now, I wonder?,.... I'm reading books all the time, even Greek... I would give all the books I ever read for a pair of lungs that would work... sitting bent down on my chair, with weary limbs and dizzy brain, worn out after another night's long agony. It is the twelfth night since my head has pressed my pillow. My feet are cold as marble; my body and head bathed in sweat... the doctor told me that the climate of Bermuda is notoriously, and excessively, unfriendly to asthmatic persons... I am suffering a daily and nightly death in life... shrunk together in my cell, dismally ill, wrapped up in coats... and it's Christmas Day. I sit constantly panting and struggling in asthma, both day and night, exposed to a damp and bitter wind, that sometimes blows out my candle at night; for the ship is old, and the porthole is much rounded away at the edges so that the casement window does not properly fit it. Of course, there is no fire... ten months' solitary confinement of a sick man in an unwholesome den... there is a danger I may not survive... I did not think I had been so ill... they have gone near to murder me!"

But relief was at hand, and due to the insistence of the medical officer, on Sunday, April 22, Mitchel was en route for the Cape of Good Hope. His health improved with the sea voyage and on July 12, he wrote of his own birthplace:

"I trust the maniacs in the North of Ireland are not cutting one another's throats today. Yet, if they are, there is one comfort in it; those whose throats are cut will not be starved to death."

Due to local opposition, the British found it very difficult to find anywhere willing to receive a shipload of convicts in their midst and he was still on board ship in April, 1850, a full year later.

"Ever since I have become a prisoner and cannot choose my company, I prefer my own society to any other. The British transportation system is the very worst scheme of criminal punishment that ever was contrived; and I seriously think it was contrived by Satan, with the assistance of some friends; there are nearly two hundred Irish amongst the prisoners, the famine-struck Irish, many who have not a word of English and most of them so shattered in constitution by mere hunger and hardship that all the deaths among the prisoners, ever since we embarked, have been Irish... I am far removed, however, from their part of the ship... now they are traversing the deep under bayonet points, to be shot out like rubbish on a bare foreign strand and told to seek their fortune there amongst a people whose very language they know not... now headed for Van Dieman's Land... I am to spend certain years there among the gum trees in grim solitude - utter solitude, for I cannot bear to think of bringing out my poor wife to those regions of outer darkness, or rearing my boys in the island of the unblessed... April 6... the mountainous southern coast of Van Dieman's Land... there, amongst these shaggy mountains, wander both O'Brien and Meagher, each alone in this forest dungeon... they have been allowed to live at large, but each within a limited district, and no two of them nearer than thirty or forty miles... surely, I shall contrive some means of meeting them once..."

Thomas Francis Meagher, a prisoner in the man-of-war brig, Swift, had been in Simon's Bay, Cape of Good Hope, a week before Mitchel in the Neptune also stopped there for provisions on April 19, 1849.

In Van Dieman's Land, his good humour and his friendliness made him popular with the settlers there, even those of English nationality, and he spent much of his time boating and fishing. The scenery around Hobart Town captivated him. "Gazing at them, we lost sight of our misfortunes... we forgot for awhile that we were prisoners destined for life to sojourn in this land...!"

Thus, Meagher married Catherine Bennett, a farmer's daughter, in Van Dieman's Land in 1851.

The comrade exiles, on the other side of the world from the country that they loved, at last managed to arrange a secret meeting, in the wilds of their island prison, which Mitchel described:

"As we exchanged greetings I know not from what impulse, whether from buoyancy of heart, or bizarre perversity of feeling, we all laughed till the woods rang around; laughter loud and long and uproariously... but even in laughter, the heart is sad; and curses or tears, just then might have become us better... he looked fresh and vigorous..."

Meagher remembered those days also: "You cannot picture to yourself the happiness which the days we have spent by that lonely, glorious lake have brought us... a small, cozy, smoky, bit of a log hut... should hearts grow faint at home... tell that here, upon a lone spot in the far southern seas, there are prayers, full of confidence and faith and love, offered up for Ireland's cause."

On May 9, Mitchel commented: "Our life here has been uniform and dull and our main object has been to kill thought by violent exercise on foot and horseback... we still go to the lakes and meet Meagher and this is our chief pleasure... I may have to live the remaining twelve years of my sentence here... I have written to Newry, inviting all my household... pray God I have done right."

Later, he wrote: "June 20. Today I met my wife and family once more... these things cannot be described... we spent such an evening as seldom falls to the lot of captives."

By this time, Mitchel had a home, Nant Cottage, and a farm of close on two hundred acres in the wilds of Tasmania. "The land is capital pasture and I am stocking it with sheep and cattle... four hours every day are devoted to the boys' lessons; then riding or roaming the woods with the dogs."

Meagher also had a dog when Mitchel met him two thousand feet up in the mountains. "Brian a noble, shaggy greyhound" and it seemed as if they had both become settlers, building up a new life in a new land. "Of literature I am almost sick, and prefer farming, and making market of my wool" wrote Mitchel then - but Meagher had other ideas!

....

In January, 1852, Meagher, after formally withdrawing his parole, rode away on his horse, assisted by some English settlers and an Irish chief constable who refused to arrest him. In a shepherd hut, he shaved off his moustache for a better disguise and, after a long journey, reached the ship that was waiting to bring him to America and freedom.

A year later, on January 13, a certain Pat Smyth arrived in Hobart Town. "Commissioned by the Irish Directory in New York to produce the escape of one or more of us." But their hopes seemed dashed when Smyth was arrested and released ill two months later. However, when he had recovered, he went with Mitchel, both of them armed, to a remote police station, formally withdrew his parole, and the few police on duty, thinking that there was a crowd of Irish convicts outside, were so slow to follow that:

- "We gave the bridle rein
a shake;
Said adieu for evermore,
my dear;
And adieu for evermore." -

Mitchel, who was also assisted by some English settlers, was now on the run, pursued by the police and waiting in vain for the ship that was due to arrive.

"I have written two letters, one to my wife at home, one to my mother in New York - a kind of provisional adieu, indeed, for I sincerely hope to meet with this ship `Don Juan'; and failing her, I shall have to disperse my party and retire from the coast again with all speed and secrecy."

Weeks later, he was still waiting, and the Don Juan had not arrived. Plans were changed, and Mitchel was to go aboard a steamer at Launceston under the name of Father MacNamara en route to Melbourne.

He rode sixty miles to the port only to find that the captain had changed his mind because the police were searching the boats. He promised to pick him up further down river instead.

In a small boat, Mitchel and his friends rowed all night but were unable to make contact with the steamer. The escape failed again. They were almost lost in a storm and had to return to Launceston in daylight.

"There is nothing like coolness. We walked quietly into, and through, the town; and the man of five feet ten, dark hair, and so forth, passed quite unchallenged through the streets."

Sheltered now by a real priest, Father Butler, fresh plans were made to have Mitchel rescued but first he had to go the one hundred and twenty miles to Hobart Town by public coach - this time disguised as the Reverend Mr. Blake. His disguise was so good that Smyth, and his other friends, did not recognize him. It was also arranged that Mitchel's wife and family should travel by the same vessel quite openly, while he should be smuggled on board at nightfall.

On July 19, Mitchel remarked: "Yesterday evening I was placed on board in the bay by moonlight... my wife was sitting on the poop with the children but did not say a word to me and Mr. Wright - his latest name - walked about as a stranger. The ship is full of passengers but not one of them knows me.

"July 23: We are off the entrance of Sydney harbour... Captain Brown produces brandy and water for the chief police officer... Mr. Wright nods a slight farewell.....and in Sydney."

His wife visits Mitchel, now known as Mr. Warren, on July 25, and tells him, "She had the kindest assistance from our neighbours in all her business arrangements, selling horses and sheep and so forth. Nant Cottage and farm were already occupied by an English gentleman recently arrived in the colony, and he took the furniture at a valued price. `Fleur-de-lis' our old favourite horse, is sold to a young lady. May her rack long abound with hay and the oats never fall in her manger... Dapple, the boy's little brown mare, has been sold and Mr. Reid promises to take care of her colt."

And thus the long convict diary of John Mitchel ends on August 2, 1853: "It is over. The man five feet ten in stature with dark hair, was recognized by no enemy... Whether I was ever truly in Australia at all, or whether in the body or out of the body, I cannot tell; but I have had bad dreams."

Perhaps, as he sailed towards freedom, his own words about the Irish came to mind: "Chased from their homes, in want and misery, seeking the bread of exiles in every land, separated for long years from home and kindred, what other race could still keep alive, deep in its glowing heart, a unanimous craving at once so tender and so fierce, so loving and so vengeful, for the hour when their long enslaved island shall be redeemed and its potent oppressor laid low in the dust...?"

....

In May 1852, Meagher had arrived in New York to an enthusiastic reception but he refused a public corporation banquet, "Whilst my country remains in sorrow and subjection, it would be indelicate of me to participate in festivities you propose."

He became a popular lecturer on Australia and Ireland, even publishing a book. "To revive in Ireland the spirit which, in the summer of 1848, impetuously sought to clear a way, with an armed hand, to the destiny that lay beyond the intervening camp and throne, may be for the time forbidden."

On October 9, 1853, Mitchel arrived to another reception in San Francisco. Iowa named an area of some four hundred square miles, Mitchel County. But the big moment came when he was reunited with his old comrade, Meagher. It seemed as if half of New York had turned out to welcome Mitchel, the unrepentant Irish felon, in an official City Hall reception. "John Mitchel was then in the prime of manhood; he was 38, a little above the middle height, with a frame compact and well-proportioned... his face was clear pale... his eyes a grey blue... one could readily understand why the London Times, the bitter and implacable foe of the Irish race, should have exclaimed that in transporting Mitchel the head and shoulders were taken from the revolutionary movement... the man was terribly in earnest, he meant every word he uttered... true, he was inferior to Meagher in the eloquence of passion, but in a clear, incisive, logical statement of facts, he was vastly superior..."

Friends suggested that Mitchel take up his old profession of law, but he preferred journalism. As in everything he did, he spared no effort and, in the next few years, published three newspapers - the Citizen and the Irish Citizen in New York, the Southern Citizen in Washington and edited three more: the Enquirer and the Examiner in Richmond and the Daily News in New York.

On January 7, 1854, the old comrades had launched the Citizen: "The principal conductors are, in the first place, Irishmen by birth. In the second place, they are men who have endured years of penal servitude at the hands of the British Government for endeavouring to overthrow the dominion of that Government in their native country. In the third place, they are refugees on American soil, and aspirants to the privileges of American citizenship... They refuse to believe that, prostrate and broken as the Irish nation is now, the cause of Irish Independence is utterly lost."

The two old comrades who had been through so much together in

Ireland, and in Australia, were now happy working together in America but their happiness was not to last very long!

....

During the course of his American lecture tours, Mitchel received such a warm reception in the South, that, in 1855, he began farming in Tennessee, where he lived with his family before moving to Knoxville to establish the Southern Citizen.

He made a hurried visit to Paris when he heard that France and Britain might go to war as he thought it might be another opportunity for Ireland - but nothing happened. He lived there for awhile, writing for several newspapers, and his daughter Henriette became a Catholic in 1861 with the Sisters of the Sacred Heart in Paris, where she died two years later. Mitchel, heartbroken, often remarked: "Poor daughter, I sometimes wish I was under the same stone..."

His other daughter, Isabel, also entered the Catholic faith and her father wrote: "There is not the least chance of my being a Catholic and so much the worse."

Mitchel returned to New York in 1862 to find that the Civil War had already broken out.

Meanwhile, Thomas Francis Meagher had been active raising an Irish company for Colonel Michael Corcoran's famous 69th Regiment and served with distinction through the first tough Virginian campaign. His horse was shot from under him at the first battle of Bull Run in 1861.

He gathered his own Irish Brigade later that year; was promoted Colonel and then Brigadier General the following year. He took part in the seven day battle of Richmond and in the battle of Antietam his horse was shot dead. He led the historic charge of the Irish Brigade at Fredericksburg where half of his men were killed and he was wounded in the leg. The remainder of his brigade were almost wiped out at Chancellorsville but Meagher escaped once again. He always had hopes that, at the end of the Civil War, he would return home with the Irish Brigade to fight for Irish freedom but it was not to be.

Meagher had proved himself a great leader and soldier for the Union and his opponent General Lee, Confederate Commander, wrote:

"Meagher, though not the equal of Cleburne in military genius, rivalled him in bravery and in the affection of his soldiers. The gallant stand which the bold brigade made at Fredericksburg is well known. Never were men so brave. They ennobled their race by their splendid gallantry on that desperate occasion."

John Mitchel already knew that his sympathies were for the South in the Civil War so he volunteered for active service with the Confederates. However, his eyesight was no longer good and he had to content himself in the Richmond City Guard and the Ambulance Service. His three sons joined the Confederate forces; James became Chief of Staff to General Gordon; John, an artillery captain, was killed at Fort Sumter; William died in the battle of Gettysburg; even his wife and daughters did hospital work for the Confederates.

Fate had brought it about that the two Irish rebels, who had endured so much together for the same cause in Ireland and Australia, were now on opposing sides in the fighting around Richmond, during the American Civil War!

....

At the end of the War, Meagher was appointed by the United States President to be Secretary of the Montana territory and in September 1866, he was acting Governor destined for a brilliant future in this new land. He had married again, very happily, to Miss Elizabeth Townsend in America and they had a son. His young Australian wife had died in 1854.

The misfortune which had plagued the country of his birth now struck at one of its illustrious sons. On the night of July 1, 1867, when Thomas Francis Meagher was forty-three years of age, he took up his official quarters in a steamer on the Missouri near Fort Benton. He went for a walk along the deck and: "A sudden slip, a splash, a faint cry, a brief struggle, and all was over... the accident was too sudden for availing assistance... the hungry water closed over him and the rapid rolling current swept away his lifeless corpse... the finished scholar, the genial friend, the matchless orator, the ardent patriot was no more. Thomas Francis Meagher was dead."

But John Mitchel had a long and bitter trail to travel still. At the end of the war, he had returned to New York and became editor of the Daily News. He immediately pleaded the cause of the beaten Confederates and hoped for forgiveness and peace among all Americans. He was arrested by order of General Grant in 1865 and imprisoned in a dark dungeon in Port Monroe. He was harshly treated and his health deteriorated.

On his release the following year, he joined the Fenians; journeyed to Paris on their behalf; but severed his connection with the movement when there was internal disagreement in the American organization. From Paris, he wrote to his wife: "I am a lonely wretch. Very little can give me pleasure except to hear about my own folk... I am a wandering Jew... I am Methuselah... It seems to me, however, I do not grow old in disposition."

Before he left Paris forever, there was a tender moment for the old revolutionary, banished from the country that he loved so much. Persuaded by some priests to visit the Irish College there, he strolled through the quiet building and came down the steps where all the students had lined up to welcome him - all young Irishmen studying for the priesthood in Paris. As Mitchel appeared, they gave three loud cheers and tears ran down his face as he exclaimed: "God bless the boys, God bless the boys, they are always right."

On his return to America, he wrote books, made lecture tours, published and edited the Irish Citizen for five years. But, because he did not give the Fenian movement any hope of success, while England was at peace, he refused the offered presidency of it, and thereby, lost many of his friends.

His health had failed, his money was gone, and he was very embarrassed when he learned that a collection had been made for him in Ireland. "As to my worldly affairs, I perceive that I am found out... I need not tell you how humiliating to me is this... "

At this time his thoughts were centred on Ireland, and his wife and family. "They are the real martyrs, not I; I am never happier than when with my family." They often observed him studying fondly a map of his native country; "An exile in my circumstances is a branch cut from a tree; it is dead and has but an affection of life."

He could stand this longing no longer and so, in July 1874, after an absence of a quarter of a century, in the company of his daughter Isabel, the old rebel landed at Cork. He spent a never to be forgotten three months meeting old friends, visiting familiar places, before he returned to America, rejuvenated and happier than he had been for a long time.

Within nine months, he was on his way back again to Ireland, this time with his son James, to stand as a candidate for parliament, although determined never to actually take his seat in the British House of Commons. "I am in favour of Home Rule; that is, the Sovereign Independence of Ireland."

By the time the boat had arrived at Cork, it was announced that: "John Mitchel of 505 Clinton Avenue, Brooklyn, United States of America, has been elected unopposed in Tipperary." The election was declared void by the British and a new date fixed for the following month.

Everywhere he went, Mitchel was received by enthusiastic crowds and it gave him great pleasure to see that the spirit of nationality and freedom was rising again in the people. But his own health was failing rapidly and he was sometimes too weak to address the meetings. "The first and greatest thing I see in this election is that it was a magnificent pronouncement in favour of the national right of Ireland, and against the usurpation of the British Parliament. The people of Tipperary elected me as the most implacable enemy of British tyranny."

Less then thirty years after the famine, Tipperary, one of the worst hit counties, was again striking for independence, and this proved his work had not been in vain.

It was now 1875, and March 11, the day of the second election was approaching. Mitchel's health grew worse and he became anxious to see his old home in Newry once more. On the day after his arrival there, he received the news that he had been re-elected, with four times more votes than his opponent. "How pleased my wife will be to hear this; how pleased my poor wife will be."

In a week, on March 20, John Mitchel died quietly and peacefully in bed. "John Mitchel died well - at home in Ireland, in his father's house, surrounded by his loving brothers, sisters and friends; after a consistently noble life, crowned with the affectionate gratitude of the people he loved and served, triumphant in every respect, over his enemies." The comrades were no more.

His lifelong friend, John Martin, who wrote those words and had shared Australian exile with him, died a few days later. The comrades were no more. On the first anniversary of Mitchel's death, there appeared in his old paper, 'The Nation', this tribute:

> "Then sleep, John Mitchel, in your
> Irish grave,
> Your name will live amid the good
> and the true -
> For when did earth behold a heart
> so brave
> And when had Chief a nobler cause
> than you?
> Your rivals in earth's story are
> but few
> Among the heroes Erin calls her
> own -
> And they are many and mighty too,
> Your equals, leader high, are
> these alone,
> O'Neill, O'Donnell, FitzGerald,
> Emmet, Tone."

But Mitchel's own words, when the death and destruction of the terrible famine seemed to have destroyed the Irish nation forever, provided a simple epitaph that the unrepentant patriot would probably prefer - for they were to come true.

"The passionate aspiration of Irish Nationhood will outlive the British Empire... No country is hopelessly vanquished whose sons love her better than life."

KEVIN BARRY

5 : AND THEN CAME NOVEMBER

It was Sunday, November 28 in Cork, when they came together for the first time. Those young, eager men, untrained but determined to learn quickly.

At 2 a.m. on the following Sunday morning, the same thirty-six picked men marched quietly from their hideout on a mission which was to strike terror in the hearts of the enemy. Six hours later they reached their destination, a bleak, lonely spot on the winding country road which turned and twisted through the boggy countryside. There was no shelter from the pouring rain. A small, stone wall, a few moss-covered boulders, overlooked the road and they took up positions there.

It was their longest day. They had no food. Their clothes were soaking with the heavy rain. Their nerves were on edge as they thought of home and the weeks gone by.

The dreaded Black and Tans, with their companions, the Auxiliaries, had been terrorizing the land. Nobody was safe. The small villages of County Cork knew too well the sound of heavy lorries during the night, the banging on the doors, the shouting, the shooting, the rape, the burning homes and the dead.

Determined to stamp out all resistance, this special force of ex-soldiers from the First World War, with a mixture of criminals and adventurers, had been given a free hand. They seemed invincible. But the little group huddled behind the rocks on that cold, wet Sunday in November, was ready for them now.

They knew their orders. There was to be no retreat. The whole country depended on them to break the legend that this new British force was invincible. Each man had a rifle but only thirty-five rounds of precious ammunition. The Commander had two Mills bombs captured in a previous raid and intended making good use of them. He had chosen their positions well. He would start the attack himself from the command post, manned by three crack marksmen, behind the small stone wall. Ten more riflemen were hidden by a big boulder which dominated one side of the road. More volunteers occupied positions behind small rocks on the other side of the road and another six were placed in a reserve position for emergencies. Three scouts had been posted to signal the arrival of the enemy and thus the minutes ticked slowly away.

They had left their camp at 2 a.m. that Sunday morning. Fourteen hours later, when it was 4 p.m., the sound of lorries came to the ears of the hidden watchers. This was the moment they had been waiting for. Some of them made the Sign of the Cross and were thankful that the local priest had heard their confessions in the secret training camp before the long march.

The sound grew louder and then the first lorry appeared around the bend in the road. Slowly it came near the small stone wall. The watchers could make out the figures in the front. Suddenly, a Mills bomb landed in the driver's seat, the commander's whistle blew, the rifle men opened fire. It was almost point-blank range for five minutes as both sides faced each other on the narrow country road. Then there was silence.

Less than fifty yards away, the second lorry was now under heavy fire, the occupants taking cover on the road, while a silent group of attackers quietly surrounded them. The occupants of the lorry shouted: "We surrender" and two I.R.A. men came out from behind the rocks to meet a hail of bullets and die there. The rebel commander gave the stern order: "Keep firing until I tell you to stop" and the battle raged again.

The blazing lorries illuminated the dark November evening as the silent raiders collected the captured weapons and ammunition. Then they vanished into the countryside; tired after their twenty-six mile walk; hungry after a day-long fast; sad about the death of their comrades; proud they had struck a blow for Irish freedom; glad it was all over.

Behind them on that lonely road lay the eighteen bodies of that dreaded force which had been terrorizing the countryside. The entire British party had been wiped out and Tom Barry's flying column of the Irish Republican Army had made Kilmichael, near Macroom, in the county of Cork, a place in history.

It was November 28, 1920 and Kevin Barry had not died in vain.

....

It was Sunday, November 21 in Dublin, when several groups of young men walked and cycled through the capital. The inhabitants of that fair city were making their way to Mass, as the young men began to arrive at private houses, flats and hotels in the fashionable south side. This was the big day they had been waiting for and they would not let "The Big Fella" down.

The big man behind this unusual Sunday morning activity, Michael Collins, had planned it carefully. His secret agents were in the post office, in military headquarters in Dublin Castle itself, and he knew every move the enemy were making. For some time he had been aware of a new development in the Irish War of Independence - a development which threatened the very existence of the Republican movement.

Months before, the Lord Mayor of Cork, Thomas MacCurtain, had been brutally murdered at home in front of his family by men with blackened faces. A civilian jury brought in a verdict of murder against the British Government. Some of the Lord Mayor's killers were later discovered, and executed, by the I.R.A.

Other murders officially sponsored by the British Government followed and letters intercepted by Collins, together with information supplied by his agents, revealed an amazing plot to exterminate all the leaders of the Irish resistance movement one by one.

Top agents of the British Secret Service and Intelligence Service had been sent from London for this purpose and, living as civilians in different parts of the city, were gathering information for their terrible work. The I.R.A. headquarters' staff decided to beat them at their own game and, through a patriotic young Irish shorthand typist working for the British, Collins learned full particulars of the secret service men in Dublin.

Michael Collins, then worth ten thousand pounds, dead or alive, made his way as usual, undisguised, through the ancient city to make final arrangements. Sunday, November 21, was the day selected. The day that was to become forever `Bloody Sunday'.

That morning, most of the undercover agents were in their beds when the I.R.A. 'execution squads' arrived. They died as they had planned the deaths of others. Fourteen dead; several others wounded; and the power of the British Secret Service broken in Ireland was the result of the I.R.A.'s morning raid. But it was a long day yet.

That afternoon, Croke Park was crowded for a big football match, most of the crowd unaware of the events of the morning. During the game, a large force of Black and Tans and British Auxiliaries surrounded the football stadium and, as a reprisal for the execution of their secret agents, opened fire on the crowd. The scene can hardly be imagined as men, women and children panicked. The hail of bullets poured into the crowded arena. More than a dozen people were killed, including women and children.

Seán Hogan, one of the players on the field, was shot dead. Almost a hundred were wounded and many more seriously injured in the stampede that followed the shooting.

That night, back at British military headquarters in Dublin Castle, three prisoners who had been arrested as I.R.A. suspects the previous evening, were bayonetted and then shot to death without trial.

It was Bloody Sunday in Dublin in this terrible war. Yet the extermination of the intelligence agents may have prompted the British Prime Minister to quickly try to ascertain the Republicans attitude to peace. It was Sunday, November 21, 1920, in Dublin and Kevin Barry had not died in vain.

....

It was Monday, November 1, in Ireland and Kevin Barry was to die. In the springtime of his life, suddenly it was November and his young life was gone. Now seventy years after his death, the haunting words of the ballad - 'Kevin Barry' - still brings a tear to the eye - and not only in Ireland where he will never be forgotten. The deep voice of Paul Robeson, the golden trumpet of Eddie Calvert, the Wolfe Tones, the Dubliners, have sent it echoing as a song of freedom around the world but, for every Irishman and Irishwoman, it has a meaning, and a certain feeling, that time cannot destroy.

Of all the men who died for Ireland during its fight for freedom which has lasted for over eight hundred years, young Kevin Barry has a special place among the most loved and most honoured. He will never be forgotten.

Kevin Barry was born in Fleet Street, Dublin, on January 20, 1902. His early life was like that of any other child of the times whose parents came from the country. He spent his summer holidays with his father's relations in County Carlow and, when his father died, lived there for a while with his mother.

At the national school and around the turf fire at night, he heard many stories of the 1798 Rebellion - for the Wicklow, Wexford, Carlow, area had been the main centre of resistance. Nearby, in the picturesque Glen of Imaal amid the beautiful Wicklow mountains, the famous rebel leader, Michael Dwyer, and his guerilla army, had defied capture for many years after the rebellion had ended. The tale of his daring escape from a thatched cottage in the picturesque Glen near the little village of Donard, in West Wicklow, made thrilling reading for any schoolboy, and Kevin Barry was no exception.

The part where the wounded rebel from the North of Ireland, McAlister, opened the door of the blazing cottage to draw the fire of the surrounding soldiers so that his leader, Dwyer, could escape before they could reload their guns, is a heroic deed that appealed to youth everywhere.

Like many a boy before him, and since, these tales of brave Irishmen who challenged the mighty British Empire at the height of its power for the sake of Irish freedom, fanned the flame of patriotism in his heart and, before he was sixteen, he had joined the Irish Volunteers.

By this time, he was attending school in Dublin at St. Mary's College, Rathmines run by the Holy Ghost Fathers and later the Jesuits' Belvedere College near Croke Park, where Bloody Sunday was soon to shock the world. Serious in himself, he was nevertheless a cheerful companion enjoying the usual schoolboy jokes and tricks "Just an ordinary person like the rest of us" remembers a school companion. A keen athlete, he was an excellent rugby player and also played the Gaelic game of hurling with great enthusiasm.

He worked hard at his studies and, by the time he was seventeen, had won a scholarship to the National University. Good at his studies and at sport, Saturday evenings, after a match, were usually spent cycling around Dublin delivering orders and messages to the members of the secret

Republican movement.

One of the youngest volunteers in the confidence of the leaders, he took his work very seriously and, even after a late dance, would always be at early Sunday morning military training.

He enjoyed life, the company of young people his own age, and made friends. When he became a medical student at the university in 1919, he was a typical youth of seventeen, fond of dances and the company of a nice girl; enjoyed playing a good game of rugby or hurling; liked to see a good play; to go 'down town' with some of his fellow students, looking at the shops and crowds; laughing and joking with his companions as if he had not a care in the world.

Yet, behind all these student activities he was always sincere and intense, never neglecting his studies or the volunteer movement which began to occupy more of his spare time. He had joined the Irish Volunteers in late 1917 when the 1916 rebellion had been long crushed, the leaders executed, and all seemed lost for perhaps another generation. The fight for independence had not yet begun and many thought it never would. But there were always other young men with the idealism of Irish patriotism hidden beneath an ordinary exterior and they too - like his fellow student Frank Flood - were to follow their ideals to the end.

Kevin Barry did not spend all his time delivering mobilization orders. He took part in several small, but successful, raids for arms and ammunition, all of which were carried out without serious incident. Soon he was promoted in charge of his own section of the Irish Volunteers and, at the beginning of June in the fateful year of 1920, played a prominent part in an important raid.

The Irish Republicans were always short of arms to carry on the fight for independence and the British forces were the main source of supply. By this time, 1920, the Republic proclaimed by the executed 1916 leaders had been duly ratified in the new Irish Parliament - in which the Irish Republican Party, Sinn Féin, had won more than two-thirds of the seats in the recent general election. The Irish Volunteers had thus become the official national Irish Republican Army (I.R.A.) fighting a war of independence against the British forces. Guerilla tactics were the only successful method of warfare for a small nation fighting a great power. Britain was then the most powerful military, naval and commercial empire in the world - and little Ireland was its nearest neighbour!

June 1, 1920, one of many such raids for arms took place in the heart of Dublin almost within sight of the centre of British power, Dublin Castle.

A British military outpost at the King's Inns was surrounded by the Volunteers. Kevin Barry was one of the first into the building and twenty-five soldiers were overpowered before they knew what was happening. Badly-needed machine guns, rifles, and ammunition were obtained without casualties and later the captured British soldiers were all released unharmed.

This successful raid in the centre of the capital had a great effect on the morale of the Irish volunteers and was to be reproduced in many different parts of the country during the next two years.

But, in Dublin, on Monday, September 20, 1920, something went wrong.

....

The need for arms was still acute. The Irish War of Independence was now in full swing and the British were being harried almost daily even in the capital, Dublin. The place selected for this September raid was a bakery in Church Street, not far from the scene of the very successful June expedition at King's Inns. An armed party of British soldiers were regular callers for the garrison's bread supplies and the plan was to occupy the bakery beforehand, close in on the lorry when it arrived, take the arms and ammunition from the soldiers and then quickly disappear in the back streets of Dublin before the nearby garrison would realize what had happened.

The first part of the plan went without incident. The bakery was occupied by the I.R.A.; all the men were at their posts in the many side streets; a van was ready to take away the captured arms. It was close to noon when the lorry appeared in the almost deserted street. Everything appeared normal. The soldiers had not thought of danger when they leisurely prepared to enter the bakery as they had done many times before. The armed escort sat around the lorry talking and then... suddenly... there was a shot, "Drop your rifles. Put up your hands." Three men with guns in their hands were standing beside the lorry. One of them was Kevin Barry.

The party in the lorry threw their rifles on the floor. The rest of the I.R.A. party moved in to cover the capture and retreat. It would be another successful raid, without incident or injury to anyone, and Kevin would be in time to sit for that important university examination in the afternoon. But one soldier did not throw his rifle down. He shot one of the three I.R.A. men in the head and when Kevin Barry raised his gun to return fire, it jammed. He took cover beside the lorry, managed to free it, fired a few shots and the gun jammed again.

One of the British soldiers was dead. Two were seriously wounded. Several of the I.R.A. were wounded and the expected British reinforcements would arrive at any minute. The I.R.A. men retreated, bringing their wounded with them and the battle, which lasted less than five minutes, was over.

The Lancashire Fusiliers arrived to support the ambushed Duke of Wellington's regiment but the fight was finished and the street peaceful once more. A crowd had appeared as if from nowhere; the wounded soldiers and their companions prepared to move off. Then a woman shouted, "There's someone under the lorry", perhaps to save him from being run over, and so Kevin Barry was captured.

He had taken cover under the lorry to try to free his jammed gun and, in the confusion, had not realized that the attack had ended; his companions had retreated unaware that he was there.

He was thrown roughly into the lorry at bayonet point and brought to the British army barracks at the North Dublin Union.

The young university student's life was almost over. His long, lonely road to martyrdom was beginning as he faced some half-dozen enraged officers for questioning. The famous ballad tells the story:

"Just before he faced the hangman,
In his dreary prison cell,
British soldiers tortured Barry
Just because he would not tell
The names of his companions
And other things they wished
to know,
'Turn informer or we'll kill you'
Kevin Barry answered 'No'."

He gave his name, address and occupation - medical student - in the accepted way of a prisoner of war and nothing else. But that was not enough and the soldiers were not satisfied.

It was much later before the whole story was known, too late to help Kevin Barry in this life. Knowing that he was soon to die, he made a solemn statement before a solicitor and a Justice of the Peace. It speaks for itself:

"...The sergeant was ordered by the same officer to point the bayonet at my stomach. The same questions as to the names and addresses of my companions were repeated with the same result. The sergeant was then ordered to turn my face to the wall and point the bayonet at my back. I was so turned. The sergeant then said he would run the bayonet into me if I did not tell. The bayonet was then removed and I was turned around again. The same officer then said to me that if I persisted in my attitude he would turn me out to the men in the barrack square and he supposed I knew what that meant with the men in their present temper. I said nothing.

"He ordered the sergeant to put me face down on the floor and twist my arm. I was pushed down on the floor after my handcuffs were removed by the sergeant who went for the bayonet. When I lay on the floor, one of the sergeants knelt on my back, the other two placed one foot each on my back and left shoulder, and the man who knelt on me twisted my right arm, holding it by the wrist with one hand, while he held my hair with the other to pull back my head.

"The arm was twisted from the elbow joint. This continued, to the best of my knowledge, for five minutes.

"It was very painful... during the twisting of my arm, the first officer continued to question me as to the names and addresses of my companions... as I still persisted in refusing to answer these questions I was allowed to get up and I was again handcuffed... He informed me that if I gave all the information I knew, I could get off. I could certainly identify the officer who directed the proceedings... and... the sergeant with the bayonet.

"My arm was medically treated by an officer of the Royal Army Medical Corps, attached to the North Dublin Union, the following morning, and by the prison hospital orderly afterwards for four or five days..." Then came the trial.

....

This period, towards the end of the year 1920, was a terrible time in Ireland. The murderous Black and Tans had been given a free hand to terrorize the people into submission and to crush all resistance. Both sides knew that it was now or never and no holds were barred.

The midnight raids; the arrests without trial; the executions on lonely roads; were all part of the planned campaign and the I.R.A. fought back with the only weapon at their command, guerilla warfare at its toughest. The British military were pinned down in the cities and towns - the country roads were unsafe as the I.R.A. were experts in the techniques of attack from ambush positions. The barracks of the armed police, who supported the British military, were being captured and burned by the Irish Republican Army throughout the country.

A high ranking British officer wrote of the I.R.A. many years afterwards: "The captains of the volunteers appear to have been almost all quite young men, farmers' sons for the most part, some of them schoolmasters, most with what, for their class, must be considered a good deal of education, ignorant, however, of the world and of many things, but, as a class, transparently sincere and single-minded, idealists, highly religious for the most part, and often with an almost mystical sense of duty to their country. The men gave to the task of organizing their volunteers their best in mind and spirit. They fought against drunkenness and self-indulgence, and it is no exaggeration to say that, as a class they represented all that was best in the countryside.

"They and their volunteers were trained to discipline, they imbibed the military spirit, the sense of military honour, and then, as now, they looked upon their army as one in a very real sense, an organization demanding implicit obedience and self-abnegation from rank to rank.

"The Irish Republican Army seems to be particularly free from ruffians of the professional type, and the killings of police and others, sometimes under circumstances which evoke our horror, were almost certainly done by members of the I.R.A. acting under military orders - young men imbued with no personal feeling against their victims, with no crimes to their record, and probably then shedding blood for the first time in their lives.

"Behind their organization there is the spirit of a nation - of a nation that is certainly not in favour of murder, but which on the whole sympathizes with them and believes that the members of the I.R.A. are fighting for the cause of the Irish people."

The British hit back with reprisals: burning villages; handcuffing hostages to lorries - and the situation grew worse, so that within a short time, Cork city would be burned by drunken Black and Tans who then forcibly prevented the fire brigade from saving it; General Cummins, D.S.O., who usually took Irish civilian hostages with his British raiding parties, had been ambushed, and killed by the Cork-Kerry I.R.A. brigades; the Cork brigade had ambushed a large military force at Crossbarry and the official British casualties were thirty-nine killed and forty-seven wounded; I.R.A. General Seán MacEoin had successfully led an attack on an eleven-lorry British convoy at Ballinalee; and later a captured British armoured car had been driven right into Dublin's Mountjoy Jail in an unsuccessful attempt to rescue him; the town of Balbriggan, near Dublin, had been the scene of terrible destruction. Late one night in September, dozens of lorries packed with British military had come from nearby Gormanstown Camp to "teach the Irish bastards a lesson". House after house was set alight; people were attacked and beaten in the streets; two innocent men were bayonetted to death as the inhabitants ran into the countryside for shelter; later, in 1921, the centre of British rule in Ireland, the beautiful Custom House designed by Gandon, beside the River Liffey in the heart of the capital, was to be set on fire by the Dublin brigade of the I.R.A. and with it perished the records of British administration in Ireland. This severe loss led to further peace moves being initiated by the British Government - but, by that time, only Kevin Barry's spirit lived on.

....

"Why not shoot me like a soldier,
Do not hang me like a dog.
For I fought to free old Ireland,
On that bright September morn.

All around that little bakery,
Where we fought them hand to hand,
Why not shoot me like a soldier
For I fought to free Ireland."

Wednesday, October 20: Kevin Barry was on trial for his life. He was the first rebel soldier captured in action to go on trial since the 1916 rebellion and the British killed in the ambush were the first of many such casualties among the regular troops. The verdict was a foregone conclusion. In spite of the fact that the Irish Volunteers were the official army fighting for independence on behalf of an Irish Parliament freely elected by the people, the British refused to recognize them as prisoners of war.

Kevin Barry and his comrades had freed the twenty-five British soldiers captured by them a few months previously, but now there was to be no mercy. He was tried by court martial and the charge was murder!

It was known that Kevin Barry had been armed with a .38 revolver and that one of the bullets taken from the soldier he was accused of murdering had come from a .45 but the military prosecutor said it had only to be proven that he was one of the raiding party, as they were all equally guilty of murder.

As the witnesses paraded before the court the prisoner took little interest in the proceedings having made his position quite clear.

"As a soldier of the Irish Republic, I refuse to recognize the court."

He thus offered no defence and, when the president of the court kept asking him if he had any questions, he grew impatient with the trial and exclaimed: "I told you I don't recognize the court. I have no interest in what anybody says here."

The trial did not last long. The verdict was not announced in court but that night, in his lonely cell in Mountjoy Jail in the Dublin that he loved, the sentence was read to him:- "Death by hanging".

> "Calmly standing to attention.
> While he bade his last farewell
> To his broken-hearted mother
> Whose sad grief no one can tell
> For the cause he proudly cherished
> This sad parting had to be;
> Then to death walked softly
> smiling,
> That old Ireland might be free."

It was October 28 when the people of Ireland heard that young Kevin Barry was to be hanged on November 1, but nobody really believed it would actually happen.

There was a strong plea for a reprieve from all shades of opinion in Ireland: Protestant, Catholic, Anglo-Irish alike. Several influential people in England also supported the reprieve and, when distinguished members of this movement had seen Lloyd George, the British Prime Minister, they were certain that the execution would not take place. Many British newspapers, clergy and opposition MPs added their weight to the campaign for clemency but within days of the execution date the I.R.A. began to prepare plans for a rescue, if all else should fail.

The Barry family, mother and sisters, gave the I.R.A. leaders every co-operation and even agreed to keep the warders from raising the alarm during a visit inside the prison, while the Republicans forced an entrance. It was also planned that two crack I.R.A. men should enter the prison disguised as priests; and, even on the last day of October, a land-mine was being prepared to blow up the prison wall for a raiding party to rush the condemned man's cell. Then it was learned that the prisoner's guards had been ordered to shoot him first, if a rescue attempt took place, and, as there still seemed hope of a reprieve, all the attempts at rescue were abandoned.

....

In the four days from the time the death sentence was confirmed by the British Government until the fateful day, Kevin Barry saw his family, relations and many of his friends. They all left him with sadness but admiration at his cheerful talk. He was still able to crack a joke about his situation and became very popular with the warders of the prison. He told his friends: "It is nothing to give one's life for Ireland. I'm not the first and maybe I won't be the last. What's my life compared with the Cause?"

Time was ticking away. The streets around the prison were full of military. Armoured cars patrolled outside the walls; suddenly Ireland realized that Kevin Barry was to die.

It was said later that Lloyd George would have reprieved him but that Sir Henry Wilson, the Chief of the Imperial General Staff, threatened to resign if he did so. For this crime, and many others, including murder committed on his orders in Ireland, Wilson himself was later to pay the supreme penalty in the centre of London from the guns of an I.R.A. execution squad.

It was Sunday, October 31, Hallowe'en, always a time of parties and rejoicing in Ireland but that year, 1920, there was no gaiety, for young Kevin Barry was to die. Bravely, his mother took her last farewell and her fond son saluted her as she sadly left him for the last time.

Brigadier General Crosier, the Commander of the dreaded British Auxiliaries, who worked alongside the Black and Tans, was so impressed by Kevin Barry, and so disgusted by the work he himself was doing, that he later resigned; as did Major Mills - who had guarded Kevin Barry - after the British forces had opened fire on the spectators at the football match in Croke Park.

It was Sunday, October 31, Kevin Barry was to die the next morning. Father Albert, the Capuchin chaplain, visited him. "He struck me as a really magnificent boy, wonderfully calm and, at the same time I could see that he undoubtedly appreciated the fact that within a few hours he was doomed to be put to death..."

When the priest asked him for a last message, he replied: "Hold on and stick to the Republic" and then, rather humanly, and sadly, remarked, when he was told his fellow university students were gathered outside the prison, "I wish I could see them just once more."

Afterwards, it was reported that later that night, Kevin Barry had been taken from his cell into the death house and told what would happen to him in the morning. He was offered one last chance to betray his comrades, offered enough money for life in any country he wished - but again he refused. He was taken back into the condemned cell and then came November.

"In Mountjoy Jail one Monday
morning
High upon the gallows tree,
Kevin Barry gave his young life
for the cause of liberty.
Just a lad of eighteen summers,
Yet no one can deny,
As he walked to death that morning,
He proudly held his head on high."

Suddenly, it was Monday, November 1,1920, and Kevin Barry was to die.

The crowd had been gathering outside the prison since dawn on that cold November morning. Those who stayed at home were there in spirit as the minutes ticked away and with them the short life span of Kevin Barry. Ireland had suddenly realized that he was to hang and, in its sorrow, there was a certain pride that one so young could die so bravely. By 7 a.m. the streets around the prison were crowded and the British troops, with fixed bayonets, stood near the armoured cars, facing the people, their eyes searching everywhere. A murmur began to rise from the silent, sorrowful people as the hands of the clock moved towards eight: "Hail Mary, full of grace..." as they knelt on the muddy road.

Inside the grim prison, Kevin Barry had slept until he was called at 6 a.m. and quietly awaited the fateful hour. At 7 a.m. the two prison chaplains entered his cell, where the prisoner had arranged a small altar the night before. They said Mass, Kevin Barry received his last Holy Communion and firmly repeated the prayers after the priests.

Then, it was almost 8 a.m. and, outside, the prayers grew louder. "Our Father, who art in Heaven..." All Ireland was praying with the assembled kneeling crowd as, in his bare prison cell, the young prisoner's arms were strapped at his sides. Then, the last, long, lonely walk began.

Slowly through the silent prison on that grey November morning, Kevin Barry walked calmly between the two priests to the scaffold, "With the most perfect bravery, without the slightest faltering, repeating his little ejaculations and the Sacred Name till the very last instant of his life." The priest, at that time by no means a supporter of the Irish fight for independence continues: "His courage all the time was superhuman and rested, I am sure, in his simple goodness and innocence of conscience. He went to die as a priest to offer a sacrifice; in all humility and submission to the Divine Will, with a full confidence that he was going into Paradise, and a hope that his death might perhaps do something to heal the wounds of his country... one of the bravest and best boys I have ever known, his death was one of the most holy."

And thus died the body of Kevin Barry, "Just a lad of eighteen summers" on that cold, sad morning, Monday, November 1, 1920. He was buried in a rough, wooden coffin in a quiet corner of the prison grounds. His body was dead but his spirit lived on.

In later years, on November 1st, since that never-to-be-forgotten day in 1920 when Ireland stood still in sorrow and then became more determined that Kevin Barry should not die in vain, students from the National University held their annual march through the streets of the capital on their way to Mountjoy Jail to lay a wreath on his simple grave. He will never be forgotten for he became a symbol of the new Ireland, a symbol of freedom, of all that is best in youth, everywhere.

The execution of Kevin Barry had the opposite effect as usual in Ireland, to what the British authorities had planned. Instead of crushing resistance, it made the Irish more determined and brought people into the Republican movement who previously had been neutral or even hostile. It gave the guerilla fighters the more active support of the civilian population for few would betray an I.R.A. man 'on the run' if it could mean he would end on the scaffold for fighting for his country's freedom.

Resistance hardened everywhere and, when Kevin Barry, taken in action, had been hanged, the rules of war no longer applied. Bloody Sunday and Kilmichael were still to come; the fight was on and the Irish Republican Army had a new meaning.

> "Another martyr for old Ireland,
> Another murder for the Crown,
> Whose brutal laws may kill the
>   Irish,
> but cannot keep their spirits down.
> Lads like Barry are no cowards,
> From the foe they will not fly;
> Lads like Barry will free
> Ireland
> For her sake they'll live and
> die."

TERENCE MACSWINEY

6 A MAN ABOVE ALL

Terence MacSwiney was born in Cork in 1879 and, like many a boy before and since, was educated by the Irish Christian Brothers. A brilliant student, he seemed set for a successful academic career, but the death of his father forced him to go to work to support the rest of their large family when he was fifteen years old. He entered a local business firm and trained as an accountant. Although he did his work well, remaining there for some seventeen years, his heart was never in his job and he soon found other outlets for his energies.

Secretly he began to study for his matriculation and later for a degree in philosophy which he obtained in 1907, without attending university lectures. After his normal day's work in the office, he would write until bedtime, snatch a few hours' sleep, rise again at perhaps 3 a.m. to study until it was time to go back to the office again. He disciplined himself to require a minimum of sleep and was happiest when working hardest. He began to write plays and poetry, to read everything he could find of Shakespeare and to contribute articles to the national papers. He also managed to teach for a few hours weekly in the local commercial school and, when he finally left the office, was soon appointed full-time teacher of commerce for Cork county.

This was more to his liking for it gave him an opportunity to move around the beautiful countryside that he loved. "To exist, the healthy mind must have beautiful things - the rapture of a song, the music of running water, the glory of the sunset and its dreams, the deeper dreams of the dawn..."

Terence MacSwiney, in his writing, showed himself a prophet and a philosopher. He was soon to show himself a soldier and a patriot.

Just before Christmas, 1913, the Irish Volunteers were formed in Cork and MacSwiney realized that this was what he had waited for all his thirty-four years. He threw himself wholeheartedly into the organization of the new movement. "We would, of whatever extraction, have lived in natural neighbourliness with England, but she chose to trap and harass us, and it will take long generations of goodwill to wipe out some memories. Again, and yet again, let there be no confusion of thought as to this final peace; it will never come while there is any formal link of dependence. The spirit of our manhood will always flame up to resent and resist that link. Separation and equality may restore ties of friendship; nothing else can..."

His close friend, Thomas MacCurtain, became the leader of several thousand Irish Volunteers in County Cork and Terence MacSwiney soon took on the full-time job of organizer. He cycled throughout the county, day and night, wet and fine, never sparing himself, bringing sincerity, devotion and patriotism wherever he went. A born leader of men, he could inspire and uplift those who had little hope left, "While we must keep alive our generous instincts, we must keep resolute in the fight; while we desire peace, we must prosecute war; while we long for comradeship, we must be breaking up dangerous alliances; literary, political, trades and social unions formed with England while she is asserting her supremacy must be broken up till they can be reformed on a basis of independence, equality and universal freedom..."

A quiet man, intent on his work, with few amusements, MacSwiney never wished to appear better than those under him but he could be strict, especially on himself when the occasion arose. "When a man takes up a position of trust, influence and honour, and, whatever the difficulty, abandons a principle he should hold sacred, he must be held responsible. A battle is an ordeal, and we must be stern with friend and foe..."

In his writings, he points out what happens to those public representatives and people in high places who are not firm in the Irish cause: "...Invitations arrive to garden parties at Windsor, lesser functions nearer home, free passages to all the festivals, free admissions everywhere... great is the no politics era, you can so quietly spike the guns of many an old politician and keep him safe. The social amenities do this. And so the strength of the old warrior is sapped; the web is woven finely.."

He goes on to make perhaps a prophecy or two over the continued partition of Ireland. "There is a dangerous tendency gaining ground of slurring over vital things because the settlement of them involves great difficulty, and may involve great danger; but whatever the issue is, we must face it...", and again "...There are errors to remove. The first is the assumption that we are only required to acknowledge the flag in places, offer it allegiance at certain meetings at certain times that form but a small part of our existence... An idea you hold as true is not to be professed only where it is proclaimed; it will whisper and you must be its prophet in strange places..."

Thus passed the years before the historic rebellion of 1916; Terence MacSwiney writing, cycling through the countryside, training the volunteers for the fight he knew must come, speaking at lonely crossroads and in tree-lined glens, raising old hopes in the eyes of old men, lighting the fire of patriotism in the youth, but always seeking perfection. "A fight that is not cleanhanded will make victory more disgraceful than any defeat... no physical victory can compensate for spiritual surrender."

But he was completely without ill-will or bitterness. "Our enemies are brothers from whom we seem estranged...For the Empire, as we know it and deal with it, is a bad thing in itself and we must not only get free of it and not be again trapped by it, but must rather give hope and encouragement to every nation fighting the same fight all over the world."

It was inevitable that the sincere, quiet man who loved literature, art, the countryside, the theatre, the sea, should love the land of his birth and its people. As he had never spared himself when his own academic and commercial future seemed important, now he never spared himself when he considered his country needed him. Rain and snow made no difference as day after day, night after night, he cycled through the city and county of Cork, encouraging the volunteers by word and example, gathering new recruits, training small groups in isolated villages, making speeches.

In January, 1916, some three months before the rebellion, he was arrested for making a seditious speech and got his first taste of prison life in Cork jail before he was freed after a few weeks.

Then came Easter 1916, a glorious week for Dublin, a week that is best forgotten in Cork. While Dublin rose against the British on Easter Monday, the confusion over orders cancelling the original day of the rebellion, Easter Sunday, with the news that the German ship, the Aud, and Roger Casement, had been captured by the British, created such consternation in Cork that the volunteers there took no part in the rebellion. A thousand men had been ready for the call but they were dismissed and sent back to their homes. It was a great disappointment for them but for MacCurtain and MacSwiney it was heartbreaking. This was the day they had been working and praying for all these years and now the opportunity was slipping from their grasp. Conflicting reports reached them from Dublin and nobody knew what was happening there. As brave men marched into the G.P.O. in O'Connell Street to strike a historic blow for freedom, confusion reigned in Cork Volunteer headquarters.

Pearse, Clarke, Connolly, and their comrades had decided to go ahead with the Rebellion in Dublin knowing their deaths would be the outcome. These brave men believed that they must fight, and even die, to raise the spirit of the nation depressed after centuries of foreign occupation. They fought now for the honour, no less than the freedom, of Ireland and history proved them right. The future was to vindicate the honour of Cork also, for it was the men of Cork, Kerry, Dublin and Tipperary, above all others, who fought and defeated the Black and Tans, the Auxiliaries, and the rest of the British forces during the War for Independence 1919-1921.

But Easter 1916 almost broke the heart of Terence MacSwiney. With his fellow officers, he occupied the Volunteer hall in Cork city and was determined to defend it if the British decided to attack. But, due to the confusion and the lack of reliable communications with the leaders of the Rebellion in Dublin, neither he, nor MacCurtain, wished needlessly to endanger the lives of the men under their command and they did not engage the enemy. Both of them were to prove their personal courage beyond all doubt in the near future.

With the end of the Rebellion in Dublin, Thomas MacCurtain and Terence MacSwiney were arrested. Dispirited men, they were soon in the company of almost two thousand other "rebels" in Frongoch concentration camp in Wales.

Studious MacSwiney contrasted with man of action MacCurtain, yet they were always firm friends and comrades for one seemed to complement the other in making the perfect leadership team. The large gathering of Irish Republicans in the same prison camp gave the Volunteer officers an ideal opportunity to re-organize, to plan, to meet one another. Thus when the general release came at Christmas that year, the men returned to their homes throughout Ireland more experienced and more determined than ever to win freedom.

Terence MacSwiney immediately set to work where he had left off and, in less than two months, was again interned, this time in England. As he had no idea when he would be freed, his fiancée, Muriel Murphy, travelled over from Cork, together with the priest, and several relations. She was twenty-five, he was thirty-eight, and, on June 9, 1917, they were married there; they were not to be together for long.

Their wedding happiness had been made complete with the news that, together with the other prisoners, he was to be released within a week.

Back in Cork, the newly-weds set up their first home together but MacSwiney had no illusions about the future, "...Let no one think we overlook that mean type of man who evades every call to duty on the comfortable plea, 'I have married a wife'..., the man so often wavers on the verge of the right path, the woman so often decides him. When they are both equal in spirit and nobility of nature, how the world is filled with a glory that should assure us, if nothing else could, of the truth of the Almighty God and a beautiful eternity to explain the origin and destiny of their wonderful existence. They are indispensable to each other; if they stand apart, neither can realize in its fullness the beauty and glory of life... Let no man be afraid that those he loves may be tried in the fire but let him, to the best of his strength, show them how to stand the ordeal and then trust to the greatness of the Truth... making in time a wonderful blend of wisdom, tenderness and courage that gives them to realize that life, with all its faults, struggles and pain, is still, and forever, great and beautiful."

Within five months of his marriage, Terence MacSwiney was arrested again for delivering another "seditious" speech. In company with other Volunteers in Cork prison, he went on a hunger strike in protest against the treatment they were receiving and they were released in a few days, back again on the job organizing the I.R.A. for the coming battle. "To defend or recover freedom men must be always ready for the appeal to arms," but he knew it would not be easy even among his own countrymen. "There will be objections on all sides; from the blasé man of the world, concerned only for his comfort; the mean man of business concerned only for his profits; the man of policy always looking for a middle way; a certain type of religious pessimist who always spies danger in every proposal; and many others."

Yet this never discouraged him as he wrote: "We fight for freedom, not for the hope of material profit or comfort, but because every fine instinct of manhood demands that man be free, and life beautiful and brave... an earnest band is more effective than a discreditable multitude... If only a few are faithful found they must be the more steadfast for being but a few."

March 1918, he was again arrested and imprisoned, this time in Belfast. While he was there, their only child, a girl, was born. He was later transferred to Lincoln and, in his absence, he was one of the overwhelming majority of Republican candidates elected to the new Irish Parliament. The Irish Republic for the whole island had now been officially proclaimed by the Irish people in that year.

Released again, and now a member of An Dáil, the Irish Parliament, he began to take an active interest in administration but did not neglect his former occupation of organizing the Volunteer army for the new State and enrolling new recruits.

In August 1919, the Volunteers became the official army of the Irish nation and the I.R.A., as it was then popularly known, was already proving too much for the regular British soldiers. The new Irish Parliament was taking over the civil administration of the country, setting up Republican courts and by the beginning of 1920, the British were getting desperate as Ireland was slipping from their grasp. They struck back with everything in the power of a mighty Empire: raids, arrests, shooting, looting, but the population, far from being terrorized, rallied more and more behind "the invisible army", the I.R.A. "flying columns", who struck fast and hard throughout the country and then disappeared.

Every ambush by the I.R.A. was followed by reprisals by the Black and Tans and the Auxiliaries, whose special job was terrorism. Many of the regular British army officers expressed their disgust at the conduct of their comrades but their Government tried to cover up the misdeeds from the world press. Ireland was in a state of war.

On March 15, 1920, in the early hours of the morning, Thomas MacCurtain who had been elected Lord Mayor of Cork, was murdered in front of his wife in their home. The Coroner's inquest, in spite of severe pressure, brought in a verdict of murder, "Under circumstances of most callous brutality," against the British Government and its officials.

Terence MacSwiney's life-long friend was gone. He stayed two nights beside the coffin as it lay in state in Cork and at the funeral said, "... No matter how many lose their lives in the cause of their duty, as did the Lord Mayor, another will always be found to take the lead."

As the weeks went by, he became more serious and sad in himself although he had been quick to remark: "Get to understand Davis, Tone, or any of our great ones, and you will find them human, gay and lovable... Our history makers were great, joyous men, of fine spirit, fine imagination, fine sensibility and fine humour. They loved life; they loved their fellow man; they loved all the beautiful, brave things of earth..."

Terence MacSwiney himself was such a man. He loved his country and its people, he loved the good things of life, the sea, the mountains, his poetry, literature, painting, music, the native Irish language, the story telling and comradeship around the turf fire in the little country cottages. He loved his wife and child, his family, relations and friends. He was not a man of war but a man of peace, yet he realized that to have lasting peace, war was sometimes necessary. He did not expect anything for himself, "A man must be prepared to labour for an end that may be realized only in another generation... we must be prepared to work in the knowledge that we prepare for a future that only other generations will enjoy... That is the task of every generation to take up the uncompleted work of the former one, and hand on to their successors an achievement and a heritage."

And as he now went about his work, organizing resistance to British rule in Ireland, he had no doubts that victory would be won, yet issued a warning which is significant even today. "That we shall win our freedom, I have no doubt; that we shall use it well, I am not so certain, for see how sadly misused it is abroad through the world today... A perfect government should seek, while careful to develop its strongest forces and keep them in perfect balance, to consider also the claims of those less powerful but not less true. A government that overrides the weak because it is safe, is a tyranny, and tyranny is in seed in the democratic governments of our time," but then his strong optimism would again shine through. "We led Europe once; let us lead again with a beautiful realization of freedom..."

He frequently told friends that, when the fighting was all over, he would like to go back to his books and his writing but meanwhile he had a job to do. Following the murder of Cork Lord Mayor, Thomas MacCurtain, - the Lord Mayor of Limerick who attended his funeral was soon to meet the same fate - the City Corporation met on March 20 to elect his successor.

The choice was unanimous in the crowded hall. The city outside was ringed with British troops and, in a voice charged with emotion, the new Lord Mayor, Terence MacSwiney, spoke these words: "... We see in the manner in which our late Lord Mayor was murdered an attempt to terrify us all. Our first duty is to answer that threat in the only fitting manner, by showing ourselves unterrified, cool and inflexible for the fulfilment of our chief purpose - the establishment of the independence and integrity of our country, the peace and happiness of the Irish Republic. To that end I am here. I was more closely associated than any other here with our late murdered friend and colleague, both before and since the opening of the Irish War of Independence, in prison and out of it, in a common work of love for Ireland, down to the day of his death. For that reason I take his place. It is, I think, although I say it, the fitting answer to those who struck him down... God is over us and in his Divine intervention we have perfect trust. Anyone surveying events in Ireland for the past five years must see that it is approaching a miracle how our country has been preserved during a persecution unexampled in history, culminating in the murder of the head of our great city. God has permitted this to be, to try our spirit, to prove us worthy of a noble line, to prepare us for a great and noble destiny...Sometimes in our grief we cry out foolish and un-thinking words: 'The sacrifice is too great'; but it is because they were our best and bravest they had to die. No lesser sacrifice would save us. Because of it our struggle is holy, our battle is sanctified by their blood, and our victory is assured by their martyrdom.We, taking up the work they left incomplete, confident in God, offer in turn sacrifice from ourselves. It is not we who take innocent blood, but we offer it, sustained by the example of our immortal dead, and that

Divine Example which inspired us all, for the redemption of our country. Facing the enemy, we must declare our attitude simply. We see in their regime a thing of evil incarnate. With it there can be no parley, any more than there can be a truce with the powers of hell. This is our simple resolution. We ask for no mercy and we make no compromise. But to the Divine Author of mercy, we appeal for strength to sustain us in our battle, whatever the persecution, that we may bring our people victory in the end..."

The new Lord Mayor then went about his duties conscientiously and worked hard to re-organize the city administration. The City Council of Cork under his guidance publicly acknowledged Dáil Eireann as the elected Parliament of the Irish people and pledged allegiance to it. The Lord Mayor took a deep interest in his new office and worked hard for the citizens of his native place; often spending twelve hours a day in his office. He also had to travel to Dublin when the Parliament was in session; he was a leader in the Irish language movement, and the industrial revival and drafted conditions of employment regulations, yet he longed to have more time to spend at home with his wife and family but devotion to duty drove him on. He seldom slept at home for there was always the possibility he might be arrested at any time and, in the Cork City Hall, secret exits from his office had been constructed in case of a raid.

It came on August 12, 1920. Hundreds of British soldiers and armoured cars surrounded the City Hall and, before he could escape, Terence MacSwiney was captured.

Included in the charges against him was a copy of the speech he made on his election and a copy of the City Corporation's resolution pledging allegiance to the Irish Parliament. His young wife, his sister and his chaplain, Father Dominic, O.F.M. Cap., were among the few people allowed at the military court martial in Cork on August 16. The Lord Mayor had taken no food since his arrest and when he faced the British officers from the dock said: "I would like to say a word about your proceedings here. The position is that I am Lord Mayor of Cork and Chief Magistrate of this city. And I declare this court illegal and that those who take part in it are liable to arrest under the laws of the Irish Republic.".

The proceedings dragged on, the accused taking little interest in them. He knew that the verdict was already determined but he made a few statements on points of importance. "... You have got to realize, and will have to realize it before very long, that the Irish Republic is really existing... as a soldier of the Irish Republic I like to respect soldiers of every kind... I ask for no mercy."

When the President of the Military Court announced a verdict of guilty, the Lord Mayor spoke again. "I wish to state that I will put a limit to any term of imprisonment you may impose as a result of the action I will take. I have taken no food since Thursday, therefore I will be free in a month... I simply say that I have decided the terms of my detention whatever your Government may do. I shall be free, alive or dead, within a month." For once, Terence MacSwiney was wrong!

His wife said goodbye; his two sisters and his brother were allowed to visit him and, during the night, the prisoner was taken from his native land to Brixton Prison in England to serve a sentence of two years imprisonment.

He had often said: "Our philosophy is valueless unless we bring it into life," and he was now to live up to his lifelong principles of freedom. He had been arrested on August 12 and, as he did not recognize the right of the British to arrest him in his own country, he was fighting them with the only weapon at his disposal, the hunger strike.

As the days went into weeks and the weeks into months, the eyes of the world were focused on the lone man in Brixton Prison. Foreign correspondents from every country poured into London; newspapers demanded his release; resolutions were passed in foreign capitals demanding his freedom; the world waited every day for news. The name of Ireland became known in places it had never reached before and Terence MacSwiney became a symbol of Right against Might. The British Trades Union Congress at Portsmouth in September adopted a resolution to telegraph the Prime Minister calling for his release.

Back in Cork, eleven of his comrades were also on hunger strike and, two died: I.R.A. Commandant Michael FitzGerald after sixty-seven days and Joseph Murphy after seventy-six days without food. The other nine, whose names should not be forgotten - Peter and John Crowley, Thomas Donovan, Michael Burke, Matt Reilly, Christopher Upton, John Power, Joseph Kenny and Sean Hennessy - carried on without food until ordered to give up the strike by I.R.A. headquarters.

From his bed in Brixton jail, England, Terence MacSwiney wrote a letter: "To my comrades in Cork; on your 56th day I greet you. I ask you to join with me in the following prayer for our people suffering such persecution in the present crisis: 'O my God, I offer my pain for Ireland... if we are to die in prison, it is Thy Will - accept our willing sacrifice for our people. May we in dying bring glory to Thy Name, and honour to our country that has always been faithful to Thee.. God save Ireland... May the liberty of the Irish people shine with Thy Glory, O my God, for ever and ever. Amen.' Comrades, if we twelve go in glorious succession to the grave, the name of Ireland will flash in a tongue of flame through the world and be a sign of hope for all time to every people, struggling to be free..." Every morning, the hunger strikers received Holy Communion and prayed together. When the first of them died, Terence MacSwiney wrote: "Not tears but joy for our comrade who was ready to meet his God and die for his country. He has joined the Immortals and will be remembered for ever. We do not know who is the second to step on the path of immortality, but by offering unreserved sacrifice we are safeguarding the destinies of Ireland. I join with my comrades in Cork in sending heartfelt sympathy to all the relatives of our revered fallen colleague." With never a thought for himself, MacSwiney had lived, and was now ready to die, for Ireland.

Only forty years of age, he now knew his destiny and lived up to the high principles he had written many years ago, his personal philosophy: "Let the cultivation of a brave, high spirit be our great task; it will make of each man's soul an unassailable fortress. Armies may fail but it resists for ever. The body it informs may be crushed; the spirit in passing breathes on other souls, and other hearts are fired to action, and the fight goes on to victory. To the man whose mind is true and resolute, ultimate victory is assured."

By the time he reached Brixton, Terence MacSwiney was in a state of collapse, having eaten nothing for five days. He was given every comfort in prison, for the British did not want him to die and so become another Irish martyr. Instead it was hoped he would give up the hunger strike and thus betray the cause of Irish freedom which was quickly gathering world support. The battle was on. One man against an empire and the brave prisoner no doubt remembered an article he wrote almost ten years previously: "Since the time of O'Connell, the cry Moral Force has been used persistently to cover up the weakness of every politician who was afraid or unwilling to fight for the whole rights of his country... a man of moral force is he who, seeing a thing to be right and essential and claiming his allegiance, stands for it as for the truth, unheeding any consequence. It is not that he is a wild person, utterly reckless of all mad possibilities, filled with a madder hope, and indifferent to any havoc that may ensue. No, but it is a first principle of his, that a true thing is a good thing and from a good thing rightly pursued can follow no bad consequence... A man who will be brave only if tramping with a legion will fail in courage if called to stand in the breach alone. And it must be clear to all that till Ireland can again summon her banded armies there will be abundant need for men who will stand the single test. 'Tis the bravest test, the noblest test, and 'tis the test that offers the surest and greatest victory. For one armed man cannot resist a multitude, nor can one army conquer countless legions; but not all the armies of all the Empires of earth can crush the spirit of one true man; and that man will prevail." Now he himself was the man who had to stand the single test. "We stand on the ground that the English Government in Ireland is founded in usurpation and as such deny its authority."

He had written this a long time ago and now he was challenging Britain alone, seeking justice for his long-suffering country.

During those weeks in the autumn of 1920, MacSwiney, one man against an empire, was symbolic of his small country's long struggle against overwhelming odds. Ireland and MacSwiney, MacSwiney and Ireland, were words spoken daily throughout the world.

A deeply religious man, he had, long before he joined the Irish Volunteers and was first arrested, become critical of some religious practices. He detested bigotry and discrimination: "When religion ceases to represent to us something spiritual, and purely spiritual, we begin to drift away from it... on all sides self-constituted defenders of the faith are troubling themselves not with the faith but with the number of their adherents who have jobs."

But the pure Christianity in the "Imitation of Christ" appealed to him and was read out to him daily by his faithful chaplain, Father Dominic, and his relatives. The great event of his day was to receive Holy Communion; he was in the prison hospital ward which had a fire and was fairly comfortable. Never one who liked the limelight of publicity, he was amazed to see international interest in his fight when a special foreign press bureau had to set up in London to issue bulletins on his progress. Once he exclaimed: "For forty years I have done nothing for Ireland. Now I have done more in a few weeks than in my whole life."

As the days passed slowly by, world reaction increased and Britain's prestige and reputation was damaged beyond repair. It was the beginning of the end for the great British Empire and this one man, from this small country, was showing the way. At home in Ireland, hundreds of thousands of people were attending Mass and Holy Communion daily; rosaries were said by the million; Catholics, Protestants, Jews, were united in protest against the detention of this brave man. But the British Government ignored them all, even the pleas from its own people.

When Terence MacSwiney arrived in Brixton Prison on August 18, after five days on hunger strike, his condition was critical and his death was expected; but, as the days went on, one after the other, very slowly, he even seemed to improve; was always cheerful with visitors, and did not like to talk about his own suffering. "People always talk about me but the others are making a greater sacrifice."

The pain he was suffering was hidden from his visitors, from his devoted wife and sisters, from his brother, his chaplain, and other friends. August dragged into September and he still battled on.

"For in our time it has grown the fashion to praise the men of former times but to deny their ideal of Independence; and we who live in that ideal, and in it breathe the old spirit, and preach it and fight for it and prophesy for it an ultimate and complete victory, we are young men, foolish and unpractical... shall we honour the flag we bear by a mean apologetic front? No; wherever it is down, lift it; wherever it is challenged, wave it; wherever it is high, salute it; wherever it is victorious, glorify and exult in it. At all times and forever be for it proud, passionate, persistent, jubilant, defiant; stirring hidden memories, kindling old fires, wakening the finer instincts of men, till all are one in the old spirit, the spirit that will not admit defeat, that has been voiced by thousands, that is noblest in Emmet's one line setting the time for his epitaph; "When my country - not if, but - `when my country takes her place among the nations of the earth',... We believe it. We know it... Liberty. Inevitable. In two words to epitomize the history of a people that is without a parallel in the annals of the world."

Never acknowledging the right of Britain to keep him a prisoner, MacSwiney soldiered on - refusing again and again all the efforts of the Home Office doctor to tempt him with food. His thoughts were frequently on the I.R.A. hunger strikers in Cork and he constantly asked about their welfare. He worried about his wife and family until assured by friends that they would be taken care of. He never once wavered from his determination to be free on his own terms; and often uttered prophetic words: "We must get men to realize that to live is as daring as to die. But confusion has been made in our time by the glib phrase: `You are not asked now to die for Ireland, but to live for her'; without insisting that the life shall aim at the ideal, the brave and the true. To slip apologetically through existence is not life. If such a mean philosophy went abroad, we would soon find the land a place of shivering creatures, without the capacity to live or the courage to die..."

September gave way to October and still the world was astounded with admiration and wonder that Terence MacSwiney was still alive. But a new enemy had now appeared. There was talk among the doctors of forcibly feeding the prisoner. Thomas Ashe, an I.R.A. officer who went on hunger strike in Mountjoy jail in 1917 in support of a demand to be treated as a prisoner of war had been brutally killed by this method. The threat of it became a worry to MacSwiney, as he lay weak and defenceless on his prison bed. The terror of it troubled his mind for he wanted nothing, even force, to break his resolve to fast until free in protest against the atrocities now being carried out by the British in Ireland. So real was the danger of forcible feeding, that his relations and friends instituted a twenty-four hour watch at his bedside. His brother Seán stayed there all through the night; one of his sisters taking over in the morning. The Lord Mayor's wife would come in the afternoon and another sister would stay until the chaplain Father Dominic arrived at night. Another brother, Peter, was also a frequent visitor, as were many friends. Several Bishops visited him and, in spite of British intrigue in Rome, Pope Benedict, finally sent his blessing and plenary indulgence.

Time was running out. It was a long, long time from August to October.

Brixton Prison, October 12, 1920: "As this is the 61st day of fast and as from this time forward every day must become more and more critical, I wish to convey through you to my Republican colleagues on the Municipal Council a last greeting and farewell lest I should not see them again. I pray that the harmony and good fellowship that existed between all of us will continue... I wish you also to convey an expression of my goodwill and esteem to our colleagues generally... I unite all now in one common blessing... Finally, I wish to convey a greeting to all the workmen and staff as it was my desire to be a personal friend with every man employed in the Corporation in whatever capacity as it gave me a pleasure to feel that every man in the municipal employ felt that he could come to me without hesitation on every matter he felt concerned in, in his day's work... I hope... that we will have no more non-Irish speaking Mayors in Cork... God bless you all and direct you in your labours. God bless and defend the Irish Republic and establish it securely in its place among the nations."

October 12: sixty-one days on hunger strike and in many capitals of the world, people were talking about this man. A few days before, he had written thus to a comrade: "Your letter went to my heart. It consoled and comforted me. God bless you for it. But I would not have you in my place for anything. I'm praying that you will be among the survivors to lead the army of the Republic in the days of freedom. I feel final victory is coming in our time and pray earnestly that those who are most needed will survive to direct it. Those who are gone before will be with you in spirit to watch over the battle helping in unseen but powerful ways... with all a comrade's love. God bless you..." This letter was to Cathal Brúgha, who was soon to die, a gun in each hand, fighting against the unjust partition of Ireland.

The Bishop of Southwark, Dr. Amigo, gave special permission for Mass to be said every morning in the prisoner's room and, as the days in October went slowly on and he grew weaker, his favourite extracts from the "Imitation of Christ" gave him continued courage. "I will fear no evil when Thy grace is with me. It is more mighty than all my enemies and wiser than all the wise."

Father Dominic would frequently read to him in Irish and discuss Irish heroes and the heroine St. Joan of Arc. "Blessed is he who has always the hour of his death before his eyes and every day disposes himself to die... Strive now so to live that at the hour of thy death thou mayest rejoice rather than fear."

The hour of death was approaching but it was not going to be easy. "He who knows how to suffer will enjoy much peace. Such a one is a conqueror of himself and Lord of the world, a friend of Christ and an heir of heaven... For him whom God will help no man's malice can hurt. If thou canst but hold thy peace and suffer, thou shall see without doubt that the Lord will help thee."

Terence MacSwiney firmly believed that God was helping him in his struggle, not for his own sake but because of the prayers offered for him and for the sake of both Britain and Ireland. He forgave those who were causing his death and never for a moment doubted that Ireland would win her freedom. He never regretted the action he had taken in the struggle for the independence of the thirty-two counties of Ireland and was living, and dying, as he intended. "True hearts lived, scattered here and there, believing still but disorganized and bewildered. The leaders were stricken down and in their place, obscuring the beauty of life, the grandeur of the past and our future destiny, came timeservers, flatterers, hypocrites, open traffickers in honour and public decency, fastening their mean authority on the land. These are the two great resting places in our historic survey; the generation of the living flame and the generation of despair; and it is for us to decide, for the decision rests with us, whether we shall in our time merely mark time or write another luminous chapter in the splendid history of our race."

These words, like almost everything MacSwiney had written over seventy years ago, are still full of meaning in modern Ireland and, like him, should never be forgotten. "Who will remember thee when thou art dead and who will pray for thee...?

It was now the middle of October, more than two months after his arrest and immediate hunger strike. His once strong and powerful body was now wasted away. He could hardly breathe and could not bear even the weight of the bedclothes on his tortured frame. Bedsores troubled him and, on Monday, October 18, three doctors visited him to inform him that unless he took some lime juice he would suffer great pain from scurvy which was breaking out all over his poor body. He refused, saying he would suffer whatever pain God sent him. "He who knows how to suffer will enjoy much peace... The perfect victory is to triumph over oneself."

He had now been fasting sixty-eight days and he began to suffer from the delusion that he was being forcibly fed and would try to move his weak body to struggle against it.

He became delirious and several times lapsed into unconsciousness. The doctor and nurse took advantage of this to force some brandy and milk between his lips but he would suddenly awaken and although feeble, would manage to prevent them. Once, when they were successful in forcing some liquid into his mouth, as he lay unconscious, his head moved from side to side as he tried to fight them off and he awoke, exclaiming: "They have tricked me." Then the liquid vomited from his empty stomach and he became unconscious again.

His wife, sisters, brothers, chaplain, and some close friends were with him through his suffering. Sometimes, his face seemed to light up with happiness. The spirit was still unconquered but the body was getting weaker and weaker; "...Not all the armies of all the Empires of earth can crush the spirit of one true man..." he had written long, long ago in Cork.

Seventy-one, seventy-two, seventy- three, seventy-four. The days passed slowly by and his agony increased. While the prison doctors and nurses showed him every consideration, the doctor sent specially by the British Home Office seemed determined to feed him by force and relatives and friends had to be always vigilant. Towards the end of that fateful week in October, they were forbidden to sit with him by direct order of the Home Office in London. However, some of them were allowed in for short periods just to see him. Time went slowly by and his young life that had been measured in years, then months, then weeks, then hours, was now finding it difficult to exist from minute to minute.

Then came the weekend and his wife and sisters were told they could not stay with him. Father Dominic and his brother Seán slept in the prison that Sunday night and, in the early hours of Monday morning, October 25, 1920, they were informed that the Lord Mayor was dying. The Home Office doctor Griffith would not allow them to telephone for his wife and sisters so Seán MacSwiney and the priest went together to his bedside.

Father Dominic watched the Irish martyr as he lay apparently unconscious, breathing with great difficulty. The priest, when giving him the plenary indulgence sent by the Pope asked him to close his eyes if he could still hear the prayers and the lids slowly shut on the invincible spirit who had defied an empire. As the prayers continued, the breathing stopped and Terence MacSwiney had gone to join his comrades, who had died for Ireland down through the centuries, after an incredible hunger strike of seventy-five days. "Let the cultivation of a brave, high spirit be our great task; it will make of each man's soul an unassailable fortress. Armies may fail, but it resists forever. The body it informs may be crushed; the spirit in passing breathes on other souls, and other hearts are fired to action, and the fight goes on to victory."

The widow, sisters, brothers and friends kept a vigil beside the Lord Mayor's body until the coffin, draped in the Irish tricolour, led the funeral procession to Southwark Cathedral. Dr. Amigo, the kind Bishop of the diocese, allowed the body of the Irish patriot to lie in state there and a huge crowd, led by bishops and priests, recited the prayers. More than thirty thousand people filed past the coffin in London before the Requiem Mass next morning. During the night, the Irish Volunteer Guard of Honour had dressed the body in his Commandant's uniform over the Franciscan habit, as the dying Lord Mayor had wished.

The Mass was celebrated by Dr. Cotter, Bishop of Portsmouth; Dr. Mannix, Bishop of Melbourne; Dr. Kenealy, Bishop of Simla, and Dr. Amigo, Bishop of Southwark Cathedral. The Mayors of Fulham, Camberwell, Stepney, Southwark and Battersea were present at the funeral procession as thousands lined the route to Euston station.

But, even dead, the British Government was afraid of MacSwiney and, at Holyhead, the Black and Tans seized his coffin. The government would not allow the body to be brought to Dublin as had been arranged and instead sent a gun boat to take it direct to Cork. The mourners continued on to the Irish capital and, next morning, with an empty hearse in the funeral procession went to the Cork train at Kingsbridge Station. Requiem Mass for the soul of Terence MacSwiney was celebrated in the Pro-Cathedral by Dr. Walsh, Archbishop of Dublin; Dr. Spence, Archbishop of Adelaide; Dr. Clune, Archbishop of Perth; and Dr. Foley, Archbishop of Ballarat. All work stopped in the silent, sorrowful yet proud city.

In Cork, British armoured cars and soldiers with fixed bayonets were ignored as a guard of honour of a hundred uniformed Irish Volunteers marched openly from the docks with the coffin on their shoulders to the City Hall. Terence MacSwiney had come home. "I shall be free, alive or dead..."

Hundreds of thousands of people from all over the country came to pay him homage. His former opponent on the question of Irish resistance, the Bishop of Cork, said, "Periodically, the memory of the martyr's death will remind a young generation of the fundamental question of the freedom of Ireland," and, in the presence of several other bishops, clergy, Lord Mayors, and members of the new Irish Republican Parliament, celebrated Mass over the coffin in the Cathedral.

Sunday, October 31, 1920, in Cork: The body of Terence MacSwiney was laid to rest beside that of his life-long comrade and friend, Thomas MacCurtain. The vast multitude who gathered there heard Arthur Griffith, representing the President of the Irish Republic, say: "We, his colleagues of Dáil Eireann, stand by the graveside of Terence MacSwiney in sorrow, but in pride. He laid down his life to consolidate the establishment of the Irish Republic willed by the people of Ireland. His heroic sacrifice has made him in death the victor over the enemies of his country's independence. He has won over them because he has gained by his death for Ireland the support and sympathy of all that is human, noble and generous in the world.

"Remember his words to you, people of Cork when seven months ago he stepped into the Bearna Baoghail - Gap of Danger - that triumph is not to those who can inflict most but to those who can endure most. He has exemplified that truth to all mankind. He endured all that the power of England could inflict upon him and, in enduring, triumphed over that power.

"His body lies here; his soul goes marching through all the ages.

"He is not dead. He is living forever in the hearts and consciousness of mankind. Mourn for him but let your mourning be that for a martyr who triumphs.

"Ireland has lost a noble son, as France lost a noble daughter when Saint Joan of Arc perished in the English bonfire.

"The sequel will be the same. Saint Joan of Arc has welcomed a comrade to heaven."

The sad yet triumphant notes of the Last Post echoed into the Irish sky; the Volunteers fired their final salute over his grave. Terence MacSwiney was dead yet his spirit lived on. His comrades were more determined that the victory he had died for would be achieved.

Tomorrow was November 1, 1920, and young Kevin Barry was to die for the same cause of Irish freedom. Many more were still to die. It was all part of a long, bitter fight for freedom that had gone on almost eight hundred years. The Irish Republic for which MacSwiney, and his comrades, suffered and died, has still to be achieved, and, in his own words;

"...It is for us to decide - for the decision rests with us - whether we shall in our time merely mark time or write another luminous chapter in the splendid history of our race."

Terence MacSwiney wrote a luminous chapter in the history of the Irish race and in the history of those who love freedom everywhere. He will never be forgotten wherever men value freedom - Right against Might - because as he said: "Every fine instinct of manhood demands that man be free, and life beautiful and brave."

He will never be forgotten by the young men and women of Ireland today for he died for them too. "We prepared a future that only other generations will enjoy."

And he gave them this reminder of their duty: "...What they left undone we must take up and fulfil. This is the task of every generation, to take up the uncompleted work of the former one, and hand on to their successors an achievement and a heritage."

TOM CLARKE

7. THE BRAVEST OF THE BRAVE

The loud bang of the heavy, iron door echoed through the silent prison like the report of a cannon. Hour after hour, night after night, for seven long years, the frail, lonely man in the small, cold whitewashed cell was not allowed to rest. During the day, he was kept at the most laborious work as a moulder of heavy castings in the iron foundry and, at night, worn out in body and mind, he was led back to the cell for the fiendish 'no sleep' torture.

"I might get a few short snatches of sleep between the inspections but the nervous system becomes so shattered that one might not be able to sleep at all. Think of the effects of this upon a man's system and no one will wonder that so many were driven insane by such tactics. The horror of these days and nights will never leave my memory. One by one I saw my fellow prisoners break down and go mad under the terrible strain: some slowly and by degrees, some suddenly and without warning, and 'who next?' was the terrible thought that haunted us day and night. The ever recurring idea that it might be myself added to the agony."

Tom Clarke, then twenty-six years old, was under no illusions when he was sentenced to: "Penal servitude for life" because he dared to strike a blow for Ireland's freedom. Yet one rule in the long litany of prison regulations startled him: "Strict silence must at all times be observed; under no circumstances must a prisoner speak."

Day after day all alike, no change, maddening silence, sitting hopeless, friendless and alone; night after night, the maddening 'no sleep' torture; all, as Clarke remarked, "Part of the system especially devised for the Irish prisoners to destroy us mentally and physically - to kill or drive insane."

He saw his companions, Dr. Thomas Gallagher and Albert Whitehead, break under the strain. "Can I ever forget the night that poor Whitehead realized that he was going mad? There in the stillness, between two of the hourly inspections, I heard the poor fellow fight against insanity, cursing England and English brutality from the bottom of his heart and beseeching God to strike him dead sooner than allow him to lose his reason."

Next it was the turn of Dr. Gallagher, but for him as for Whitehead, insanity was no escape. Daily they were punished for every minor transgression against the rules; daily they were made to work and were confined alone in their cells although they had both long lost the use of reason. For eight years before they were released, the authorities refused to admit these men were mad and stated that they were shamming but, when they arrived in America, they were both pronounced hopelessly insane and placed in an asylum; Dr. Gallagher died there in New York without regaining his reason and is buried in Calvary Cemetery, Long Island.

The story of Tom Clarke is the story of one man's fight against torture and insanity and of how he lived to strike another blow for the freedom of his country.

Thomas J. Clarke was born in Hurst Castle, Isle of Wight, on the 11th of March 1857, of Irish parents, although his father was a soldier in the British army. Within a few weeks, the family were in South Africa where the regiment was posted and he was ten years of age before he saw Ireland, the country he grew to love more than life itself. Dungannon, in the County Tyrone, became his home town and he attended St. Patrick's national school, where he later became an assistant teacher.

Mixing with the local people in this busy, country town, young Tom heard many terrible stories of the famine and the mass emigration that cut Ireland's population by almost half a few short years earlier and he saw for himself the continued brutality of the landlords and British soldiery as they kept the people in subjection. That was the deliberate policy to wipe out this ancient nation. He came to believe that the only hope for Ireland's survival was to break the connection with England but his father tried to change this viewpoint. "You cannot hope to fight the British Empire, son," he would say frequently for, in those days, Britain ruled the world and countries a hundred times larger than Ireland, and thousands of miles further away from London, were proud possessions of the invincible army and navy of England.

The Fenians, after their unsuccessful rebellions in the 1860's had re-organised and, on August 14, 1880, Tom Clarke, then 23, was sworn in as a member of the Irish Republican Brotherhood, (I.R.B.), whose aim was to free Ireland from British rule. Meanwhile, the attendance at the local school had declined and Tom, out of work, decided to go, with a few local boys, to seek his fortune in America.

He became a night porter at the Mansion House Hotel in Brooklyn, where his big task was to light, and mind, some fifty fires every day. He was described then as: " A bright, earnest, wiry, alert, young fellow," and, within a couple of years - as could only happen in America, 'the land of opportunity', he was offered the post of manager at the new Brighton Beach Hotel. However, Tom now had other things on his mind. A call had gone out among the Irish-Americans: "Single men wanted as volunteers for dangerous work for Ireland," and he had answered.

Earlier he had been sworn in as a member of the Napper Tandy Club in the Clan-na-Gael organization in New York City, run by men who were determined to have vengeance for the British atrocities in Ireland. These Irish emigrants were now conducting, from America, a dynamiting campaign on public buildings in England and it was for one of these missions that young Tom Clarke had offered his services although he did not know this at the time.

Thus, he gave up the opportunity of becoming manager of a luxury hotel and instead, in 1883, sailed for England. Ships were always unlucky for him. On the way to South Africa with his family, they had been involved in a collision and almost drowned; on the way back, the ship caught fire; and, this time, the boat from Boston struck an iceberg and he was very fortunate to be picked up by a passing vessel.. He was landed at Newfoundland, where he gave his name as "Henry Hammond Wilson" an Englishman returning to his native land!

Dr. Thomas Gallagher and Albert Whitehead, two Irish-Americans who were organizing the dynamite plots, had already arrived in Britain, shadowed all the way by British secret service agents, who had lost track of Tom Clarke through the shipwreck. The famous Carlton Club in London had been blown up previously and, at the trial of Dr. Gallagher, it was alleged that he had pointed to Big Ben and the British House of Commons, exclaiming: "This will make a grand crash when it comes down."

By now, the police had been following "Wilson" although not aware of his real identity and, on April 4, the three Irishmen were arrested. Their trial opened at the historic Old Bailey, London, on Monday, June 11, 1883, and the prisoners were described as: "Dr. Gallagher, aged thirty-three, physician; Henry Hammond Wilson, aged twenty-two, clerk; Albert Whitehead, aged twenty-three, painter," and they were charged with, among other things, "Levying war against our most Gracious Lady, the Queen, in order to compel her to change her measures and counsel and in order to intimidate and overawe both Houses of Parliament... " all under the notorious Treason Felony Act of the Famine year, 1848, introduced so that arrest, banishment, or execution could be given the appearances of legality without the burden of providing substantial proof of guilt.

The government, and the British press, now wanted blood. The Fenians and the rest of the Irish rebels must be crushed without delay, so the trial was just a formality. The prisoners pleaded "Not guilty" and Henry Hammond Wilson, conducting his own defence, stated that he had not committed any such act as alleged.

On Thursday, June 14, the three conspirators, and John Curtin, (34), engineer, who was tried with them, were all sentenced to: "Penal servitude for life," which they were told must mean at least twenty years in prison. They immediately got their first prison haircut. "These scissors at work every weekday to barber about fifteen hundred men were blunted and most of them with the rivets loose; a pair of scissors of that kind in the hands of a clumsy operator made a terrible torture for the victim who was being trimmed. It was a sight to see the havoc that had been wrought, regular ridges of cuts in many cases, where the skin had been clipped away."

They were put into prison dress, with arrows and a number on the back, but this did not deter Clarke either. "I wore this convict garb with a certain amount of pride and took satisfaction in the thought that with all her laws, and with all her power, this great England could not force me, one of the mere units of the Irish rank and file - to regard myself as one of the criminal class, any more than I could ever be forced to regard myself as English."

And so began the long battle of one man against an empire, a battle that lasted for more than the fifteen long years he was to spend in an English prison cell. The "silent system" had first to be conquered, for Tom Clarke knew that; "No matter who the man may be, educated or illiterate, no matter how hopeful his disposition or how physically fit he be, no matter what strength of will power he may possess or what determination of character may be his to `see things through' in man's fashion, it will avail him nothing: he will inevitably be driven insane if only kept long enough under that silent system. It will gradually wear him down and shatter his nervous system and destroy the normal tranquillity of his mind to such an extent that a point will be reached when the mind becomes thoroughly exhausted and left in a state of frenzied unsettlement, having nothing to feed upon except such gloomy thoughts as will be dictated to him by his wretched environment. The end, insanity, for that poor mortal is then near at hand."

Tom Clarke refused to be driven insane although he admits that: "The worst my imagination could picture of British brutality was outdone by the horrors of Chatham Prison and had anyone told me that it was possible to endure what the Irish prisoners have endured there and come out of it alive and sane I would not have believed him. It has been a source of perpetual surprise to me that I was able to get through it all."

The ordinary rules governing the treatment of criminals were set aside and the officers in charge were given a free hand to persecute the prisoners, just as they pleased, with a scientific system of perpetual and persistent harassing, morning, noon and night.

Clarke, and two other Irish prisoners, John Daly and James Egan, although each in solitary confinement in small, dreary cells, were determined to fight the "silent system" which could drive them insane and the way they did it was remarkable.

First, Clarke got hold of a needle from the prison tailor's shop and, on a sheet of brown paper, perforated a code of dots and dashes to correspond to the letters of the alphabet, something like Morse. "It took two days to write the note with the vigilant eye of the officer peeping every now and then into my cell... I concealed it in my stocking when going out for the weekly bath... managed to get it into the next compartment to Gallagher... and, within a week, we were able to converse freely through the wall dividing our cells by producing two different kinds of knocks on the wall, one made with the knuckles, the other a sharp sound made by a button, to correspond with the dot-dash code as set out in our note."

It was by this system of "conversation" that he first realized that both Gallagher and Whitehead were changing and slowly losing their reason. Although he several times drew the attention of the Governor to this fact by writing to him, these poor men who had become insane were still subject to the same inhuman treatment and not released for another eight years.

It was soon afterwards that Clarke, Daly and Egan began to pass written notes to one another when Daly had got a supply of lead pencils from the carpenter's shop. This was later discovered, so Clarke made pencils by baking stove blacklead and clay under the eyes of the guards in the prison iron foundry, but they were not satisfactory. Then he got hold of some graphite and they were in business again.

He always realized that if he "let go" of himself, madness was inevitable, so he gave his mind to many strange occupations. "Looking back on these times, memory shows me a picture of myself in that whitewashed cell of mine, sitting with slate and pencil devoting hours and hours to all sorts of calculations. Not only have I counted every brick in my cell and every bolt that studded the ironclad doors, and every perforation in the iron ventilators in that cell, and calculated the weight of the bricks used in building it, and also worked out the number of bricks used in building the entire prison and figured out the total weight. Yes, many an hour I spent turning that prison inside out and upside down, re-arranging the bricks of it into a pyramid one time or into a square and calculating dimensions."

When he had exhausted all the possibilities of the prison building, he turned his attention to the inmates, "As a result of calculations, I could at one time have told the total number of buttons on the clothing of the entire population of that prison or the number of 'broad arrow' marks that were stamped on their clothing."

When he "knew" everything about the other prisoners and could not find anything else to keep his mind busy, he turned his attention to himself. "I have taken clippings of my hair for several weeks from the weekly cuttings and measured these samples... and calculated that over six feet of hair has been cut off my head during thirteen years."

On one occasion, he had an unexpected stroke of luck getting hold of a book which contained lessons in shorthand, which he soon mastered.

"Then, by way of practice, I set to work on the Bible. Starting at the beginning of the Old Testament, I worked my way right through the whole book to the end of the New Testament, stenographing every word of it from cover to cover. That finished I started again and went over the same ground a second time."

But this did not satisfy him and, proof that his mind was still normal, he became very curious to know what speed he had obtained. "I waited till the clock started to strike and simultaneously I started to write something from memory at my best speed and came to a stop when the clock finished striking. Counting the number of words I had been able to write I made a note of it. Next night I was again ready waiting for the clock but this time with my finger on the pulse of my wrist. When the clock began striking I began counting the pulse beats and noted how many beats were made while the clock was striking... assuming that my pulse was beating at the rate of a normal, healthy man... I was able to calculate the number of words per minute I could write."

Although always in solitary confinement, always subject to the rule of silence and always watched, "Impossible to tell whether or not the officer's eye was at the spy hole in the door," Clarke, Daly and Egan carried on regular "conversations" during the night. "Telegraphing could be carried on between two prisoners though four or five cells might intervene .. provided the fellow receiving the message pressed his ear against the wall making, as it were, an airtight connection... the slightest sound with the finger nail could be distinctly heard."

Daly, for many months, had a companion in his cell that helped him to pass the time. It was a black spider which he tamed and trained to do many little tricks. Clarke was asked "by telegraph" to capture as many moths as possible to feed Daly's pet.

Not satisfied with the effects of the inhuman prison treatment, officials tried more drastic measures to rid themselves of Daly and Clarke. The former was more than once given doses of Belladonna poison in the prison and ended his life as an invalid.

To Clarke's sufferings there seemed no end. During the deadly silence of his lonely, prison cell, they even tried the drip, drip, drip of the water tap to drive him mad. Once, he thought they were succeeding, "There commenced a loud buzzing in my ears, and nothing I could do would remove it or ease it... all night long it kept buzzing away, and, with a queer, sickening feeling, the thought came to me that I was nearing the insanity mark."

For days, the buzzing lasted when he was inside the cell and then he noticed the cause. A fresh telegraph wire had been fastened to the ventilator outside his cell and, "The cell looked less gloomy that evening."

The Irish prisoners were kept at the toughest of hard labour every day and Clarke was subjected to jeers, scorns, sarcasm and insults, as he tried to learn new trades. "No sooner had I arrived at the point of being as good a tradesman as any other man in the shop, and thus become free, to some extent, from continuous nig-nag, then I would be shifted off to another shop to make a fresh start to learn another trade to the full accompaniment of incessant harassing... I learned iron-moulding, stereotyping, japanning, stencilling, carpentering, joinery, tinsmithing, woodturning, pattern-making - a continuous performance for almost sixteen years."

The officers of the prison left nothing undone to make life miserable for the prisoners, harassing them day and night, year after year."In the preceding winter, I underwent some forty days' special punishment. It had been an exceptionally cold winter, and after taking from me portions of my clothing, I was put into the coldest cell in the prison, one that was known as the Arctic cell... some degrees below freezing point. I got forty days starvation and solitary confinement in that cell. Talk of hunger and cold. Many a time I was forced to chew the rags I got to clean my tinware in an effort to allay the hunger pangs."

But the prisoner survived and the forty days of cold and hunger were over. "The officer came and let me out and then stood looking over the corridor railing, apparently interested in the ward below... my heart gave a great jump... there on the floor beside one of the cells were several pieces of broken bread. I was absolutely starving and could have eaten it ravenously, but like a flash, a revulsion of feeling came, and in my impotent rage and misery, I uttered curses fierce and bitter against English villainy."

This was one of the few times that Clarke gave vent to his feelings for he had seen the officer watching him slyly in the hope that he would pick up the bread and could then be put back into the solitary confinement of the Arctic cell for another forty days of cold and hunger. But the effect of even one period there had been frightening. "By the time I had finished that terrible forty days, I was so weak and exhausted that I was unable to straighten myself or to stand upright and I could not walk without staggering like a drunken man. My application to the doctor to be put on light labour for a while was refused and, exhausted as I was, I kept at hard labour and had to work out my salvation as best I could."

Several times during his fifteen years of imprisonment, Clarke was offered concessions, and even freedom itself, if he would give information about the Irish revolutionary movement and name those connected with it. When the torture and cruelty failed to weaken his determination, bribes and friendliness were tried briefly, and then it was back to the brutality again for his answer was always the same: "If a single word of information would get me out of here tomorrow, sooner than give it, I'd prefer to remain here till the Day of Judgement. Please take that as final."

His spirit could not be broken. He even succeeded in sending out notes in packing cases leaving the prison workshops asking for newspapers and, when the empty crate was returned, it was full of them but there was one thing that really offended his manhood and caused him great suffering. Four times a day, the prisoners were subjected to a "rub down" search for which all clothing had to be unbuttoned and the officers carefully felt all over them. "I have been obliged to complain to the prison authorities of the indecent and hurtful way some of the officers mauled us while subjecting us to this search... part and parcel of the game to try to debase the mind and sap the self-respect."

But these routine daily searches were nothing compared with the terrible "Special Search" which was carried out twice a month through all his years in prison. Tom Clarke's own words describe it best: "On these occasions we would be stripped stark naked and subjected to the minute examination of our person - so minute that often times the bull's eye lamp was used. Had this search stopped short at a minute examination of the hands and between the fingers, of the soles of the feet and between the toes, of the mouth and inside the jaws and under the tongue, it would be disagreeable enough; but it went further and to such a disgustingly indecent extent that I must not do more than imply the nature of it".

Clarke carried on this fight "against fearful odds" for more than fifteen years, while most of those who had been arrested with him, had died, or been released crippled or insane. Alone, the sole occupant of the special "Treason Felony" section of the penal cells, there was no let-up in the inhuman treatment. When he was not in solitary confinement, that is, when he was working in the prison shops, wearing the prison uniform, mixing with hardened criminals guilty of every crime in the calendar, he never forgot that he was there for striking a blow for Irish freedom. "England might force me to associate with the dregs raked in from the gutters, might shave my head like theirs, and stamp the government broad arrow all over me, humiliation might be heaped on me with an unsparing hand and punishments, diabolically brutal, measured out for years, but never for one minute did I forget I was an Irish Political Prisoner and, in spite of it all, never felt any degradation. The struggle for Irish freedom has gone on for centuries and, in the course of it, a well-trodden path has been made that leads to the scaffold and to the prison. Many of our revered dead have trod that path and it was their memories that inspired me with sufficient courage to walk part of the way along that path with an upright head."

In September 1898, after serving fifteen and a half years, Tom Clarke was released due to growing pressure of public opinion and, his two former prison companions, John Daly and James Egan, both freed years earlier, crossed to London to greet him. The first thing Clarke ate when he was brought to a house for breakfast was a pot of mustard which happened to be on the table, "The first food with any worthwhile taste I have had for many a year."

He came back to Dublin and settled down quietly with his mother and sister in their home near Kilmainham Jail.

On March 2 the following year, Tom Clarke was given the Freedom of the City of Limerick on the motion of the Mayor, John Daly, who had shared much of his prison life. While in this ancient city, Tom Clarke stayed with John Daly and his widowed sister-in-law, who had eight daughters and a young son. He returned there in the summer and accompanied the large family to the seaside of Kilkee, where they had taken a house, and thus romance came into his life for the first time.

Young Kathleen Daly had a romantic admiration for the brave Irish felon Tom Clarke long before they ever met, but this soon blossomed into love when he came to visit them. With such a large number in the family, there were few chances for the couple to be alone and they had a regular date at 5 a.m. every morning on their holidays when they would slip quietly from the house and walk up the hills to enjoy the sunrise. The romance remained a secret until the couple decided to get married.

On the advice of "Uncle" John Daly and the family, it was agreed that Tom should first get a job and that young Kathleen be given more time before making such an important decision. Finding a job was not easy for an Irish patriot who had spent more than fifteen years in an English prison and disappointment followed disappointment. "I am living in a fool's paradise. I built my hopes of having a home..."

So in the winter of that year, 1899, Tom Clarke again sailed to America alone, and soon had two jobs, one as a clerk, one as a pattern-maker, which brought him a total of fifty dollars a week, a good sum in those days. But the girl he loved was back home in Ireland and friends there were trying hard to get him a position in his native land.

In 1900, they prevailed on him to come home urgently as a job was waiting, but when he arrived, it had gone to someone else and he was very disappointed. He wished to get married then before sailing back to America but again Uncle John insisted on more time, promising that Kathleen could go to America later in the year. So it was that in July 1901, at the church of St. Augustine, New York, that Kathleen Daly and Tom Clarke were married, the ceremony performed by the Reverend J.A. Talbot and the best man being Major John MacBride.

Living in a flat in the Bronx, the happy couple often laughed at how Kathleen had lost her luggage containing her wedding dress on arrival in New York and had to get married in Tom's sister's best clothes. They laughed, too, about the first time she heard of the "Irish Troubles". She was only six years old when four Scotland Yard officers arrived at her home in Limerick to "arrest" a large doll given her by her Fenian Uncle, John. They carefully took it back to London and when it was eventually returned the child noticed that it had been beheaded. The detectives had suspected that the doll was a new type of Irish revolutionary time bomb!

Life was good in those days when their first son was born but, before he was six months old, Tom had lost his pattern-making job and Kathleen took a job in a sweet shop where she worked from early morning until late at night, while Tom walked the streets looking for employment.

One day, to pass the time, he sat for the Civil Service examination and was surprised to see that he passed at the top of the list. But he was advised that as he was an alien free on a ticket-of-leave from a British prison, he would be deported if he presented himself for an American Government position. This was incorrect, although he had been released provisionally with the following official document: "License to be at large, dated Whitehall, 21st day of September 1898... Her Majesty is graciously pleased to grant to Henry Hammond Wilson, alias Thomas James Clarke, who was convicted of Treason Felony... her Royal License to be at large..." and this was followed by four conditions which must be observed if the license was not to be forfeited. The one that amused Tom Clarke most after his life in a criminal prison read: "He shall not habitually associate with notoriously bad characters, such as reputed thieves and prostitutes."

Now, in New York, things were so desperate that one day he even tried for a job as a street sweeper without success. That night, the great will that the might of England could not bend almost gave way. He came home a dejected man and it was the only time that his wife saw him without hope. A man of few words, he whispered, as if to himself: "Would I not be better off in prison where I never had to beg for work?"

Now his wife was not in good health. He saw starvation facing his family, but Kathleen managed to comfort him in these moments of agony. The next morning, he left the house early on the usual search for work and this time was lucky.

The old Fenian John Devoy engaged him to organize and launch a long-proposed Irish Revolutionary newspaper in New York and, in September 1902, the "Gaelic American" made its appearance with Tom Clarke as Assistant Editor and Manager. So well did Devoy and Clarke organize Clan-na-Gael, and the Irish-Americans generally, that they were twice able to prevent the Americans signing an alliance with Britain. Clarke organized Irish dancing classes and Irish language classes, published Irish journals and contributed greatly to the revival of Irish literary and cultural activities among the exiles. But he never forgot his Fenian principles and, on January 1, 1906, was appointed Regimental Adjutant of the Clan-na-Gael Irish Volunteers in New York.

Shortly before this, on November 2, he received his certificate of naturalization and the Irish felon was now an American citizen, with a bright future in the new world.

But Ireland was still the country that he loved. Early in 1907, there were rumours that England was looking for an opportunity to go to war against Germany for commercial supremacy and when Tom Clarke heard this, he became anxious that Ireland might be drawn into fighting England's battles instead of striking for her own independence. Almost every day, he spoke to his wife about returning to Ireland and she tried to dissuade him. They both knew what returning to Ireland would mean but he had set his heart on it and finally Kathleen agreed. December 1907 saw the Clarke family arrive back in Ireland, a fateful decision that was to have tragic consequences.

He took a small tobacconist shop in Amiens Street and later another at Parnell Street and, in March the following year, a second son, Tom, was born. In business as a tobacconist and newsagent, with the family living over the shop in Amiens Street, the Clarkes looked a typical family. Standing for hours behind a shop counter selling papers and tobacco, exchanging jokes and talk about the weather with his customers, the lean figure of Tom Clarke, older than its years, was a familiar sight to people of the locality. Dublin became his home.

Many of his "customers" were interested in more than papers and tobacco, for his shop soon became a rendezvous for leaders of the Irish Republican Movement from all parts of the country. A member of the Supreme Council of the Irish Republican Brotherhood, since his arrival back home, he formed a close friendship with Seán MacDiarmada, a national organizer for that movement. Shy of publicity, Tom wished to direct operations from behind the scenes and had no time for petty jealousy or personal ambition. "It's all for Ireland; nothing else matters," he told his companions often. Never a man to waste words, his speech was direct and to the point, a trait which the young men found refreshing after the volume of words with little real meaning they had become accustomed to hearing from politicians and those playing at soldiering. Soon, the younger generation began to look to him for leadership. "He would support every proposal which the other men of his generation would try to obstruct," and he backed their efforts to have a paper that would make known the Republican ideals.

After much work, the paper, "Irish Freedom" was launched in November 1911 and left no doubt as to its purpose. "We believe in, and would work for, the independence of Ireland and we use the term with no reservation; we stand for the complete and total separation of Ireland from England and the establishment of an Irish government."

One by one, men who were later to play leading roles in Irish history came to Tom Clarke's little shop and thus took the first step on a road that led to a soldier's death, Pearse, Mellows, MacDiarmada and many others.

When the King of England visited Dublin that year to the welcome of a big crowd, the Irish Freedom editorial, and the poster outside Tom Clarke's shop, read: "Concessions be damned, England, we want our country."

In 1912, the serious business of organizing and drilling was put in hand by the I.R.B., through their Club na Fianna Eireann (boy scouts) and the Cumann na mBan (women's association), the Gaelic Athletic Association, and the Gaelic League. The Fianna Eireann youth movement was ideal for the purpose of revolution, "We do not see why Ireland should allow England to govern her either through Englishmen as at present, or through Irishmen under an appearance of self-government," said its manifesto. While the majority then favoured Home Rule under the British Empire, this small but growing band of men, led by Tom Clarke, was secretly organizing to establish the Irish Republic by physical force.

Yet these were happy days for the Clarke family. Apart from the freedom of Ireland, Tom had no interest in life except his wife and family. If he was absent from his home, he would always write to his wife every day he was away. By now they had three sons, the youngest Emmet, and he loved to play with them in the evenings, sometimes exclaiming: "It would be wonderful if they could grow up in a free Ireland."

He never lost the prison habit of sitting erect, his hands resting on his knees, head erect and staring straight in front of him, but, at home, he relaxed with the family and enjoyed himself so much that he sometimes remarked, "Are we not too happy?" The children loved to see him take his handkerchief from his sleeve in the shape of a rabbit and keep repeating this trick again and again for their amusement.

If his dinner was not ready when he returned from the shop, he was delighted, for it gave him the opportunity of slipping out to the garden to admire the flowers. When he saw the first snowdrop or the first rose, "He would rush in like a delighted child to bring the news.". After spending Christmas at home with the children, he wrote to "Uncle" John Daly, his prison comrade who was always his close friend, remarking, like many a father: "What an obstreperous kid I discovered Emmet to be." Always cheerful when in his garden, he found that there was less and less time for it, as more and more young men came to talk rebellion in his shop; men like Pearse, who needed his assistance and guidance toward their destiny.

He was in favour of the Irish language movement though not actively connected with it and the same can be said of his attitude to the Labour movement, but he felt no doubt about his feelings over the

1913 lockout troubles. "Nothing I know of during my career can match the downright inhuman savagery that was witnessed recently in the streets, and in some of the homes of our city, when the police were let loose to run amok and indiscriminately bludgeon every man and woman and child they came across..."

The Irish Volunteers were launched that year, controlled behind the scenes by the I.R.B., which naturally included Tom Clarke. There was much secret jealousy in the various Irish organizations, some of whose members would be content with a limited form of "Home Rule" under Britain and others who would talk of rebellion but never really meant it.

To the I.R.B., 1914 meant the beginning of Ireland's opportunity to strike for freedom. The landing of one thousand six hundred Mauser rifles, with ammunition, in July was an indication that the Irish Volunteers meant business and the following month the Supreme Council of the I.R.B. decided, "To work for an insurrection in arms against England to be launched at the earliest possible moment..."

While thousands of Irishmen, including some of the Volunteers, went to die in the British army fighting for the freedom of small nations held by the Germans, others trained secretly at home to fight for the freedom of their own small nation held by the British.

By now the British were aware that Tom Clarke was engaged in some conspiracy and he was "shadowed" by their secret service. Sometimes he found it difficult to attend meetings of the I.R.B., but always managed to lend his guidance, with the help of his trusted companions, MacDiarmada, Pearse, Ceannt, Plunkett and many others.

On the 29th of June, 1915, one of the best known of the old Fenians, O'Donovan Rossa, died in America and when Pádraic Pearse asked Tom Clarke how far he should go in the graveside oration he was preparing for the hero's homecoming, he was told, "Make it hot as hell, throw all discretion to the winds." Pearse's speech at the grave in Glasnevin cemetery became one of the classics in a long line of many famous Irish revolutionary orations and was an inspiration to all who heard it then... or since.

The stage was almost set. The characters were coming together, Clarke and Pearse and the I.R.B.; James Connolly and his Irish Citizen Army who were ready to fight when asked; Eoin MacNeill, Chief of the Volunteers, who was to let down the revolutionaries at the last critical moment; the British and their secret service agents who were getting ready to arrest them all.

The general public seemed on the side of Britain for the much-promised "Home Rule" so the British did not take the Volunteer parades too seriously, looking on them as a harmless pastime for men who did not want to fight in the World War.

St. Patrick's Day, 1916, saw such a parade of the Irish Volunteers throughout the centre of Dublin city, the first time in centuries that such a thing had happened. Yet the British played a cat and mouse game of watching the leaders and waiting to pounce on them all together. They did not know that this "harmless parade of idle men" on St. Patrick's Day was almost a dress rehearsal for the parade planned for the following Easter Sunday but with a different finale. That parade would be a camouflage for the Volunteers marching to various points in the capital city and then occupying them for the rebellion before the British realized what was happening. Dublin was to be taken over by 6.30 p.m. and orders were sent to the country to start at the same time.

The long awaited day had almost arrived and the best organized, and the most secret, of the many Irish rebellions was about to begin. Suddenly the rumour began to circulate that the British intended to disarm the Volunteers and arrest their leaders, but the I.R.B. command decided that there would be no change in the plan for the insurrection.

Easter 1916; the most famous date in Irish history; Dublin, Cork, Galway, Limerick, Wexford and all the other provincial centres had their orders and were eagerly awaiting Easter Sunday. Then 'The Luck of the Irish', in other words, often terrible misfortune, happened again.

In that day's "Sunday Independent", there appeared an order from Eoin MacNeill cancelling all the Irish Volunteer parades for the Easter weekend. For some reason, still somewhat a mystery, he had decided against a rebellion at the last moment and thus threw confusion into the ranks of those who had planned this moment for years. The thousands of armed Volunteers throughout the country did not know what was happening and those who had assembled, with few exceptions, disbanded and went home.

Tom Clarke was dumbfounded, yet at an early morning meeting of the military council, he argued for the rebellion to take place, as arranged, with the men available, saying: "If Dublin strikes now as planned, the country will conclude that MacNeill's orders are a hoax and the men will carry out the original orders." He was overruled in this but only as to the day for it was agreed at the fateful meeting in Liberty Hall, "To strike on Easter Monday at noon with as many men as would follow."

Everything was ready and the curtain was about to go up on one of those dramatic moments in history that live forever.

Tom Clarke, who looked older than his fifty-nine years, frail in body but strong in mind, was genuinely surprised and deeply moved when the other leaders of the rebellion insisted that he should have the honour of being the first to sign the Proclamation of 1916, Ireland's Declaration of Independence. He did not think himself worthy of the honour but, to a man, they insisted, that he had always been their inspiration and their leader; they would sign only after him. Thus,

Tom Clarke is the first of the seven heroic names to come after this memorable document.

"We declare the right of the people of Ireland to the ownership of Ireland and to the unfettered control of Irish destinies,... six times during the past three hundred years they have asserted it in arms... we hereby proclaim the Irish Republic as a Sovereign Independent State and we pledge our lives and the lives of our comrades in arms to the cause of its freedom, of its welfare and of its exaltation among the nations."

At that same meeting it is said that Tom Clarke was elected the first President of the Irish Republic and Pádraic Pearse the Commander-in-Chief.

Easter Monday, 1916: Tom Clarke left his home that morning at 9.45 a.m. never to return. He met the other leaders at Liberty Hall and inspected the men and women assembled there.

Outside, the crowds were setting out to enjoy the Easter Bank Holiday, some were going to the races, others taking a tram to the country. They spared but casual glances for James Connolly as he marched forth at the head of one hundred and fifty armed men to challenge the most powerful empire in the world.

Almost at the same time, the other leaders, Tom Clarke, Seán MacDiarmada, Pádraic Pearse, Joseph Plunkett, approached the General Post Office which was to be their headquarters. As the armed volunteers entered, Tom Clarke ordered the staff, and people inside, to evacuate the building. He locked the doors, handed the Proclamation of the Irish Republic to Pádraic Pearse to read aloud and the Irish Republic was born.

Thomas MacDonagh had occupied Jacob's Biscuit factory, accompanied by John MacBride; the other signatory, Eamon Ceannt, and the remaining Dublin officers had also taken up their allocated positions. The fight was on.

By the following day, Tuesday, close on a thousand volunteers had come to man the strategic positions but, because of the confusion over the countermanding orders, there still were not enough men to carry out the original plan. Tom Clarke was heard to whisper to a friend: "The game is up. We have lost."

British reinforcements were arriving all the time; a gunboat came up the Liffey to shell Liberty Hall and other rebel positions; half-a-dozen brave men on Mount Street Bridge held off successive charges of several hundred British troops arriving from England and prevented them reaching the leaders in the city centre; Connolly was wounded in the G.P.O., Plunkett, already in bad health, took ill, the Post Office was badly damaged and, by Friday, the leaders were discussing whether they should surrender to save their comrades, the general public and the total destruction of the capital city.

Tom Clarke tried to persuade his comrades to die fighting as he knew they would be executed if they surrendered. The men smashed their way from house to house along Moore Street, after several had died, including The O'Rahilly, in a charge under heavy fire across the city streets.

They still held out, with Tom Clarke rallying the men and narrowly escaping death a dozen times. To the very end, he wanted to fight on but, good soldier that he was, he accepted the decision to surrender when it was made on Saturday afternoon and, with his men, followed Commandant General Pearse to lay down their arms.

They were marched off to a space in front of the Rotunda Hospital at the top of O'Connell Street, and there, under heavy guard, spent the night without food or bedding. A British officer, Captain Wilson, selected Tom Clarke and his brother-in-law, Ned Daly, for more indignities and, having them stripped naked, made them submit to the terrible "special search" of their person so dreaded by the old Fenian in his prison days.

Detectives Barton and Hoey were also particularly vicious against the rebels and both of them, and the British officer Captain Wilson, were later executed by the Irish Republican Army.

On May 2, Tom Clarke was brought before the court martial and sentenced to death, having told the court that, were his life spared, he would act for Ireland in the future as he had acted in the past. The same day, a large party of British soldiers terrorized Mrs. Clarke in her home for two hours before arresting her. At 1 a.m. she was handed an urgent message that Tom was in prison at Kilmainham and wished to see her. She was taken there under escort and, for the last time, saw her brave husband.

More than half a century later, still active, still firm in the ideals of Tom Clarke, this frail, white-haired lady in her late eighties, was sitting beneath a picture of the 1916 leader and vividly remembering for me that fateful meeting.

"It was a tiny cell, a plank for a bed, a small table and a stool. He told me he hesitated to send for me in case I might break down and asked did I realize that this was the end. He said, 'I am to be shot at dawn. I'm glad that I can die like a soldier. I feared hanging or imprisonment. I have had enough of prison.' When I saw him in that bare, stone cell in Kilmainham, I agreed with him that death would be better than this for life. We were not so sad that night. The sadness came afterwards."

They talked of recent events and of the future, "We have saved the soul of Ireland," he told her.

On May 3, 1916, Tom Clarke walked proudly from his cell and the long journey of an Irish felon had come to an end. He quietly yet proudly faced the firing squad and died as he had lived, a brave man, the bravest of the brave!

To the lonely woman he left behind with three young children, there were further agonies. The following day she said her last farewell to her only brother, Commandant Ned Daly, the youngest of them all, before he, too, faced the firing squad, as did the best man at her wedding, Major John MacBride. The uncle whom she loved had been publicly excommunicated from the Catholic Church for being an Irish Fenian and, due to his inhuman treatment in the British prison was an invalid for the last years of his life. Her mother, sisters and herself were terrorized regularly in their Limerick home by the dreaded Black and Tans after the only three men in the family, her husband, her brother and her uncle had been disposed of. Yet, this frail woman, like her husband, never faltered, and until her death some sixty years later, was still a true Irish Republican.

On her way from the prison after saying the last goodbye to her only brother who had spoken of his comrades and said: "We shall have a glorious meeting in Heaven," Mrs. Kathleen Clarke met a member of the British firing squad which had shot her husband the previous day. "He died a very, very brave man. I never saw a braver man and I have been in many a firing squad in my life." She never doubted that, for she knew Tom Clarke.

As Tom Clarke proudly walked to face the firing squad, after making his peace with God and sacrificing his life for Ireland, for freedom everywhere, for you and me, there may have come to his mind some verses of the short poem he had written to his friend John Daly in that lonely English prison cell, long, long, ago:

"Another year,
For Ireland dear,
We've spent in these drear
cells,
Where England strives
To blast our lives
With torments fierce as hell's.

But their worst we scorn
For we're Fenians born
And, by Heaven, the same
we'll die;
No slaves are we,
We bend the knee
To none but God on high!"

8: IRELAND UNFREE SHALL NEVER BE AT PEACE

These words of executed 1916 Rebellion leader, Pádraic Pearse, are still valid today and will remain so until the last British soldier withdraws from the island of Ireland.

Ireland's history, all the true stories in this book, the regular reports of violence in the part of Ireland still occupied by the British, prove this fact without any doubt.

When the 1981 Northern Ireland hunger strike, during which Bobby Sands and his comrades died, was in progress, Mrs. Thatcher, the British Prime Minister, met Cardinal Tomás Ó Fiaich, then Primate of Ireland and Archbishop of Armagh, at 10 Downing Street, London, in the hope of reaching some compromise. As they sat down to tea, Mrs. Thatcher showed the same lack of understanding of the Irish question which had been responsible for so many deaths over the years she had been in power.

She asked the Cardinal how, after many wars between Britain and Germany, they could now be friends yet Britain and Ireland couldn't - "Because Madam," replied Cardinal Ó Fiaich, "if you want a simple answer, you are no longer in occupation of the Ruhr!"

When the Treaty establishing the six-county state of Northern Ireland was signed in London in 1921, with the British agreeing to leave Ireland's other twenty-six counties (which later became the present Republic of Ireland), President Eamon de Valera had said: "I am against this Treaty not because I am a man of war but because I am a man of peace. I wanted a document that would enable Irishmen to meet Englishmen and shake hands with them as fellow citizens of the world."

Michael Collins and other Irish Republican leaders of the time admitted they had signed, marooned in London, under threat of immediate and terrible war, as well as the promise of a Boundary Commission which would make the new Unionist state unworkable and nonviable. It became instead simply the exact area necessary to ensure a permanent pro-British majority which has no historic, cultural, political or geographical basis. But those six of Ireland's thirty-two counties still remain under British rule and are now Western Europe's main trouble spot some seventy years later.

In that small North-eastern area of Ireland only, specially selected by the British in 1921, the Loyalist / Unionists / Protestants, as planned, still have a majority over the Nationalist/Republican/Catholic inhabitants who have been subjected to reigns of terror of varying intensity during the past 70 years. They have been denied the basic human rights of fair employment and housing, while being harassed by British army and police raids which regularly wrecked their homes in the middle of the night; by internment or arrest without trial; by one-judge, non-jury courts; by beatings, shootings, strip searches and every indignity which could be devised.

In 1978, Britain was found guilty, by the European Court of Human Rights, of "inhuman and degrading treatment" of Irish people imprisoned without trial. Little has changed. Britain was again found guilty by the European Court in Strasbourg in November 1988, ten years later, of breaking the Convention of Human Rights, a decision which Mrs. Thatcher then tried to ignore. New allegations that people detained in Northern Ireland were again being ill-treated by the British forces were also included in a report to the United Nations Commission on Human Rights at Geneva in February 1989, in April 1991, and so it goes on and on.

Only some of the more recent cases of British injustice against the Irish are well-known, including the Guildford Four, the Winchester Three, the Maguire Seven and the Birmingham Six. There are many more. Will Britain ever learn or even understand? Perhaps if England had been occupied by the Germans, or the Japanese or even the Russians during World War II, things would now be different.

What if, with the British and American Allies later victorious, the Germans or the Japanese, or the Russians , had agreed to evacuate all but 20% of England and remain permanently in, say, Devon and Cornwall or even Hampshire and Finchley? Within these carefully selected areas, they would have created an artificial permanent majority by driving enough of the original local inhabitants out during the war years and giving their land, jobs and houses to their own people. What if they created their own heavily armed police force with a large army garrison of foreign troops there to keep the local population in submission?

This minority of less than 20% of the population of England would then give allegiance to a foreign power and refuse to unite with the rest of the country. Would Mrs. Thatcher, if she did not send in the British Army to get them out, understand it if other Englishmen and women, even her own son Mark, took up arms to drive out the occupying foreign force and re-unite their own country, England, once again?

Can any British Prime Minister honestly answer that question and then justify the refusal to leave the six counties of Northern Ireland where Britain is an occupying power against the wishes of the majority of the Irish people?

Does her successor, John Major, or any other British Government Minister understand it any better? Would even prime minister Neil Kinnock understand the Irish problem and bring about the only lasting solution?

How often, on British television and in the press, do we see "heroic" stories of how British agents landed behind enemy lines in occupied France, helping the gallant French resistance shoot unsuspecting German sentries or blow up whole barracks full of soldiers while they slept? That was war, so they tell us, but even Mrs. Thatcher admitted that there is a war in Northern Ireland also. She condemned murder, as we all do, and has been heard to point out that "Murder is Murder is Murder", but that condemnation, like ours, must not only include the IRA's bombing of innocent shoppers in Oxford Street or Knightsbridge in London, but also the shooting of thirteen innocent Civil Rights marchers in Derry on Bloody Sunday 1972 by the Parachute Regiment and the daylight murder of three unarmed young Irish people in Gibraltar in 1988 by the SAS.

Like de Valera, the leaders of the last great Irish rebellion against British rule in all Ireland in 1916, which led to independence for 26 of the country's 32 counties, were men of peace. They were teachers, poets, writers, trade unionists, farmers, shopkeepers, students; there was hardly a soldier amongst them. Yet they challenged an Empire at the height of its power.

The young men and women who are now dying because of the continued unjust partition of Ireland and the existence of the six-county Northern Ireland state, which could not survive a year without huge British support, were not born people of violence either. They went to school, played football, went to discos, enjoyed the good life, like other young people everywhere.

Yet, for some, as in all other countries, living under a foreign flag and daily seeing armed soldiers of a foreign power patrolling your streets, searching and questioning you at every corner, often bursting down the door in the middle of the night to search and wreck your home, has, together with a natural longing for the unity and freedom of their country, driven them to take up arms, as it did other Irishmen in other generations, particularly after fifty years of pressure for political change had yielded no result. To the young and not so young republican nationalist people living inside the six counties of Northern Ireland today, the situation does not appear much different to that when all Ireland was occupied by the British - for them the struggle for independence has never ended.

Inevitably and unfortunately, as in every war situation, there are horrific atrocities and casualties among the civilian population, and some people, on both sides, become habitual killers with terrible consequences for the whole community. These inhuman acts sicken and disgust us all, they horrify and shock us, these callous murders of innocent people bring sadness to our hearts and degrade us all. They can and must be stopped.

What is needed now is not the posturing of petty politicians, but a statesman of the calibre of de Gaulle who had the courage to withdraw the French from Algeria against fierce opposition and was proven right in the end. The British, with the assistance of the US, the UN, the European Community and many other countries, including the Government of the Republic of Ireland, whose jurisdiction extends over 26 of Ireland's 32 counties, could initiate talks with all parties concerned in, and with, the troubles in the last remaining six counties under British control. They could agree a timetable for an orderly withdrawal with adequate security during the transitional period and economic aid to enable the new independent united Irish nation guarantee peace, justice and reasonable prosperity to all its citizens.

What is the alternative in a war which both sides admit they can never win? Do we want to leave this problem to our sons and daughters and their families in Ireland, in Britain and even in other countries as well?

Do we want to take the easy way out of peace at any price and peace in our time by talking about, once again, so-called 'solutions' which have been tried before and have failed? Power-sharing, Devolution, Direct Rule, call it what you like, are only temporary measures which everyone knows will not solve the real problem which is the British presence in part of Ireland.

Now that the international climate for change is favourable as never before, why avoid this real problem - the British presence in Northern Ireland - and why not, instead, work out the only lasting solution, which will guarantee peace with justice and freedom, the planned British withdrawal, so that all the people of both countries can live together as friends and neighbours for the rest of time.

As recently as Easter 1989, the then British Prime Minister, Margaret Thatcher, urged Israel to start talks with the Palestine Liberation Organisation and said the South African Government should have talks with the banned African National Congress - organisations she had branded as "terrorists" and "murderers" in her earlier years. She made her South African-PLO plea at a dinner with President Robert Mugabe of Zimbabwe and President Joaquim Chissano of Mozambique as part of an African tour during which she met many leaders who were once also branded as "terrorists" by her Conservative colleagues and the British media.

During the same visit, she welcomed and gave her full support to the United Nations role, particularly that of the Soviet Union and the United States, in the peaceful solution to the long-standing Namibia problem. She said that this was the way to resolve outstanding areas of conflict in the world and stated - "Nothing was ever lost by exploring the views of one's opponents."

So why did she and other leading British politicians have a blind spot regarding the problem on their own doorstep - the six counties of Northern Ireland occupied by Britain against the wishes of the majority of the Irish people at home and overseas? Until an IRA mortar bomb landed in the back garden of No. 10 Downing St. in January 1991, shattering the room where the British Gulf War cabinet was in session, did new Prime Minister John Major even think of Ireland at all?

Opinion polls over the past ten years, not only in Ireland but also in Britain, show a consistent majority in favour of withdrawal of British troops - so why does it not happen?

The old excuses are usually trotted out - the same excuses which were used to keep almost half the world, including Ireland, within the long-dead British Empire, which now happily only exists on atlases and globes in museums and libraries, with the colour red covering America, Canada, India, Australia, the best parts of Africa and Asia and, of course, little Ireland.

Margaret Thatcher said there would be Civil War if the British leave Northern Ireland, yet admitted there is war there now and for the past twenty years! She suggested religious discrimination against the Protestants there if the British leave, ignoring the centuries of discrimination against Catholic Nationalists, which she still clearly supported as evidenced by the millions of dollars spent in the U.S. by her Government to try to prevent the MacBride principles becoming law and thus guaranteeing equality of employment in Northern Ireland for people of all religions.

The record of the Republic of Ireland since independence in 1921 shows that, in a State that is more than 90% Catholic, there have been two democratically elected Protestant Presidents, and in the capital city of Dublin, there have been two Jewish Lord Mayors. This is in marked contrast to Britain itself where even marriage to a Catholic automatically disqualifies Royal heirs to the throne.

An impartial excellent British book, "Northern Ireland - the Political Economy of Conflict" (Polity Press 1988) by Bob Rowthorn, Reader in Economics at Cambridge University, and Naomi Wayne, a trade unionist, who has worked for the British Government's Equal Opportunities Commission in Northern Ireland, describes the situation there and shows how the British withdrawal can be achieved - "As the second decade of the present 'Troubles' nears to its close, few believe there will ever be a primarily military solution to the Northern Ireland conflict. Even the most optimistic British Government Ministers rarely speak about victory nowadays. Catholic hostility of British rule remains widespread. The IRA has not been defeated, nor, in spite of fluctuations in its levels of support and occasional severe setbacks, is it likely to be.

Since nothing else has worked, and deaths on all sides continue to mount, it is surely time to re-examine the old nationalist solution to the Northern Ireland conflict. Should not Britain withdraw from the province, re-unite Ireland and thereby reverse the historic mistake of partition? Nowadays this possibility rarely merits any consideration amongst politicians and the media, where, if mentioned at all, it is usually dismissed out of hand as completely impractical or politically unacceptable. However, public opinion polls indicate that withdrawal commands consistent majority support amongst the British population, and as IRA attacks on British soldiers continue, this support is likely to grow.

Perhaps the most common objection to British withdrawal derives from the assumption that it would be impossible to secure Protestant consent, and that without such consent, there would be a general bloodbath, with very large numbers, both Catholic and Protestant, being killed. Outside Republican circles, this perceived danger is taken so much for granted, even among people who would otherwise support withdrawal, that it is rarely subject to any scrutiny whatsoever.

Were Britain simply to pull out and dump the North, cutting off all aid and abandoning responsibility for what followed, the result would be chaos. The province's already bankrupt economy would finally disintegrate, and there would be a bitter struggle by the rival factions battling for supremacy. Tens of thousands would flee and the Republic would eventually be forced to intervene and single-handedly pacify the region.

Such behaviour would clearly be a gross abdication of Britain's moral obligation. However, simply dumping the North is by no means the only option available. Perfectly feasible instead would be a phased and responsible withdrawal.

To begin with, by making a firm, unequivocal decision to leave, and an equally firm commitment to a united Ireland, Britain would cause a profound crisis in the Northern Ireland Protestant community. For the first time in their history, the Protestants would seriously have to contemplate life without Britain.

The certain knowledge of British withdrawal would itself produce confusion and disunity. To ensure and to capitalise on this Protestant disarray, Britain would need to act decisively, getting the process of withdrawal clearly under way, organising the transition to a United Ireland and making it absolutely clear that, no matter what, the decision to go home was irreversible.

Immediately, of course, Britain would also have to take steps to minimise the potential for violent resistance from the Protestant community. In particular, this would mean disbanding the UDR, thus greatly reducing loyalist paramilitaries' access to official weapons arsenals. The RUC might require disbanding and/or disarming too, but not necessarily. It would depend on whether the RUC's discipline held, which would be more likely to happen if the future employment and pension rights of those who obeyed orders were to be guaranteed by the British and Irish governments.

Such measures would still leave many light weapons in Protestant hands. Even so, it is unlikely that a significant number of Protestants would actually fight. Most Northern Protestants are opposed to British withdrawal, and they recognise that their best bargaining counter to prevent it is the threat of massive bloodshed. But to threaten is one thing, to deliver when the time comes is quite another. In fact, more relevant here than the Protestants' military strength are likely to be two quite different factors: war weariness and economics.

Many Protestants are heartily sick of the violence. If genuinely convinced that Britain was going, some Protestants would emigrate, while many would accept re-unification as a fait accompli. Those who genuinely wished to fight would be relatively few in number.

The economy of Northern Ireland is utterly dependent on British aid and goodwill. To destroy a breakaway Protestant state would require no military campaign by Britain - merely a few weeks concerted economic sanctions. Northern Protestants know this already, and if the British Government decided to withdraw, it would have to make absolutely clear in advance its willingness to apply such sanctions if required. Such a threat would itself be a powerful deterrent, both discouraging militants hoping to block re-unification and undermining their support in the Protestant community at large.

Equally important would be the positive side of the re-unification process. Northern Protestants would need reassurance about the kind of future they could expect if they co-operated. They must actually be welcomed into the new state, with specific guarantees over such matters as civil and religious liberties, employment policy and the future of the Northern economy.

Thus, simultaneously with the threat to use her economic power as a weapon to undermine resistance, Britain should offer to deploy her economic resources to help shore up the new state. Provided she received guarantees that the money would be spent on the

North, and that satisfactory arrangements would be made for the future employment and civil liberties of Protestants, Britain should offer substantial aid for fifteen to twenty years, until the economy of the North had been re-built.

Were Britain to act in the responsible manner here described, the risk of a widespread bloodbath would be reduced to almost negligible proportions. The risk of a short spate of sectarian killings would have to be weighed against the virtual certainty that thousands more will die in the coming years if Britain remains in Northern Ireland.

Catholics have refused to accept Northern Ireland for nearly seven decades, would not Protestants forced into a united Ireland be equally disaffected? If this were true, the violence would not end. Enforced unity would simply mean replacing Catholic guerillas by Protestant ones. This comparison, though widely made, is quite spurious. Many Northern Catholics are prepared to support armed struggle because they have a clear objective to aim for and some prospect of success. They want to unite with a State which already exists alongside them, and which will continue to provide a goal to which to aspire. With some justification, they can reason that if they keep up the struggle long enough, Britain will lose heart and leave.

The struggle of Northern Protestants within a united Ireland would be radically different. What would they fight for? Having actually withdrawn from the North, Britain would not return, as every Northern Protestant would realise. The most the Protestants could do would be to try and set up a new and smaller statelet in the most north-easterly corner of Ireland. However, this new and independent state could not survive without British economic support," concludes Bob Rowthorn and Naomi Wayne, two British experts on Northern Ireland affairs, in their highly recommended book.

The guarantees which both Bob Rowthorn and Naomi Wayne feel important for the peaceful re-unification of Ireland have not only been offered many times by all Irish Governments and Opposition Parties, but also by Gerry Adams, President of Sinn Féin, when MP for West Belfast, who is regarded by the international media as spokesman for the IRA. As recently as October 3, 1988, he declared: "A new all-Ireland constitution must also include written guarantees for those presently constituted as "Unionists". It must grant them real security instead of tenure based on repression and triumphalism. The British state has always needed to exclude Catholics and attempts to change this situation, to modernise the state, have been unsuccessful. The state was custom-built. It had a special purpose. So too, an all-Ireland state must be custom-built. One of its special purposes must be to include all its citizens, not to exclude any of them.

In the face of grave injustices, Irish republicanism has never abandoned the principle that the domiciled people of Ireland, those who live on this island, have the right to shape Irish society provided only that they accept full and consistent equality and freedom for all.

But we cannot rely solely on legislation and judicial decrees to resolve our difficulties though such measures are a necessary and most important element in regulating behaviour and in setting an example of what is expected by a society for and from its citizens. The ultimate solution lies in the willingness of the Irish people to leave aside their fears and prejudices, to forgive and be forgiven, and to embrace each other as neighbours in building a new society which reflects the diversity of our nation. Our northern Protestant neighbours are part of what we are. We are divided at present because of differences carefully fostered by an alien government which divides a minority from the majority and by the obstacles which have been erected upon these differences.

The removal of that government's influence and the difference it fosters will create a settlement based on Northern Protestants throwing in their lot with the rest of the Irish people. It is upon such a settlement, based on the conditions for peace and justice which will be agreed through the process of decolonisation and dialogue, that a peaceful and stable Ireland will emerge" - concluded Gerry Adams, the Sinn Féin President.

In many, if not most, democracies, including Britain and the Republic of Ireland, often almost 50% of the population have not voted for the government which comes into power after any general election. Yet they live peacefully and happily under its rule when it is fair and just to all citizens equally. The Protestant Unionists from the six counties of Northern Ireland have nothing to fear from a United Ireland in which they would play an important part and which offers them real opportunities. They would elect their representatives, like everyone else, to the new Parliament for the whole island of Ireland, which would operate under a new Constitution guaranteeing equal rights for all citizens. For the first time, the Unionist businessman and industrialist would be able to take their rightful place in the political and economic life of the island on which they live, and play an important role in its affairs. It is likely that some former Unionists would become Ministers in future Irish Governments and represent their country at European and international level. Their well-known political and business expertise would ensure their prosperity in a United Ireland and, as in any other modern democracy, all their civil liberties, with particular emphasis on their right to their religious beliefs and practices, would be guaranteed under the new Irish Constitution. The old fears encouraged by religious fanatics in Northern Ireland and by the British who wanted to keep Ireland divided seventy years ago when naval bases there were important for Britain's Atlantic defences, should now be exorcised forever. The Republican Nationalist in a United Ireland are prepared to give Protestant Unionists any guarantees they feel necessary to enable them to take their rightful place in the economic, political and social life of the country in which they live. The British no longer have need for naval bases as one mega-nuclear bomb would wipe out either island. So Britain has to face up to this problem it created over the years for its own ends and, once and for all, bring peace to Ireland and to Britain itself.

A definite date for a carefully planned phased British withdrawal, officially declared now - why not for 1998, two hundred years after the United Irishmen's Rebellion of 1798, which was led by many Irish Republican Protestants? - would be realistic and the only hope for lasting peace in Ireland and between Britain and Ireland.

The United Nations could be called in to supervise the disarming of all sections of the population there and to play an active peace-keeping role for an agreed period. Not alone did the UN owe Ireland some £14m. in 1989 for services rendered in other world trouble spots, but it is also time that this international organisation repaid its moral debt to the soldiers of this small nation who have given their lives for peace, justice and freedom in many other lands. Now it should be Ireland's turn.

An international campaign should be mounted without delay throughout the world to put sustained pressure on Britain to bring lasting peace and justice to Ireland and end the only war in Western Europe. This campaign needs to be conducted by professionals and could be financed by the Irish Government - it is already costing them more than £100m. a year in security and customs to maintain a border they do not want - and by the Irish overseas, with the help of the U.S., France, Germany and other friendly countries and international organisations. What any of the major advertising and public relations agencies could do with such a campaign directed particularly at the ordinary British voter! While the English man-in-the-street may be aware that almost 3,000 people have died in the present outbreak of violence in Northern Ireland, he will only become interested in doing something about it when it affects him personally in his own country and in his own pocket. He needs to be forcefully reminded that it will soon be costing the British taxpayer almost £3,000m. a year - about £8m. a day - and rising rapidly to keep control of a small part of Ireland which is yielding him nothing but trouble in return and which he does not want. Effective pressure on all British politicians for withdrawal from Northern Ireland would soon come from their own constituencies, from the people who put them in power, as happened with the Poll Tax.

A good publicity campaign would hit home with the benefits of more money in their pockets if the British were to withdraw, which even the opinion polls in Britain already support, and would encourage the voter to take action to see that it actually happens. This will become even more effective very soon when British belt-tightening becomes necessary as the recession bites, as North Sea oil begins to run out and increased imports and immigrants pour into Britain from 1993 onwards.

British citizens know that their Government has set a date for leaving Hong Kong - as it did in many other former colonies - and it was not the end of their world. The millions of pounds a day spent in direct and hidden subsidies to keep the British flag flying in the small north-eastern part of Ireland will not seem worth it nor will the lives of the British soldiers being killed there, and even in their own country and on the Continent of Europe - for what?

Another positive argument for a British withdrawal is that the people of Britain and Ireland get on very well socially, as tourists, in business and in sport - an Englishman, Jack Charlton, managed Ireland's very popular 1990 World Cup team and returned to Dublin for a hero's welcome from almost 500,000 people in July 1990, more than double the number that greeted the English team in London.

Why should a small majority calling themselves Unionists and British Loyalists in the six counties of Northern Ireland, but who represent only about 1% of the total population of the two islands, remain the only barrier to even closer and much more friendly relations between the two neighbouring countries of Britain and Ireland? Why should this 1% seriously affect the daily lives of almost everyone else on the two islands?

- "The current state of relations between the two countries is never static, there's always some new development, some new element of strain. As I've said before, as long as there is the Northern Ireland problem, Anglo-Irish relations will never follow the same smooth pattern which should take place between two friendly neighbouring democratic states" - stated Irish Prime Minister, Charles Haughey, after his European Council meeting with the then British Premier Margaret Thatcher at Rhodes in December 1988.

Pressure from voters could be organised by Irish people living in every constituency in Britain, supported by funds and professional assistance from the Government in Dublin. As Britain has, for centuries, interfered in Irish affairs, the Irish are now certainly justified in conducting an open democratic campaign in Britain with the praiseworthy objective of peace and justice between the two countries. In Britain, like everywhere else, members of Parliament, and those who hope to become members, will be forced to listen, as politicians do when an election is near. The European Community and the United Nations - most of the members of both these organisations would support the Irish objectives - would also be encouraged to put pressure on Britain to fix a date for withdrawal and even help to organise an international conference to work out the timetable and other details. The active political and financial support of the U.S. would be invaluable.

It would no longer be just the opinions of such eminent British people as historian A.J.P. Taylor, actress Julie Christie, Lord Gifford or Clare Short, Birmingham M.P., who have stated many times that a majority of the British public have expressed support for withdrawal from Northern Ireland in a series of opinion polls over the past ten years, but that now is the time to actually do something practical about the situation. Even Tory spokesman, the late Sir John Biggs-Davison stated: "I do not apply the term 'British' to the island of Ireland, in law particularly. There is the Nationality Act. The people of Northern Ireland are British subjects. This is a technical term. So are the people of Hong Kong. The people of Northern Ireland are Irish but part of Her Majesty's dominions."

Since he made that interesting statement, the British Government under Mrs. Thatcher did a deal with the Chinese People's Republic which alters Hong Kong's links with Britain and will transfer sovereignty, and its 'British' citizens, to China in a few years time.

So what's stopping Britain doing the same thing with the six counties of Northern Ireland?

The problem will not go away. Seán MacManus, chairman of Sinn Féin which supports the armed struggle of the IRA against the British in Northern Ireland has said: "Sinn Féin takes no pleasure in the deaths of British soldiers in Ireland, who are dying in a war they don't want, their families don't want, a majority of the British people don't want and which their generals admit they cannot win." He called on the British Government to have talks with the Republicans as they did in 1972 when another Conservative Prime Minister, Edward Heath, authorised William Whitelaw, the British Secretary of State for Northern Ireland, to fly IRA leaders by RAF jet to London - the first time the IRA had negotiated directly with the British Government since 1921. Although the Unionist/Loyalists, with the help of a section of the British army and police, helped to engineer an end to that particular ceasefire, surely now is the time for another serious practical attempt at the only realistic peaceful solution, a united Ireland.

On American Independence Day, 4th July 1990, a man was greeted at the door of 10 Downing Street, London, by the British Prime Minister, entertained to a three hour luncheon and then posed for the usual smiling handshaking photographs with Mrs. Thatcher. This man was the founder, and still acknowledged leader, of the ANC, an organisation described as "terrorists like the IRA and PLO" - by that same lady only two years earlier.

After their meeting, that now world-famous statesman, but still guerilla leader, Nelson Mandela said:- "There were a number of points on which we do not see eye-to-eye, like the use of violence as a method of political actions". He had joined the long list of those the British had called "murderers and terrorists", Kenyatta, Mugabe, Nkrumah, Begin, Collins, de Valera and many more, who were later to be entertained by British Prime Ministers because of political, economic or financial expediency. Almost at the same time Margaret Thatcher was having lunch with Nelson Mandela, her spokesman and other British Government ministers were stating: "We do not talk to terrorists and do not negotiate with them ever".

Mandela had already created a political storm in London following a press conference in Dublin, when he was made a Freeman of that city in recognition of his lifelong struggle for his country's freedom, when he said: "What we would like to see is that the British Government and the IRA should adopt precisely the line we have taken in regard to our own internal situation. There is nothing better than opponents sitting down to resolve their problems in a peaceful manner. It seems to me that it is wrong for anyone to suggest that force will bring about a solution in conditions of this kind. The only way to resolve the problem and stop the mutual slaughter between various population groups is to sit down and talk without any pre-conditions. What I am concerned about is a peaceful solution. The British Government has involved itself in negotiations of this kind before."

Popular national columnist Gene Kerrigan put the British criticism of Mandela's speech in context in the 8th July 1990 edition of the "Sunday Tribune", when he wrote:- "Wasn't that shocking stuff Mandela came out with, about how everyone should sit down and discuss the Northern war? Who does he think he is - Willie Whitelaw? Didn't it occur to any of those howling that the British Government would never sit down with the IRA, that that is precisely what Whitelaw and the Heath Government did in the early 1970's?

It was while mulling over this stuff about men of violence that I tuned into "Open Space" on BBC2 last Tuesday. It was about the

British Government and the arms trade. Thirty million (30,000,000) people have died in over 100 little wars since 1945. In 1989, Britain sold military equipment to 84 countries, including those massacring civilians. All done with Government support and approval. In East Timor, the Indonesian Government which gets arms from Britain, has killed 200,000 - a third of the entire population. With impeccable impartiality, Britain sold arms to both sides in the Iran-Iraq war. In 1990, Britain will sell an estimated £4,000m. worth of arms.

Some of us have qualms about Mandela sitting down to talk with such people." concludes Kerrigan's article.

In the same edition of the same national newspaper, respected political columnist J.J. O'Molloy's article was headed: "They Always Talk To The Terrorists In The End."

Perhaps if all the Republican Catholic people living within the confines of the six counties of Northern Ireland under British rule had been BLACK and subjected to the same unjust treatment they have received at the hands of the WHITE British and their Unionist Loyalist supporters there, over the past seventy years since the country was partitioned, things would have been different and there would have been such a world outcry that Ireland would have been united years ago?

Why does the British Government not initiate meaningful talks now with the stated objective of arranging an orderly withdrawal from the North of Ireland inside ten years? Why do not the international community, including the USA, the Soviet Union, the EC, the UN, and, of course, the Government of the Republic of Ireland, all combine to bring lasting peace and justice to the whole island of Ireland? Why?

This book is a plea for real lasting peace in Ireland and between all the people of Britain and Ireland, which can only be achieved by the British Government opening negotiations with everyone involved with a view to fixing a date for the orderly withdrawal of all British troops from the island of Ireland, while seeking the support of the powerful countries and international organisations already mentioned to make it all happen. It can be done.

The vast majority of the people of the two islands of Ireland and Britain want an end to the killing and the atrocities now. A united Irish Republic would bring peace and prosperity to all its citizens and lasting friendship between the people of the two countries. Everything else has been tried and has failed.

The years 1989/1990 have seen the beginning of the end of more than half the armed conflicts and wars around the world. Soviet soldiers left Afghanistan, Cuba agreed to quit Angola, South Africa left Namibia, Libya left Chad -why do the British not leave Ireland? Does John Major want to imitate Saddam Hussein?

Those two years also saw U.S. disengagement from several countries in South America, Iran agreed to a ceasefire in its bloody war with Iraq, the Berlin Wall, which seemed set to divide Germany forever, disappeared, even the mighty Soviet Union agreed in principle to the phased freedom of the Baltic States with unity and independence promised to the small republics. The Russians, in 1990, also paid the British £28m. for damage done to British property during the Communist revolution of 1917! So withdrawals and compensation are not that unusual.

July 1990 also saw an historic meeting of the Heads of State and Governments of the sixteen NATO countries, including Britain, proposing the signing of a joint declaration with their former Warsaw Pact adversaries, including Russia, to build a new European security framework based on a new era of friendship and co-operation. In 1991, Britain entered the Gulf War to force big neighbour Iraq to get out of little Kuwait. What about nearer home?

Why should Britain be perhaps one of the only countries in the world to continue its present policy of occupying part of a small nation against the wishes of the great majority of its people at home and overseas? Must little Ireland, the first country and the nearest, to strike for its freedom against the then mighty British Empire in the 20th. century, be the last to achieve it?

Why should any British Prime Minister and Government, who now have the unique opportunity of going down in history as the ones who finally settled the Irish Question, miss this chance?

Until the British Government commences negotiations with a view to setting a reasonable date for the complete end to any British presence in the six counties of Northern Ireland, its Prime Minister and that Government must bear a large share of the blame for deaths in Northern Ireland and for related deaths in Britain and other countries. Britain is the cause of the problem in Northern Ireland, Britain created the problem, and only Britain can solve the problem.

A declaration of intent now to carry out a phased withdrawal, over the next few years, from Ireland, together with organising the international support necessary to assist the successful establishment of the new thirty-two county Irish Republic, would settle the problem peacefully in a short time, forever. Why should people like Ian Paisley and his pro-British followers, who represent only about 1% of the total population of the two islands of Britain and Ireland, continue to prevent this inevitable peace which would be followed by friendship, happiness and prosperity for all the people of both countries? Is there a statesman in the House?

The one and only real alternative is, and always will be, as Pádraic Pearse said more than seventy-five years ago - "Ireland Unfree Shall Never Be At Peace".

WHY - 75 years after the 1916 Rebellion -
"IRELAND UNFREE SHALL NEVER BE AT PEACE".

"As long as the problem of Northern Ireland lasts, there will never be normal civilised relations between Britain and Ireland. Only in an all-Ireland context will a permanent and lasting solution to the problems of the North be found"
"Northern Ireland is a failed entity. I wish to assert my conviction that a solution guaranteed to last, to end conflict and tragedy and to bring peace and stability can only be found in a new political structure accommodating safely and securely the two traditions in Ireland. A unitary state, achieved by agreement and consent, embracing the whole island of Ireland."
Charles Haughey, Taoiseach,
Irish Prime Minister, 1988

"This used to be one nation and as far as I'm concerned, it still is. Britain is trying to protect an artificially created majority in Northern Ireland and you know as well as I do that the British have no right occupying the North of Ireland."
Joe Kennedy,
U.S. Congressman, 1988

"The Loyalist/Unionist people in the six counties of north-east Ireland at present occupied by the British against the wishes of the vast majority of the Irish people, in common with all other citizens, must be given firm guarantees of their religious and civil liberties following the British withdrawal from the six counties of the national territory which must precede a real and lasting peace."
Gerry Adams, President of Sinn Féin, regarded by the media as spokesman for the IRA, 1988

"It just seems to me that the continuing presence of troops is a continuing provocation. The British should take their troops out of the North."
Cardinal John O'Connor,
Archbishop of New York, speaking in Ireland, 1988

"I am appalled by the killings that have gone on there and I believe that, ultimately, Britain will have to withdraw from the North of Ireland. I believe the British should set a timetable for their departure. If the British decline to set a departure date, the Irish government should set the date and then initiate a worldwide campaign to compel the British to leave."
Mayor Edward Koch of New York, following a visit to Ireland in 1988

"Ireland's right to sovereignty, independence and unity are inalienable and indefeasible. It is for the Irish people as a whole to determine the future status of Ireland. Neither Britain nor a small minority selected by Britain has any right to partition the ancient island of Ireland, nor to determine its future as a sovereign nation".
Seán MacBride, Nobel and Lenin Peace prize winner and former United Nations Commissioner for Namibia, 1987

"The whole thrust of the guarantee is that it is a sectarian guarantee, a unilateral guarantee, and an unconditional guarantee. It is a guarantee of perpetual sectarianism. When the state came into being it was set up on the basis of a sectarian head-count. That having been done, the British government then said, `We guarantee you can stay with us as long as the majority want to.' By doing that they trapped the unionist population into perpetual sectarianism, because in effect what they were saying is, `In order to maintain your power and your privilege you must behave as a sectarian bloc.' And that's exactly how unionism has behaved. No other group of people in the same circumstances would behave any differently.

If one is to break down sectarianism, one has to remove that guarantee...British policy should be: `There are no guarantees for any section of this community any more. Our policy, the reasons we are here, is to promote the coming together of the people of this island in a manner and form they can both agree to.The British should join the ranks of the persuaders."
John Hume MP, 1986

"Ireland is the first example of British imperialism and it will undoubtedly be the last. What would have happened if an imperialist Ireland had taken over Britain and eventually left but clung on to Lancashire. Obviously the British would have something to say in such a situation...The partition of Ireland and the creation of the border was a disaster from the beginning and it has created a whirlwind..."
Martin Flannery, British Labour MP,
House of Commons, 26 November 1985

"The present policy of the British government - that there will be no change in the status of Northern Ireland while the majority want British rule to remain - is no policy at all. It means you do nothing and means that the loyalists in the north are given no encouragement to make any move of any kind. It is an encouragement to sit tight...I would like to see that British policy changed into a positive form. I would like them to say, `Just as we brought British colonialism to an end in other parts of the world we are not going to be in Northern Ireland ad infinitum. Our presence in Ireland, which was based on conquest in the past, is now a post-colonial situation, and ultimately we would like to see all Ireland ruled by Irishmen. While we are waiting to move out we would like to use our good offices to try and bring Protestants and Catholics together.'"
Cardinal Tomás Ó Fiaich,
The Universe, 19 November 1985

"If England is out for the cause of small nations, she should prove it by giving Ireland freedom.... Until the full account is paid to the last penny, the Irish people will never be satisfied. We will do our best in our lifetime. We shall not sell our birthright for a mess of pottage. If we do not succeed, we will pass on the fight as a sacred duty to those who come after us."
Eamon de Valera, 1917

"It would sorrow Tone's heart not to have the whole nation united. Let us have the hope and courage that Wolfe Tone had. Let us work to see that his ultimate ideal will be realized."
Eamon de Valera,
President of Ireland, 1967

"Those who make peaceful revolution impossible will make violent revolution inevitable."
President John F. Kennedy, 1962

"Article 1.
The Irish nation hereby affirms its inalienable, indefeasible, and sovereign right to choose its own form of Government, to determine its relations with other nations, and to

develop its life, political, economic and cultural, in accordance with its own genius and traditions.

Article 2.
The national territory consists of the whole island of Ireland, its islands and the territorial seas.

Article 3.
Pending the re-integration of the national territory, and without prejudice to the right of the Parliament and Government established by this Constitution to exercise jurisdiction over the whole of that territory..."
Present Irish Constitution, enacted by the People in 1937

"We declare the right of the people of Ireland to the ownership of Ireland, and to the unfettered control of Irish destinies, to be sovereign and indefeasible. The long usurpation of that right by a foreign people and government has not extinguished the right, nor can it ever be extinguished except by the destruction of the Irish people. In every generation the Irish people have asserted their right to national freedom and sovereignty; six times during the past three hundred years they have asserted it in arms. Standing on that fundamental right and again asserting it in arms in the face of the world, we hereby proclaim the Irish Republic as a Sovereign Independent State, and we pledge our lives and the lives of our comrades-in-arms to the cause of its freedom, of its welfare, and of its exaltation among the nations."

"The Irish Republic is entitled to, and hereby claims, the allegiance of every Irishman and Irishwoman. The Republic guarantees religious and civil liberty, equal rights and equal opportunities to all its citizens, and declares its resolve to pursue the happiness and prosperity of the whole nation and of all its parts, cherishing all the children of the nation equally, and oblivious of the differences carefully fostered by an alien government, which have divided a minority from the majority in the past."
From the Proclamation of the Irish Republic read by Pádraic Pearse at the General Post Office in Dublin at the start of the 1916 Rebellion against British rule in Ireland.

"To break the connection with England, the never-failing source of all our political evils and to assert the independence of my country - these were my objects. To unite the whole people of Ireland, to abolish the memory of past dissensions, and to substitute the common name of Irishman in place of the denomination of Protestant, Catholic and Dissenter - these were my means."
Wolfe Tone, 1798

IRISH HISTORY AT A GLANCE

The first known inhabitants of Ireland date from about 7000 BC and were mainly hunters and farmers. The spectacular complex of megalithic passage graves still to be seen around Newgrange in the Boyne Valley date from about 3000 BC and remains of pottery and bronze ornaments come from a thousand years later. Iron was brought to Ireland about 300 BC by the Celts who were to make a lasting impression on the country.

AD
432 St. Patrick arrives to convert Ireland to Christianity.
600/700 The golden age of the Irish Celtic Christian civilisation when art and literature flourished and produced such masterpieces as the Book of Kells and the Ardagh Chalice.

795 Arrival of the Vikings (the Danes), who were attracted by the wealth of Ireland and its importance in Europe. They began to conquer the country.

1014 Brian Boru, High King of Ireland, finally defeated the Danes and drove them out of Ireland following the battle of Clontarf, outside Dublin.

1169 The English King Henry II sent a force of Norman soldiers to land in Wexford and, by 1172, he was claiming sovereignty over Ireland. However, by the 15th century, the Anglo-Normans had lost control of most of the country outside an area around Dublin which was then known as the Pale.

1507 Henry VIII became King of England and Ireland was soon in rebellion again.

1558 Elizabeth 1, then ruler of England, sent more troops to Ireland where unrest continued.

1595 Hugh O'Neill, Earl of Tyrone, leads a rebellion against the English.

1598 O'Neill inflicted a heavy defeat on the English army at the Yellow Ford, near Armagh, and English rule in Ireland was in danger.

1601 A Spanish fleet landed in Ireland to help O'Neill and his ally Hugh O'Donnell, the two great Irish Chieftains from the province of Ulster, to get the English out of Ireland. On Christmas Eve, the Irish and Spanish armies were defeated in the Battle of Kinsale, Co. Cork.

1607 The Flight of the Earls, O'Neill and O'Donnell, which was followed by the plantation of English and Scottish settlers on their confiscated lands. James 1 had become King of England in 1603, and English law again began to be enforced throughout Ireland.

1641 Major rebellion against the English led by Owen Roe O'Neill, a nephew of exiled Hugh O'Neill, who came from Spain to command the rebel forces, and was almost successful in driving the English army out of Ireland.

1649 Cromwell arrives in Ireland and puts thousands to death in Drogheda, Wexford and other cities, giving the Irish population the choice of "To hell or to Connaught" as his huge army sweeps through the country.

1690 The Battle of the Boyne - The Dutch Protestant King, William of Orange, defeated the English Catholic King, James 11, on the banks of the Boyne river in Co. Meath, Ireland.

1691 Patrick Sarsfield and his Irish army surrendered under the Treaty of Limerick and were exiled as 'The Wild Geese' to fight again, against the English, in the armies of France, Spain and many other countries.

1695 The Penal Laws were enacted. They prohibited the Irish Catholics from publicly practising their religion, from buying land, entering a profession, even writing their names in their spoken native Irish language. The result was that, although making up the great majority of the population, by 1714 only 7 per cent of the land of Ireland was owned by the Irish Catholics.

1782 Henry Grattan established an Irish Parliament in Dublin but it was under the control of the English Government in London.

1798 The United Irishmen, founded by Wolfe Tone to break the connection with England, are forced into premature rebellion and defeated at Vinegar Hill in County Wexford. Wolfe Tone heads French attempt to defeat English Army in Ireland.

1800 The Act of Union which abolished the separate identity of Ireland and created the United Kingdom of Great Britain and Ireland was passed by the British Parliament.

1803 Irish nationalist rebellion led by Robert Emmet defeated.

1829 Daniel O'Connell succeeded in having the Catholic Emancipation Act passed to repeal most of the Penal Laws.

1847 The Famine begins and at least three million Irish, about half the population, die from starvation or emigrate to America within two years.

1848 The Young Ireland rebellion is suppressed.

1858 James Stephens founded the Irish Republican Brotherhood (IRB).

1867 The Fenian rising is defeated, but the secret Irish Republican Brotherhood survives to plan another rebellion.

1875 Charles Stewart Parnell elected MP and begins to work for Home Rule for Ireland.

1879 Michael Davitt established the Land League with the intention of winning back property rights for the people and to resist evictions.

1893 The Gaelic League was founded to restore the native Irish language and culture.

1905 Arthur Griffith forms Sinn Féin to promote the cause of Irish Independence.

1912 Home Rule Bill for Ireland passed by British Parliament. But the Ulster Unionist, Sir Edward Carson, with the aid of the British Conservative party, imported arms from Germany for the Ulster Volunteer Force he had formed to resist it.

1913 The Irish Volunteers and the Irish Citizen Army were founded to support Home Rule and ultimately Independence for Ireland.

1916 The Easter Rebellion. After a week holding Dublin against superior British forces, the fifteen leaders, who surrendered as prisoners of war, were executed.

1918 In this, the last general election to date held in the entire 32 counties of Ireland, Sinn Féin which stood for the 32-county Irish Republic, declared in the proclamation read at the General Post Office in 1916, won 73 of the 105 Parliamentary seats.

1919 The new Irish Republican Parliament (Dáil Eireann) meets in Dublin, under Eamon de Valera. The Irish Republican Army (IRA) now the official army of the People, declares war on British rule in Ireland.

1920 The Black and Tans and the Auxiliaries arrive from England to terrorise the Irish people. War of Independence continues.

1921 IRA burn Dublin Custom House, the British Administration Headquarters. Truce declared. Anglo-Irish Treaty signed under duress in London.

1922 Treaty accepted by small majority in Dáil Eireann. Civil War begins. Nationalists split on continuing British control over part of Northern Ireland, Oath of Allegiance to the King, and occupation of Irish ports.

1923 Ceasefire declared. Irish Free State Government now in control of 26 counties, with William Cosgrave President of Executive Council. The other six counties remain under British rule.

1926 Eamon de Valera founds Fianna Fáil, dedicated to achieving a 32-county independent Irish Republic.

1932 Fianna Fáil elected to Government and proceeds to dismantle the provisions of the 1922 Treaty which gave Britain continued involvement in the 26 counties of Ireland, which were later to be declared the Republic of Ireland in 1949.

1937 Irish Constitution enacted by the People.

1939 The IRA begins campaign in Britain to force British withdrawal from the Six Counties in Northern Ireland.

1956/62 New IRA campaign in the Six Counties of Northern Ireland against British rule there.

1968   Unarmed Civil Rights marchers brutally attacked by Royal Ulster Constabulary in Derry while campaigning for voting rights, fair allocation of housing and equal job opportunities.

1969   Civil rights marchers attacked by RUC at Burntollet Bridge near Derry in front of world media. "B Specials" and RUC conduct reign of terror on the Nationalist population in Belfast and Derry.

1970   Provisional IRA formed by some members of the Official IRA to protect the Nationalist Catholic population against the police and to wage war against the British army in the Six Counties of Northern Ireland.

1971   British introduce internment without trial. Over 1500 Nationalists arrested.

1972   13 unarmed civilians shot dead by British army in Derry on Bloody Sunday. 'No-Go' areas established. On-going warfare continues to date.

1981   Bobby Sands, MP, Republican prisoner and nine of his comrades die following their hunger strike for political prisoner status.

1991   Some 3,000 people - British soldiers, police, IRA members, civilians - have died in the Six Counties of Northern Ireland since the present troubles commenced in 1969.

BIBLIOGRAPHY

Ireland-A History by Robert Kee; Weidenfeld and Nicolson, London, 1980.
The Divided Province, edited by Keith Jeffery, Orbis Publishing, London, 1985.
Ireland-Past and Present, edited by Brendan Kennelly, Gill and MacMillan, Dublin 1986.
The IRA by Tim Pat Coogan, Fontana, London 1980.
Northern Ireland-The Political Economy of Conflict by Bob Rowthorn and Naomi Wayne, Polity Press, 1988.
A Short History of Ireland by J.C. Beckett, Hutchinson, London 1966.
The Green Flag by Robert Kee, Weidenfeld and Nicolson, London, 1972.
Eamon de Valera, the Irish Times, Dublin 1976, edited by Peter Tynan O'Mahony.
Ireland-A Cultural Encylopaedia, edited by Brian de Breffny, Thames & Hudson, London, 1983.
Mitchel (John) - Jail Journal. Ed. by Arthur Griffith, Dublin, Gill, 1913.
The Trials - inc. speeches of Mitchel and Meagher, New York Nation, 1849.
Barry (Kevin), by Seán Cronin, Cork, National Publs. Committee, 1965.
MacSwiney (Terence), Dublin, by Brian O'Higgins. n.d.
MacSwiney (Terence) Lord Mayor of Cork, New York, Dutton 1921.
Barry (Commandant General Tom) Dublin, Irish Press, 1949.
Casement (Roger) Life and Times of, by Herbert Mackey, Dublin, Fallon, 1954.
De Valera (Eamon) Ireland's Stand. Gill, Dublin,1946.
The Irish Republic by Dorothy MacArdle, Gollancz, 1937.
Collins (Michael) In the Fight for Irish Independence, Batt O'Connor, Davies, 1929.
Tone (Theobald Wolfe) The Life of; Sales & Seaton, Washington 1826, also Whittaker, Treacher, 1831.
Clarke (Thomas James) by P.S. O'Hegarty, Maunsel, 1922.
Emmet (Robert) Dublin Wolfe Tone Memorial Assoc. 1921.
Meagher (Thomas F) Orations of; The Nation, 1852.
Pearse (Pádraic H.), Collected Works of: Dublin, Maunsel & Robert, 1922.
The Pursuit of Robert Emmet by Helen Landreth. Browne & Nolan, Dublin. 1949.
The Young Irelanders by T.F. O'Sullivan, The Kerryman, Tralee 1944.

Principles of Freedom by Terence MacSwiney, Irish Book Bureau, 1921.
My Fight for Irish Freedom by Dan Breen, The Talbot Press, Dublin 1924.
With the Army of O'Neill by T.A. Finley, S.J. Educational Co. of Ireland.
Life of Eamon de Valera by David T. Dwane, Talbot Press, Dublin 1922.
The Forged Casement Diaries by Dr. Herbert O. Mackey, Apollo Press, Dublin 1962.
Brendan Behan's Island, Hutchinson, London, 1962.
Facts about Ireland, Department of Foreign Affairs, Dublin.